MATILDA,
MY DARLING

NIGEL KRAUTH

MATILDA, MY DARLING

A GROLIER COMPANY

FRANKLIN WATTS
NEW YORK   TORONTO   1985

First published in 1983 by
George Allen & Unwin Australia Pty. Ltd.
First published in the United States
in 1985 by Franklin Watts, 387 Park Avenue South,
New York, New York 10016

The lyrics from "Waltzing Matilda,"
words by A.B. Paterson, music by Marie
Cowan, are reprinted by permission of
Carl Fischer, Inc. Copyright © 1936 by
Allan & Company, Australia. Copyright
© 1941 by Carl Fischer, Inc., New York.

Library of Congress Cataloging in Publication Data

Krauth, Nigel.
Matilda, my darling.

1. Paterson, A. B. (Andrew Barton), 1864-1941, in
fiction, drama, poetry, etc. I. Title.
PR9619.3.K72M3 1985   821   84-29135
ISBN 0-531-09782-X

AN HISTORICAL NOTE

In the 1890s the six Australian states were separate colonies of the British Empire. During the decade there developed a crisis situation in Queensland (the large northeastern state) which brought the Australian states closer to civil war than did any other historical event.

The main issue at stake was the contract system of shearing. The Pastoralists (the big sheep station owners) wanted to set the rates for shearing. The shearers did not like this idea at all; they wanted the freedom to negotiate the contracts. Organizing themselves into unions, the shearers began to use strike action as their political weapon. The Pastoralists retaliated by forming their own associations and importing non-union labor from other states. The Unionist shearers who had gone on strike then settled into camps throughout rural Queensland and from these strongholds mounted raids on the sheep stations. They set fire to grazing lands, derailed trains carrying non-union labor, and burned down wool sheds where non-union labor was employed.

The Queensland colonial government supported the Pastoralists, sending police and military troops to protect the non-union workers and Pastoralist property. The Unionists responded with threats of civil war aimed at overthrowing colonial rule and establishing an Australian republic. The two largest flare-ups occurred in 1891 and 1894, when massive strikes and military-style activities crippled primary industry in Australia's eastern states. Civil war was only narrowly averted.

By the end of the decade the opposing groups had managed to carry their differences into parliament. There the direct consequence of the Great Shearers' Strikes was the formation of the major Australian political parties—the Country Party (bastion of rural wealth and conservatism) and the Labor Party (upholder of unionism, intellectualism, and republicanism).

The 1890s was the major decade in the development of modern Australia's political character; its events established the conflicts and animosities which were to plague Australia's politics thereafter. And in other areas of development—social aspirations, literature and culture—the 1890s were seminal in the formation of Australia's national character.

PROLOGUE

Until his death, Andrew Barton Paterson ('The Banjo') refused to speak of one particular period in his life. That was a period of several weeks in 1895 when he travelled from Sydney to Central Western Queensland to visit his fiancée, Sarah Riley. She was staying with her brother, Frederick Whistler Riley, in Winton, where Riley was employed as the Town Clerk. During the period of Paterson's stay, two important events occurred. The song 'Waltzing Matilda' was composed; and the engagement between Paterson and Sarah was abandoned. Paterson's collaborator in the writing of 'Waltzing Matilda' was Christina Macpherson, the sister of the three Macpherson brothers who owned and ran Dagworth station, outside Winton. Paterson's only comment on his time at Dagworth was that it held 'sad memories'. Paterson refused to acknowledge his authorship of 'Waltzing Matilda' for many years, and did not publish it until after he was married to Alice Walker, in 1903. At his death, he left the original inspiration and personal associations of his— and Australia's—most famous song shrouded in mystery.

Several books have been written on the subject of 'Waltzing Matilda's' origins. One of them is extremely good, based as it is on information handed down through Central-West Queensland families. My own aunt, a spinster, kept a large box of papers bequeathed to her by her aunt (my Great-aunt Sarah), who was herself a spinster. As you can see, there has been something of a tradition of unmarried women in my family. But there is no spinster niece in the next generation for me to leave the box to, so I have decided to make a book of the papers it contains.

The following story is my imagined account of events. Things may not have happened this way, but Great-aunt Sarah's diaries, and her collection of letters, photographs and newspaper cuttings, suggest to me that this was how it must have been. Similarly, I cannot promise that the historical characters who have their counterparts in my reconstruction were anything like what I say they were. But I have tried to be true to Great-aunt Sarah and her life work, which was the gathering and recording of evidence against the cad who misused her. Bartie!

Yet I have not been hard on Bartie. For example, we've all heard that he lisped badly. It was that nose which pulled his top lip up and prevented his teeth from getting out of the way of his tongue. Australia's heart-dear poet—a lisper! It is too much. I left it out. Nor have I suggested at all strongly that Paterson may have been in Winton on unsavoury political business. His book, The Man From Snowy River, had just been published and was taking the country by storm. It is possible that the pastoralist axis saw 'The Banjo' as potentially ideal for the role of publicist in their cause. Certainly 'Waltzing Matilda' has remained the most powerful single piece of propaganda ever produced in the Australian bush.

With Great-aunt Sarah's character, I cannot deny that I have been particularly sensitive. At the end of her Winton ordeal she locked herself into a room and never re-emerged, except for personal necessities, such as her return to the family home in Camberwell. It is said she was always happy and sociable on those occasions when she had to show her face to others. On the question of her self-incarceration (which lasted forty years) she wrote simply in her diary: 'What else can a woman do in this day and age?' Behind her closed door she amassed a wealth of artefacts of her era, all delivered via the post and her family; and she became wealthy in another way too, several of the family estates being left to her. I believe Bartie lived for the rest of his life in fear of what she might come out and say about him; but she said nothing. In 1933, at the age of seventy, she allowed one visitor into her room—a Brisbane woman, a widow by the name of Mrs Rowena Niall.

My aunt (Sarah's niece) continued the tradition of self-imposed exile, and thereby inherited all that was Sarah's. When *it came my turn, I improvised. I chose the solitude of vast spaces. I lived my life as a grazier. (Lady-grazier? Curse the thought. I was a grazier full stop.) Only a small place, naturally. But I made it a success. I was thought of as eccentric; I didn't mind. On the contrary, I encouraged the notion. My Christmas dinners were famous. I always carved and served dressed in but two tea-towels. Two different tea-towels each year. I kept it up until a surprisingly late age, I am proud to say. I never got a man in to do anything on the place that I could do myself. I sold out recently and came to the Gold Coast.*

I cannot help mentioning (before allowing you to get on with the real story) that the sickness Hammond Niall tried to nip in the bud in 1895 now flourishes around me. Surfers (or Sufferers') Paradise is a high-rise geriatric ward. The decrepit come to stay, briefly, then pass on; the young fly in and out to visit. Estate agencies and surgeries do roaring trade. The resorts (as our homes are called) get higher and higher. Mine has two swimming-pools, two games rooms, a squash court, a sauna, a spa, and a tennis court with plastic grass—none of which I am physically able to use. In fact, no one much seems able to use them. I live on the twentieth floor. The lift is unreliable. I have fire sprinklers dotting the ceiling. I can look down on the beach or into the canyons formed between the tall buildings. I find difficulty accepting this concrete alpine landscape. My eyes have never really left the flat, vast Western plains. Everything here seems so close, so tall, so cluttered, so glossy, so new. There is nothing I can see which bears the patina or the cracks of usage, except the people.

It is raining on the plastic grass of the tennis court. Niall failed.

CHAPTER

1

Queensland, 1895
Hammond Niall lit the gas-lamp and checked his watch. He removed his coat and tie, and his collar. He straightened his braces. Then he turned to the wall of the office where the two steel rings hung down. He grasped them, one in each hand. He began tugging alternately with each arm, in a sort of boxing motion, making the wires sing in the pulleys, making the weights rise and fall on their guides against the wall. Outside the open window the hot night smouldered.

Niall's mind jerked back and forth with the movement of his arms. One-two. One-two. One for his wife. Two for his clients. One for the city. Two for the bush. He felt the sweat begin in his armpits and crotch, and under his moustache. One for the shearers. Two for the graziers. One for the nation. Two for himself. The sweat on his skull was turning his hair to rats'-tails.

The argument with his wife had been no satisfactory farewell. They had stood in the bath together with the new-fangled plumbing squirting a shower over them. They had yelled accusations through facefuls of water. They had scalded themselves because out of spite neither would turn the valves to control the shower's heat. They had stood there foolishly, surrounded by their status-symbol bathroom, enmeshed in their status-symbol plumbing, their skins getting raw, their minds travelling the maze of their argument, their eyes filling with tears indistinguishable from the water washed down the plug-hole. They were of the emergent Brisbane middle class, those who had bathrooms to argue in and clean bodies to spill tears

1

down. They were the suburban pioneers — the newly well-washed society who had discovered that cleanliness was next to keeping up the insurance payments.

But now, in his office a few hours later, Niall could not recall the reasons for the argument. He knew what had precipitated it — his wife's proposed activities during his forthcoming absence — but he could not recall his own exact reasons for disputing with her. Undoubtedly his chronic jealousy had something to do with it; whether that jealousy was due to mistrust of her or of himself he could never decide. Since he had met her — indeed, first seen her — the magnet of her beauty prickled the iron in his soul, telling him two things he had not known before: how near perfection was, and how far. It was a damnably marvellous situation. He was married to the woman he worshipped. He was the luckiest tortured man in the world.

He jerked at the training weights. He made the wires whine for mercy in the pulleys. He hoped that if he pulled cruelly enough he might cause sparks, might even set fire to the office or the whole building. Its timbers had survived last year's floods; perhaps they would burn better.

It was like shadow-boxing, this exercise. Most appropriate, he thought, for the project in hand. His opponents were not yet palpable. He was not entirely sure who his enemies were. One-two. One-two. One for the workers. Two for the pastoralists. One for the nation. Two for himself.

The trouble with his wife was that other men worshipped her too. She was the stuff all men's dreams were made of. The first time he had seen her was on a rather naughty postcard advertising the delights of the Queensland seaboard. She was seated astride a dolphin (a soggy papier-mâché one, he learnt later) at the water's edge at Humpybong. Her bare limbs protruded from her swimsuit with an exuberance undiminished by the long series of chemical transformations her image had undergone in becoming a bookstall-counter fantasy. He had bought the postcard — captioned 'Seaside Nymph, Humpybong' and 'Queensland Welcomes you' — after the photographer who took the shot was murdered. Niall had been retained by a prominent politician to make a fuss over the photographer's private life while the political dirt in the affair was swept under the parliamentary carpet. The politician had been particularly

2

concerned about the photographer's connection with brochures illustrating rich Queensland pastures which were not the lands advertised in the accompanying prospectuses and sold at scandalous prices.

Niall had been successful in his brief in that case. It had gained him some professional notoriety, a lot of business inquiries, and an uneasy conscience. His only reason for agreeing to participate in the first place had been his sighting of the Humpybong Nymph on the postcard. The woman had fascinated him. She still did. He knew of no other husband so committedly jealous as he was. And he was jealous because he was deeply (perhaps out of his depth) in love. By contrast, the jealous husbands of his acquaintance were jealous only about their possession of their wives. That kind of jealousy had no effect on their attempts to broach other women's stays — especially his wife's, it seemed. Nor did it cause them to resent the outlay in Fortitude Valley's flasher houses after their advances were spurned.

At the root of the matter, Niall suspected, lay the simple fact that these other men's wives had not been on the stage or in the circus or wherever it was imagined a woman picked up exciting disrepute. But Niall's wife had. She was always the Nymph on the Dolphin. To other men the Nymph on the Dolphin could be satisfied only by themselves in their own personal fantasies. It was these fantasies — the delusions of his friends, his neighbours, the anonymous males in the street — that Niall lived with, slept with, ate with. When he reached out and touched his wife, he touched a public property, and other men's guilty dreams. Or so he believed in his lowest moments, which were the moments when he forgot how often she told of her devotion to him.

The training weights leapt and plummeted without smoothness or rhythm. Niall's body felt annoyingly out of joint. A lively work-out had at times calmed his agitations, but not this evening. He let go the rings. The weights shot to the floor with a clatter. The mess on his desk needed tidying before he left. His make-up needed attention too. Also his sweat-patched clothes. The instructions he had placed in Harris's desk-tray should be run through in Harris's presence, to insure that the synchronisations planned for the next three weeks would be effective. But Niall had no stomach for ordering the details of the project.

3

Behind the narrow barred window the Brisbane night lay hot and swollen in Little Roma Street.

He sat at his desk and decided to think about money. It was hardly a soothing topic, but the threshold created by his other worries was so high that it provided some relief. The money associated with the present case would be exhausted after twenty-one days. Most of the expense would be in travel. Most of the time would be spent in travel, too. He would have to try to extend the contract because (as he had explained to his clients without success) the case was a delicate one and likely to involve weeks, maybe months, of undercover work. The clients had not been impressed. They insisted that surprise was the key element and that a swoop and snatch operation was the requirement. So they offered a fee accordingly. He had accepted the unsatisfactory contract only because the case appealed to his professional vanity. Like the surgeon who had felt the lump and thought he knew what it was — but dared not be certain until the body lay opened on the table — Niall was willing to start out on an investigation only because he believed he knew where it would lead. To the tiny bud of a canker. To the germ of a national epidemic.

What was the case? As far as Niall had been informed, it concerned recent events in the Queensland outback. His clients — a group of rough-hewn men who dropped their aitches — had spoken of pay-packets, politics and police, of exploitation, intrigue, harassment. Each had coupled 'murder' with 'civil war' in determined, unflinching phrases. There had been four of them, granite-fisted, fierce-mouthed. He had met them in an anonymous room sufficiently far removed from the Trades Hall to avoid surveillance. In consequence, Niall was off to the bush. There he would investigate and report on the circumstances surrounding one obscure incident — the disappearance of an itinerant pastoral worker. Niall would be expected to use identity covers as required. He would link with the agents of his clients' network. He would need to be wary of the dirty tricks of the opposition's network. There would be a lot of boring travel.

Niall had found in his past experience that investigations led to puzzles, not solutions. Therefore the Swagman Affair, as he had come to think of the case, was as promising as any in terms of likely complications and surprises. His fledgling profession, Niall had found, involved scratching through blank walls to

4

discover not exits and vistas but mazes of walls beyond.

Yet the maze which most concerned him at this urgent hour was the maze of his relationship with his wife. It was singular, this maze, in its never-ending capacity to provide another promising avenue and another false turn. He did not run in this maze in search of the exit. Had he seen an exit he would not have taken it. He searched instead for the maze's centre, for the beast there whose brainchild the maze was. Niall was not so naive as to suspect that the beast was anything other than his own imagination, but he had not yet proved that point conclusively. If there was something wrong with his marriage he was perfectly willing to accept it was due to his own foolishness. But he had always failed at investigating his own case. As inquisitor unto himself he was soft and dishonest. As his own suspect he lied and prevaricated under interrogation. It was beyond him to admit that he was not the man to solve his own problems. What addict could honestly question the source of his bliss? He praised her, blamed her, suffered the side-effects. But he had no intention of ever giving her up.

From Little Roma Street rose the night's first gust of cool air. It came laden with the dark stench of rotting fruit and the raised voices of two merchants arguing over a price for Jerusalem artichokes. Niall stood by the window, gripping the bars. They were still warm from the day's heat. Into the window's narrow line of vision wandered a driverless horse and cart. ('Australia's Choice' it had painted on its tail-board — an advertisement for a brand of flour.) Its creaking, hoof-knocking progress linked one gas-lamp's circle of light to the next. Niall unclasped his hands, feeling them gritty and sweaty. He wondered about his nerves. He was never happy about being nervous. He liked to think that nerves were the affliction of others — stage actors, petty criminals, executioners. Why should an investigative agent be nervous? An Aboriginal man slid upright down the street. In the obscure light Niall thought for a moment the man was walking on air, or being transported through it by some dreaming trick of levitation. Then, with the sound of soft-slurring wooden wheels in the street's dirt, Niall realised the man was on roller-skates. Yes, why should the sleuth be nervous? Surely the pursuer had the least worrying position. Unless, of course, the pursued turned. Unless the quarry turned on the hunter, with a

5

weapon, or a word. A child ran past the window, a horse-whip in his hand. He called: 'Come back here, you crawly old bastard.' He disappeared down the dog-leg of the street where the horse and cart, and the skater, had gone. 'When I catch you I'll make you suffer,' the piping child's voice called to the night.

Harris arrived. He was dressed in a policeman's uniform. 'Evening,' he said. He took the helmet from his sweating head and looked round the office. He did not approve of the jungle of potted ferns and palms cluttering the room. They were unprofessional, he maintained. The tropical pot-plants turned Niall and himself into a pair of sweating monkeys peeping at clients between the greenery. Niall had let his wife do the decorating. 'I like it. They're creative,' Niall had said. Harris wanted to get rid of them: 'It's a rainforest,' he had argued. Harris wanted to wash the walls, too, but Niall would not allow it. A foot from the ceiling was the high-water mark of last year's floods. Below that the walls were stained in brownish streaks. 'If we wash them we invite another flood,' Niall had said. The logic of it escaped Harris: 'By that reasoning,' he had replied, 'the city should not rebuild the Victoria Bridge.' Harris preferred the quick horse-drawn tram journey to work. The ferries were too slow. The river cut the city in half. 'We are not bursting to expand like the city,' had been Niall's argument. 'If we don't expand, we'll go under,' had been Harris's. 'You'll afford no more fancy plumbing then,' he had added. Harris could not yet afford a bathroom at his place. He had to stand and slop cold water on himself in the lean-to wash-house out the back.

'You don't look good,' said Harris, hanging the policeman's helmet on a hook.

'I know.'

'You don't look prim. That's what Clohesy should be.'

'I know. I'll be right in a minute.'

'The train leaves at ten thirty.'

'Plenty of time. You picked up the tickets?'

Harris tossed them onto the desk. 'Want me to make you up again?' he asked.

'Plenty of time. I'll be right in a minute. I put the schedule in your tray. There are three programmes, depending on circumstances. It's self-explanatory.'

'Then you'd better explain it to me,' said Harris.

6

Niall sighed. 'I'll be Clohesy to the town,' he said, 'and Laver to the pastoralists, if they find me out. Then I'll simply be myself, should the worst come to the worst. I'll be depending on you, Edgar, to squeeze our clients for an extension, and to get to me anything you hear of importance.'

Harris sorted through the file of papers. Whenever he frowned his ears moved forward. 'What's Tindall's Electric Bath House got to do with it?' he said.

Niall bit at his fingernails. 'Rowena's new job. She starts as a masseuse there tomorrow. I thought you might like a course of treatment on the firm's account.'

Harris shrugged. 'I don't believe in hydropathics. All that water and electricity running around together. Positively dangerous.'

'Have a Turkish bath, then.'

'They're segregated, you realise. If I'm to keep an eye on your wife . . . .'

'Discreet inquiry will suffice. I'm not asking you to spy on her. I'm concerned, that's all. She wants a career; I want her to be happy.'

'Not much status in bath-houses, I'm afraid.'

'Tindall's is absolutely respectable. All the latest apparatus.'

'Gimquackery.'

'Electricity will run the world soon, Edgar. You might as well get used to it. Besides, I am sure it will do you good. Very relaxing, the high-frequency.'

Niall lifted a suitcase to the desk and opened it. Its contents were mainly clothes in a somewhat unfashionable style. 'Clohesy would wear pyjamas, I suppose,' he said. 'Probably a night-cap, too.'

Harris shrugged. 'Not in that climate. Not the night-cap.'

'Spectacles?'

'Absolutely. And a cane.'

'But not too boring, Edgar. Why don't I make him a hypochondriac? Lots of patent medicines. Pills, ointments, oils —'

'Too expensive. Small budget, didn't you say?'

'He needs an eccentricity.'

'Make him a vegetarian.'

'Very droll, Edgar. He's a vegetarian already.'

Niall took a revolver from the suitcase. He checked its

chambers. It was a police-issue Colt. He settled it back amongst the clothes.

'You should wear that on you,' suggested Harris.

'It's only a bona fides. I have no intention of using it.'

Harris broke a leaf from one of the fountaining fishbone ferns. If he had had the advantage of a wealthy family he, too, would have opened his own agency. It would have run on strict rules. It would have enshrined Discipline as its mentor and motto, not Imagination, as Niall preferred. Harris's would have been a tidy office with a sign on the inside of the door saying, 'Don't be a fool — it's not a game out there', or some such terse reminder. He would have had a filing system that worked and a safe for documents. He would not have kept the business in stacked fruit-cases as Niall did. And he would have kept a variety of weapons, well-oiled. A large variety. For it seemed to him that trusting to reality, rather than to theatrical devices, was where the future of the profession lay. Niall's notion that crimes were, at conception, works of fantasy, had in Harris's opinion nothing to do with the fact that the investigator's unravelling was of strands of actuality. Harris had no intention of reading Shakespeare, as Niall had suggested, to discover the plots of the Four Basic Crimes. Nor did he eagerly await the sea-mailed issues of the *Strand Magazine* for its crime features. Conan Doyle was an idealistic *naïf*, in Harris's view. Harris's combined trust lay in Wallace Burton's *Ancient Concepts of Wrong* (the unabridged, three-volume edition) and in the *London Metropolitan Police Force Advanced Operations Manual*. In Harris's mind, crime, like war, was a function of history, not a work of art. He kept his revolver fully loaded and holstered handily by his heart. He also carried a serviceable truncheon tucked in his left boot, and a stiletto was strapped to his thigh. He never went without a pocketful of change. It is best to hit a man with your fist full of coins.

'I hope you don't blame *me*,' Harris said, 'when you come back with a squatter's bullet in your throat. Or a shear-blade in your rump. There's no suspension of disbelief in the outback. Once you're seen through, you're done.'

'I have my contingency plans.'

'I see no reason for the bush to suffer lightly a city prank like this. They've not shown themselves to be particularly civilised out there thus far. "Queensland's ulcer" the newspapers called it.'

'It won't be healed with a bullet.'

'Especially not a stage-property one.' To emphasise his point Harris tugged at the tight trouser-band of the police uniform which, under Niall's instructions, he had purloined from the costume department of the Opera House in Queen Street. 'This, for example, is a London Peeler's getout,' Harris complained.

'No one will know in the dark.'

Harris thought this typical of Niall's irresponsibilities. The Niall family money, Harris never forgot, was made in circuses and magic-lantern displays — a flotilla of travelling tent-shows which worked every city exhibition and outback goldfield. Harris's own forbears and relatives were honest cedar-cutters. They had not made enough money to send any of their sons south to the university for a liberal education.

'I'm not sure I'm happy with this moustache,' Niall said, articulating his upper lip towards a table mirror set on the desk. 'The ends droop a little. Clohesy would have them trimmed up, I feel. Neater.'

'I don't believe he knows anything about the ends of his moustaches. He's not conscious of fashion.'

'But he is conscious of appearances.'

Harris thought a moment. 'Is he in love?' he said.

'Good God! Do police inspectors fall in love?'

'Never.'

'So. He's not in love. What does he do with the ends of his moustaches now?'

'He leaves them alone. He has more important matters to consider.'

In response Niall pouted Clohesy's upper lip close to the mirror. 'No, you're wrong here. If Clohesy's not in love he'll shave it off.' Niall tore the moustache from his face and put it back in its box.

Harris retrieved it. 'You should wear it,' he said. He took a pair of scissors from the box and trimmed the drooping ends. 'It changes the shape of your face. Narrows it down. Makes you older. Absolutely necessary, in my opinion.'

Niall reapplied the moustache, using glue and a brush. He grunted into the mirror. 'A goatee, perhaps?'

9

'Too dramatic.'

'I can't do him if he's not dramatic.'

'If he's too dramatic he won't be a police inspector.'

Harris held the pinewood box on his knees. The moustaches were pinned in neat rows on plush like a collection of butterflies. When the box lid opened the tiered display drawers rose and separated, like so many mouths yawning to expose their claret-soft interiors. The paint-sticks, the powders, the brushes, the tweezers, the puffs, each had their own compartments. Niall selected a powder. 'Reality is dramatic, Edgar,' he said. 'All the world's a travelling circus.'

With a paint-stick Niall re-darkened his eyebrows and accentuated the hairs sprouting from his ear-lobes. He applied more Macassar oil to his hair and brushed it down firmly, with the part on the right side. Then he rose from the desk. He put on tie, coat and hat. He picked up the spectacles and adjusted them on his nose. Finally he selected a cane from the umbrella-stand and took several surprisingly light steps round the room. 'I like Clohesy,' he said. 'Clohesy is an enigma.'

'Be careful he's not vaudeville.'

With the end of his cane Niall snapped the police helmet from its hook on the wall and flicked it towards Harris. 'Clohesy is a surprise packet,' he asserted. He gave a quick salute to Queen Victoria's stolid portrait peeping from behind the fronds of a six-foot potted palm. Then he sauntered to the door. In a voice not his own he said, 'Bring the suitcase, Sergeant. I have a train to catch.'

The city steamed and fretted in the stale glow of its gas-lighting. It was an eager, sweaty city. It was keen to try new things. It throbbed with the drive of strange urges in its secret places. Mr Trackson was at work on a steam carriage in his Ascot backyard shed. Bland Holt, 'The King of Melodrama', sat in the wings of the Theatre Royal designing a ramp by which he could get live horses on stage. W. J. Byram's lecture to a small audience of the Royal Society linked a droplet of Breakfast Creek water to the Beginning of Life. With the aid of her father, an armless child in a Spring Hill boarding-house practised the letter 'A' with a pen stuck between her toes. These were the sparks shooting in dim places. The city was keen to explode into bright lights, fast movement, mad fads, bizarre entertainment, new science, mixed sports, women's education, unionism, party politics, birth control. These were the sparks of a new century.

Inspector Clohesy and his aide emerged from the darkness at the corner of Little Roma Street. They hailed a cab, but it trotted on. It headed, as all traffic seemed to be headed, towards the Exhibition ground. There a much-publicised Aboriginal corroboree was the night's attraction. They walked on briskly through the market area. A tram rocked westward, its horse sweating and farting. They crossed Roma Street and tackled the hill towards the station.

'You have horse-shit on your boots,' said the Inspector kindly.

'So I have,' said the Sergeant.

The station building was functional, not attractive. It was a long half-cylinder lying down — an outsized drum of curved iron. It was a railway tunnel with no mountain on top. Inside its ribbed arch one had the feeling of being in the stomach of a whale; especially so at night when the gas-light and the steam brooded in the high girders. In the day it was a relief to sit in the structure's shaded breezeway. But at night the iron skin and rib-cage released the heat accumulated during the hotter hours in sickening eddies. They combined with the puddles of light and steam to create the impression that one had just walked into a whale's burp. Thus the refreshment rooms were heavily patronised. It was to these that Clohesy and his aide headed, after having found carriage and compartment satisfactory, and lodging for the suitcase on a vacant rack.

The station platform was restless with a languid bustle. The engine hissed steam in a lazy way. Passengers looked confused or regretful or hopeful, but none was angry or panicked or afraid of missing the train. Clohesy and the Sergeant sat at a table. They sipped sodas and watched the crowd.

'They're blowing up railway bridges in the north,' said Niall. 'No one here takes it seriously.' He sucked on his straw meditatively.

'No bridges went, in fact. Just scare tactics. It's all died down now,' Harris replied.

'Not necessarily. When did a war ever end with so few bullets fired?'

11

'When did a war ever start over the shearing of a sheep?'

'They've started for less than that. Locks of women's hair are the most notorious of history's war-starters. A dead horse started the Dorian wars. A foreskin, which later proved to be a fake, started a holy war which raged for thirty-two years.' Niall's history had come from popular books.

'But politics is the ace war-starter these days,' said Harris.

'Politics and poverty keep a modern war going, but it takes a murder to start one. The first death is always a murder. After that come the casualties.'

Brraghh!! An explosion of gaiety. A champagne-popping crowd of young men and women spilled through the station gate. Their scarves and boas were flying. Those in front walked backwards, not wishing to miss any of the back-slapping and glass-clinking at the centre of the group. They surged along the platform, a rolling collage of straw hats, lace frills, tweed and leather, snatches of song and spirited laughter. They funnelled into the refreshment room. They whirled around the tables for a time. Then they settled, as a large animated puddle, at the room's centre. Drinks, chairs, sandwiches, glasses, headache powders were called for. There was a maximum of clamour. One reveller, the central figure of the group, missed his chair and sat on the floor. He was grabbed by a dozen strong, sun-tanned hands. He was lifted and tossed high into the air. He hung there for a moment, his fingertips outstretched towards his toes, his confident neck thrust forward. A broad mouth full of strong teeth shouted a grand 'Coo-ee'. 'Ride boldly, lad,' someone shouted. 'Never fear the spills.' On the way down he was caught and placed squarely on his chair. Coins spilled from his pocket. They rolled away on the floor. There was great cheering. No one cared to go after the coins.

And no one cared to give the two obvious policemen a second glance. They swept their confident gazes by. Young and well-to-do, this crowd was. Their tweed and pearls, their cultured voices, would keep any police at bay. However, one dizzy young woman on the outskirts of the group came to sit with Clohesy and the Sergeant. She continued to applaud the launching of the young gentleman, then confided an 'Isn't he wonderful?' to the Sergeant's ambushed ear. She drank from the Inspector's straw, and touched him, by way of thanks. She wriggled her

12

little rump when the group burst into a chant about hard-riding bushmen. She shook her head and made her ringlets shiver. She was having a fine time. 'What a pity he's going,' she said. There was real tragedy in her voice. 'He's the poet,' she added reverently. She got up and danced towards the next table, to drink from the straws there. All the world was her party.

Niall felt in his pocket for his watch, suspicious that the girl might have stolen it. He checked the time. He nodded to the Sergeant. Together they left the refreshment room. It was the only grotto of light and laughter in the cavern of the station. They moved away from it like two dull fish leaving the brilliance of a reef for the murkier waters beyond. They boarded the train. In the narrow corridor of the carriage the Sergeant saluted his superior and wished him well. Then he turned on his heel and left. Striding across the platform towards the exit gate, Harris looked back once to catch a glimpse of the Inspector's profile, seated in the first-class carriage, looking straight ahead.

The bell rang. None of the revellers heard it. The station-master shuffled into the refreshment room. With a fat hand he waved the clanging bell in the midst of the noisy party. They hesitated momentarily under the impact of the ringing, but soon gathered their forces to lift to shoulder height the previously tossed reveller, the centre of their attentions. They carried him across the platform and through the first-class carriage door. Past Clohesy's suspicious gaze they surged, roaring on-wards down the corridor till they filled it to rocking with a smothering tide of back-slapping and sweaty hand-shaking. Then they retreated, leaving the object of their attentions abandoned like a piece of driftwood on the shore of his first-class seat. Visibly pale beneath his suntan, the young man rested his head back and closed his eyes. His admirers poured out the carriage door, milled on the platform for several indecisive minutes, then swept towards the exit gate.

The train whistled. The well-wishers on the platform shrank back. The carriages moved in reverse for several feet inexpli-cably. Then, with a jolt, they departed in the correct direction. Clohesy's compartment was suddenly filled with smoke. He slammed the window shut. Slowly the station moved away, sucked back into the darkness.

13

In the night Niall woke in his berth. Or he thought he woke. The carriage had stopped swaying. It sat sighing. The creamy-grey light seeping round the edges of the window-blind indicated a station outside. Niall heard the clatter of a window opening in a compartment farther down. An odd tremolando chanting came through the walls, punctuated by soft, hollow collisions. When he moved the blind to peer out he saw figures in a mist brandishing mallets. They knocked the mallets against the ground, and against the train's side. And they howled, these figures, in ululations. Then several horses galloped the length of the train. They were phantom horses, or else horses dressed in flapping sheets. And the horses seemed to Niall to be almost silent in their galloping. They swept past his window and cleaved the group of mallet-wielders farther down. Cleaved them, maybe passed right through them if they were indeed insubstantial. Then as the train began to move again the ghosts or men or figments of his imagination lay themselves down on the ground in tortured rigid poses with their mallets beside them, and Niall heard the window farther down the carriage clatter shut. And as the train picked up speed the demon horses and riders returned, and the riders waved their mallets high, and galloped beside the moving train for a stretch. Then they faded away into the darkness, and Niall sank back to sleep in the rocking of his berth.

At Bundaberg the passengers and luggage were transported from the station to the wharf in wagonettes. The rail link between Bundaberg and Rockhampton was still not complete, so that section of the journey had to be undertaken on the government steamer *Lucinda*. She was a sturdy paddlewheeler built as a replica of Queen Victoria's royal yacht. On the train Niall had had the compartment to himself, perhaps surprisingly considering it was December and the holiday period was approaching. On the boat he found he shared a cabin with a morose, middle-aged man who wore a smart cotton suit and American boots. The man, immediately he entered the cabin, borrowed five shillings and left, grunting something about the lounge bar. Not normally a lender of money, Niall was taken by surprise. That a traveller in a first-class cabin should ambush one for a grog-loan was an interesting mystery. So after having briefly observed the effects the man left in the cabin (which amounted to no more than a clutch-bag with a cheap lock holding a single change of moleskins and singlet, along with two frightfully sharp mechanical shear-blades) Niall made his way through the ship to the lounge. It was not crowded. He easily spotted his cabin companion. He was seated at a table talking with the young man who had been propelled into the air at the station the night before.

When Clohesy walked up to them they broke off their conversation. The morose man seemed less morose now that he had a whisky comfortably in his hand. 'Ah. You are my cabin mate,' he said, not inviting Clohesy to sit. 'Mister — what was it?'

'Clohesy.'

'Mr Clohesy. This is Mr Paterson. My solicitor. As coincidence would have it, he is a fellow traveller. I had no idea I was to be so fortunate. We are making use of the opportunity for a brief business discussion. If you don't mind. . . .'

Clohesy apologised and began to move away.

'No, no, no,' said the solicitor. He seemed quite desperate for another to join them. 'Stay and talk with us. We would appreciate it.'

The morose man was put out. He fidgeted with a hibiscus flower he had taken from the squat vase at the table's centre.

'Truly,' said Clohesy. 'It's my mistake—'

'Not at all,' protested the solicitor. He grasped him by the arm. 'Here. I insist.'

While the solicitor gently forced Clohesy into a chair, and called for the steward to come to the table, the morose man ripped off the petals of the flower one by one, leaving the naked stamen. The solicitor seemed intent on ignoring his client.

'Are you from Brisbane?' asked the solicitor, drawing his chair closer to Clohesy's. 'I like Brisbane. It's a town of contrasts. Don't you think so, Battenbridge?'

'Yes, Mr Paterson,' the morose man agreed. Niall had the feeling that he would have said yes, albeit surlily, to whatever was suggested.

'Aye, a town of contrasts,' Paterson continued. He was warming to a lengthy speech, obviously to avoid any subject his client might raise. 'Take Indooroopilly Bridge, for example. A splendid piece of engineering. It will probably last for centuries.

And where is it? Out in the middle of nowhere. Who has ever been and viewed Indooroopilly Bridge? I ask you. Yet it's famous on postcards. Everybody knows it from postcards—its suave span, its muscular arches, the broad sweep of its triumph over the savage Brisbane River. What has Sydney to compare with it? Nothing, I assure you. Or what about Alderly? A stone's throw from the city centre—the suburbs, in fact. And what's there? A thriving Aboriginal camp in all its prehistoric glory. Bora-grounds, totem cemetry, even a palace of sorts for old King Billy. How far from Parliament House and the Acclimatisation Gardens would you reckon? And then, of course, there's Humpybong—'

The steward came with drinks. The morose Battenbridge wanted to pay but Paterson insisted that he shouldn't. They wrangled for a little, causing the steward to stand back politely. One of the arguments Battenbridge used to support his case was that the nature of his situation had no bearing on the reputation he wished to maintain. He looked across at Clohesy resentfully. Finally Paterson let his client pay.

'What was I saying, old man?' Paterson asked, with a frown puckering the crow's-feet at the corners of his eyes.

'You were itemising the delights of Brisbane,' said Clohesy. 'You were down to Humpybong.'

'So I was. But of course the city cannot match the bush in two vital commodities. What are they now? Come on . . . what does the bush excel in?'

'Men and horses,' said Battenbridge, with surly confidence.

'Horses certainly,' agreed Paterson. 'Horses is one of them. What's the other, then?'

'It must be men.'

'My dear Battenbridge. Use your imagination.'

'Droughts? Floods? Bankers' agents?' Battenbridge was getting annoyed.

'Women, man! Women, of course.' Paterson sank his tonic water in a gulp. He smiled across the table. 'Am I wrong?' He had a handsome face and he knew it.

Battenbridge took another hibiscus and tore one of its fleshy leaves, slowly. Niall could have sworn he heard it rip. 'The bush is a bastard,' said Battenbridge. 'But I wouldn't expect a city toff like you to know that, Mr Paterson.'

Battenbridge pushed himself away from the table, almost upsetting it.

'Good night, Mr Clohesy,' Battenbridge said. 'And I hope you sleep well too, Paterson.'

After Battenbridge had lurched his way through the lounge doors, Paterson sank into his chair. 'There's no such thing as a holiday from business,' he said wearily. 'The client's claims. The public's clamour. No consideration for the man beneath the professional mask.' With a slightly cramped motion of his left arm, he brought his hand to his shut eyes and pressed with thumb and forefinger against the eyeballs. 'I'm beginning to feel positively haunted,' he said.

They took their drinks onto the deck. Paterson wanted the open air. They walked to the bow of the boat where the beating of the paddlewheels was not so loud. Niall looked out to sea. Paterson leant his elbows against the rail and faced back at the boat. In spite of its calmness the dark sea was slashed where the smallest ripples picked up light from the night sky. The two men were illuminated from the sea below by shifting gashes of silver which threw their playing shadows onto the deck canvas above them.

'Lots of reefs in these waters,' said Clohesy.

'Don't I know it,' answered Paterson. He was not referring to the sea. He was thinking about something else.

'Are you really a solicitor?'

'Yes. Unfortunately.'

'Difficult job.'

'I'm compassionate by nature, Mr Clohesy. But clients like Battenbridge strain the patience. The first thing I said to him tonight was that I was on holiday. He took no notice.'

'Financial troubles?'

'He's a sunken squatter. The banks broke him a month ago. He's off to shearing now. There's nothing else he can do. He hates everyone at the moment. Even himself. Had to send his family to Sydney. His wife has work in a tomato sauce factory. The children will roam the streets, I suppose. There's really no excuse for my being so harsh with him, nor for my having taken advantage of your arrival at our table, but I am feeling besieged at the moment. I'm trying to escape suffocation. Do you understand?'

The two men continued to look in opposite directions. As in the confessional, there was no need for them to see each other.

'In fact,' continued Paterson, 'although Battenbridge doesn't know it, my own father lost his property—not just once but twice in a row. Not his fault, of course. I was a kid, so I know the feelings, at least from the child's point of view. Shunted off to aunts. Hearing of one's father going grey overnight. Well, in my father's case going grey wasn't the problem. It was his teeth falling out. The first two landed on his dinner plate one night and lay there, staring up accusingly at him. He was meticulous about his teeth. Used to keep them in brilliant order with charcoal and a pen-knife. I think he took the loss of the teeth worse than the loss of his land. And that's saying something.'

'Bad times,' offered Clohesy.

'Not as bad as they are now,' said Paterson. 'Nor as bad as they're likely to get. Battenbridge won't be the only swagman with a photograph of a homestead and a solicitor's unpaid bill in his pocket.'

A scented breeze blew over the ship. The moon had risen at the sea's edge to chrome the water.

'One degree north and we'll be in the tropics,' said Paterson. 'I adore the tropics. They remind me of love.'

'They remind me of bath-houses,' said Clohesy. 'I think I'll retire to my berth, Mr Paterson, if you don't mind.'

'So early?' Paterson struggled with his thoughts. 'But you've not told me a thing about yourself, have you?'

Clohesy smiled. 'You haven't asked.'

They turned to look at each other, Paterson with surprise, as if his eyes had been suddenly unblinkered. He laughed. 'I'm sorry, old chap. Too damned wrapped up in my own troubles. It gets you that way, doesn't it...life?'

They shook hands and parted. Niall headed for the stern, but did not descend to his cabin. Instead he stopped just aft of the churning paddle. He watched the moon teasing the wheel-thrashed water.

Niall leant on the rail there looking down at the sea, thinking of the reefs fretting beneath the surface, like cancers. His mind circled and paced, treading tip-toe round the image of his wife, as if she were a priceless sculpture in a museum and he a worshipping art student. One night away from her, he thought, that's all it takes. He wished she could have come with him. He wished he could have said good-bye to her with a smile and a generous hug. He wished he could see their relationship objectively without having to go away from it.

They had everything, he and Rowena, except calm sailing. They had vitality, creativity, adventure, yet they argued — not hating each other, but loving each other more desperately as the argument scorched them deeper. The arguments were not collisions, for the two were never opposed in their views or desires. Rather, the arguments seemed between two people on adjacent courses who realised only later that their parallel progresses led to the same destination. Yet Niall did not want a separate course, and he suspected she felt similarly. He wanted them to share the same progress so that there would be no argument at all. Beneath him the lacy water frothed back like a parting gown. It crossed his mind that suicides probably saw the water that way.

Then it occurred to him that while the paddles clashed with the water, the boat made headway. Without friction they would be adrift. A silly analogy, perhaps, but it comforted him. Then the night and the sea seemed better, quite healed. He left the empty whisky glass, which he still held in his hand, on a fire bucket box, and went down to his cabin. There Battenbridge was asleep in the top bunk. Niall undressed in the dark, giving little grunts of effort. Then he lay down on the sheet in the lower berth. Above him the other man tossed and groaned in the private purgatory of his dreaming.

At breakfast the next morning Niall found the dining-room alive with chatter and the clatter of crockery. A story was doing the rounds of the tables. It seemed to cause spoons to leap out of hands, and teacups to collide against saucers. It gave to the dining-room a general air of fuss and excitement, as of an ants' nest stirred up.

Niall sat at a table by himself. Sleep still clung to him, putting him at odds with the room's buzz. He ordered a slice of fresh pawpaw, toast and tea. He was half-way through the pawpaw, cutting into its pink flesh with a spoon bearing the government's crest, when a woman, remarkably ancient-looking and severe, came to sit with him. For Niall she had the air of the professional traveller, one who did nothing other than move from here to there. One who accosted strangers at any hour of the day or night to impose upon them memories of the last annoying time she made this particular crossing, or the time before that, or, better still, a ripe piece of irritating gossip from the present voyage. Niall would have preferred to have been left in peace. She refused food when the steward asked for her order. She was not in the dining-room to eat.

She sat straight-backed and silent. He spooned the last of the pawpaw to his mouth. He gave his moustache a gentle pat with the napkin. Then, without preliminaries, she spoke:

'He broke loose,' she said.

'I'm sorry—?'

'He broke loose, didn't he?' She said it with a nervous relish, an odd mixture of fear and triumph, as if it were the essential piece of evidence for the proof of an entire—and horrifying—principle. 'And in consequence we are running late. Disgraceful, isn't it?'

Niall had no idea what she was talking about.

'Broke out of the brig. What else could I mean? Against all Christian principles. A shame on law and order. There'll be talk in the Parliament, I'll be bound. There are women and children on this ship. Now, I for one never sleep without the cabin door locked. But there are other women less cautious in their habits. What an alarming business it might have been. What a scandal!'

Her gaunt frame suffered a visible shudder. Looking at her across his pawpaw rind, Niall had the bad grace to wonder about her sanity.

'Who broke loose?' he asked gently.

'Oh dear,' she said. 'The Unionist, of course.'

The story then burst from her like a flood, the words at times running together like tears. It transpired that during the early hours of the morning a lone prisoner, on his way to court proceedings at Rockhampton, had broken from the lock-up and roamed the ship for an hour before any alarm was raised. He had been unable to achieve much during his brief period of relative freedom, for he was manacled at the wrists. Nevertheless he had found his way to the galley where he had purloined the cook's entire and surprisingly large supply of

20

lemon essence. Being forty per cent alcohol (a fact confidently asserted by Niall's informant) the lemon essence had been quickly disposed of by the rampant escapee. When he was discovered on the floor of one of the lifeboats and taken again into custody, there was added to the list of charges against him Theft of Non-Recoverable Government Property; and — because the ship had been stopped while the captain supervised the search — Disruption of the Progress of Her Majesty's Royal Mail.

Niall thought the story laughable, but kindness prevented his saying so. The dear old woman was in no doubt as to the serious nature of the outrage. While she was telling the story her hands twittered at her breast and throat, and the vulnerable folds beneath her chin shook with fearful tremors. Each time she mentioned the word 'Unionist' she might have been saying 'Jack the Ripper'. She considered no one on the ship safe while that modern monster breathed in the labyrinthine depths of the hull. She intended to inform her brother who was a member of parliament. She saw no reason in decent law-abiding citizens being exposed to the ungodliness of Unionism. The incident had left an indelible stain on the quality of her entire life. Niall suggested he pour her a cup of tea. She accepted gratefully.

At Rockhampton, later in the morning, the *Lucinda* was moored in the Fitzroy River opposite Quay Street. A nervous knot of women and children gathered on deck to board the first boat off to the jetty. A set of stairs was lowered and a boat arrived, but the women were prevented from descending. Way was made for the prisoner, who appeared along the deck between two policemen. He was chained hand and foot. His movements drew forth female shrieks. Children's faces were hidden in the folds of dresses. He made a miraculous descent to the bottom of the stairs without tumbling. From there he was helped into the boat by the police and the oarsmen. Had he slipped, the weight of his chains would have taken him directly to the bottom of the river.

His preferential treatment was due to his being late for his trial. Once seated in the boat, he looked up at the deck where the relieved gallery of passengers twittered in cautious triumph. For Niall he provided a pathetic sight. He looked yellow and haggard, and still somewhat drunk following his lemon essence spree. He was bruised in the face, and one eye seemed spoiled by a blow. It occurred to Niall that here, in the figure of the Unionist caught in the web of Her Majesty's chains, was the ultimate picture of impotence. Thinking this, he also thought of Battenbridge, who had woken Niall during the night by calling a woman's name from the depths of some nightmare. Battenbridge and the Unionist were symptoms, Niall realised, of the malady he had set out to diagnose, perhaps to cure.

Along with the prisoner and his escort in the rowing-boat there was room for a few passengers. Only the males considered going. Ultimately it was Paterson — with a wave to the women — who led the way down the stairs. He was followed by Clohesy and Battenbridge. The rest of the passengers watched as the boat pulled away towards the jetty.

I am writing this in a particular style chosen (I am sure you realise) from a particular book on a particular shelf of the Golden Casket Newsagency. It is the nearest newsagency—just around the corner. For me that is a thirty-minute walk—to the lift, to the gate, down The Boulevarde, and into Sunrise Avenue. Usually I send the gardener (his name is Vincent) if I want the Financial Times *or the* Land *or something similar. Vincent is a sprightly sixty-seven, so he leaves me for dead (as they say these days).*

But I made the journey myself to consult the fiction shelves, and while my choice of style may have proved doubtful at least it has got me started. The problem with it is that I don't feel it allows me to be especially close to my characters. I mean, I'm not sure that I can hear them breathing, or smell them sweating: let alone tap their dreaming. Perhaps that is due more to their youth than anything else.

Bartie was only thirty-one at the time, and dear Hammond a year or two younger, I suspect. They were gay young men ('gay' in their own day's sense), and bristling with energy, I am sure. Perhaps they shared that youthful tendency to play with life on occasions, but the ways were clearing within them for shocks and despairs to percolate deeper. I hope I am getting that across. And the world itself was priming up—tautening back like a bow-string, gathering back like a shore-wave—to hurl its force at them, to pierce and swamp, to test them. And a lot of others with them, too.

I have a photograph of the Lucinda *before me, mid-stream on the Brisbane River, scuttling past the Customs House. She was a small vessel, but she had a racy, raked-back appearance. Also I have a photograph of Central Station: not at all a pleasant-looking place in those days. I have a panoramic view of the city's market area snapped in 1898 — a little late in date, but it has sufficed. More importantly, I have copies of these two letters, both of which were posted in Rockhampton. Possibly both were written as the* Lucinda *manoeuvred her way gently up the brown flow of the Fitzroy River.*

J.W. Street & A.B. Paterson	Waltham Buildings
Solicitors	Bond Street
	Sydney, . . . 18 . . .

Box 788, G.P.O.
Telephone 1197

HMSY *Lucinda*
4 Decr., 1895

My dear J.W.,
    A spot of bother. Please be so kind as to check the Battenbridge, Robert Adrian file and ascertain the exact financial situation of the man and his family. He accosted me on this yacht and has insisted upon hanging about my person. He begged money from me, which I gave him, but I am not pleased with the affair. He has not shown me the least kindness in my desire to avoid the strains of our profession during this all too brief leave. He says he will travel further north seeking work. He had better stick to his word. I do not want him bothering me any more.
    I sincerely trust that office work proceeds more smoothly than my wretched holiday.
    Yours,
    A.B.

Queensland Police Dept.
S.I. Branch.
All at sea
4 December '95

Spectacular Angel!
    What more can I say than that I am mortified to think we parted angrily. You in tears trying to penetrate

my stupid fears and imaginings, and me too damned foggy to grab and crush you in what could have been (God spare it) our last embrace. My splendid woman, please forgive me. It was entirely my fault. You have every right to a career of your own choice, just as you have every right to my absolute trust in you. I am desperately sorry that I cannot have you contact me during the next three weeks, but it could easily spoil the whole project. Nevertheless, as per usual, I will set my head to catch the electricity on that mental telegraph you say runs between us. Send me messages, my mate, and I will pick them up from the air!

By the way, I have already some surprising tales to bring back to you. I have as a travelling companion (wait for it) one of your favourite poets, 'The Banjo'!!! In his real-life masquerade as a solicitor, no less. But everyone is onto him. You should see the receptions he is getting along the way. One stir, a pantomime at Geebung Station in the middle of the night, was remarkable. Seems he wrote a poem about the polo club there and they have taken it to heart. But more about that later, my splendid animal. The bell is ringing so I must end now.

Your True Mate,
H.

CHAPTER

2

Niall woke with the new day sun licking about the rattling compartment, so like a fire that he thought of grabbing for the emergency brake. He lay for a while, blinking. Then he struggled from the berth and dressed. Paterson was still asleep in the top bunk. It had seemed a pleasant idea for the two men to share a compartment on the continuation of the journey westward. They sensed a compatibility — an absence of latent hostility towards each other. Neither was particularly anxious to have company at all, in spite of the length of the train journey to Longreach. But a bond had been established between them — a minor one, but a bond nevertheless — for both had lent money to the now-departed Battenbridge, and both had offered a kind word to the defeated Unionist in the rowing-boat. They acknowledged the bond by not mentioning it, each seeing in the other a man who could keep a confidence wisely.

Niall left the compartment stealthily, not waking his companion. He made his way to the W.C. It was engaged, as the little revolving sign above the latch indicated. He stood in the clattering corridor watching the land move beyond the window. The early slant of the sun raised colours in the trees — all the greys, blues and russets of the Australian green. Among the lower scrub there were tart greens, too, very tropical and lolly-poisonous. But mainly it was the blue leaves and black trunks of the countrywide droop that looked like softness but wasn't. Dry sand watercourses, trees not too close together, groups of them forming arches and naves — silent alcoves for dry death — and occasionally a fallen branch regrowing. Some birds flew with

25

monumental slowness—waterfowl and crows. The scrub birds had a fussier flight. The most obvious feature of the passing landscape was the low ant-hills, like ragged tombstones dotting the bush. They grew, earth-coloured, amongst the trees, accusatory fingers of earth. And the earth was puce and liverish in the morning light, a collage of pinks and oranges and reds that were mixed by the rush of the train to another blue, like the trees, hardly a blue at all, an earth-blue. And amongst it Niall saw an abandoned homestead, with its tilted shed half-toppled, and its fences down, and the bougainvillea thriving, invading the veranda. And Niall began to see that the deadest trees in the landscape were the most eloquent—their nude boughs cramp-clutched, like the visual expression of a scream. Tragic sculptures. Yet some of those dead trees seemed quite gay, bowing their end-branches to the ground, comically elaborate, as if they might begin to spin, as skeletal carousels, inviting people to board them, to take rides.

To Niall all this was new. He had never before travelled so far inland. He was seeing the land wake in the new dawn as a man sees a woman wake for the first time beside him. All seemed vivid and intimate, delightful and alarming.

The lavatory door opened. The emerging passenger was a squat man in his fifties, clutching a satchel to his chest. He pressed past Niall in the corridor. He apologised as he went. Niall entered the cubicle and closed the door. He removed the spectacles and looked at his face in the mirror. He pushed at the moustache with his forefingers and rubbed the palm of his hand over his chin. He wondered could he afford to wait until Longreach before shaving. The lurching of the carriage seemed more pronounced here in the cubicle. He did not at all fancy the notion of taking to his cheeks and throat with an open razor.

Suddenly there was a juddering of the door-handle. Niall mistook it for part of the general clatter at first. Then he realised it was someone trying to get in.

'Occupied,' Clohesy shouted.

At the mirror Niall quickly oiled and brushed down his hair. He resituated his spectacles. Then he stepped into the corridor.

'The Australian bush is not a homogeneous entity,' said Paterson, leaning comfortably against the seat cushion at the corner of the compartment. 'Not like the European or American forests. In fact, the Australian bush is quite like the Australian people: a mixture of many varieties, all in together, each and every individual an eccentric — bent, disjointed, leaning this way or that, undisciplined, a bulge of growth here, a forgotten, leafless branch there, a sort of skew-whiff calendar of the seasons showing the regular hopeful out-reach and the inevitable die-back. But subdued, all of it. No real joy. Just the gentleness that comes from submission.'

Niall looked out the window, too. They were past Barcaldine, edging towards the plains. They saw an emu with a line of seven chicks bobbing through the dry grass, snaking away from the train. The chicks followed the mother like train carriages.

'It appears to me,' said Clohesy, 'that the Australian bush is a vast system of fortresses. Each hard tuft of grass is a little fortress. Each tree, each ant-hill. That emu was built like a moving fortress. A man would have to be a fortress, too, in this country, like the lizard, and the defiant stump it poses on....'

There was a screeching and shuddering. They were lifted forward from their seats. The couplings of the carriages clashed together. The train was brought to a fighting halt. After a moment of silence the consternation of the carriage's passengers expressed itself in an outbreak of questioning conversations and opening windows. Niall stuck his head out of the carriage. He looked ahead. The smoking engine was surrounded by a group of men. The engine-driver was descending from his cabin. There was excited shouting. Most of the group on the ground were Aborigines. Niall realised it was a police detachment that had stopped the train.

Niall was one of the first passengers to get out. He moved towards the engine. The red-nosed conductor hobbled up and down trying to get the passengers to return to their seats. The police officer in charge of the native troopers came along assuring the passengers that there was no danger. 'Simply a routine inspection. Probably a hoax,' he shouted.

The conductor took issue with him. 'Bloody hoax, all right. Probably started it yourself,' he said. He seemed a little drunk, Niall thought.

The police officer kept his voice up for all those hanging out the windows to hear. 'There's a bridge up ahead,' he shouted. 'Some suspicious types were reported in a gathering there.

27

Probably Unionists. We have to check no tampering has been done.'

'If the line's booby-trapped, we all know who done it,' the conductor shouted. He waved an accusing finger at the police officer.

'We'll try not to disrupt your journey for too long,' said the police officer. He looked with distaste at the conductor and turned on his heel.

Niall moved up with the police officer. Paterson joined them. They walked along the railway line. They stepped from sleeper to sleeper. The three men had their hands in their pockets, but they studied the taking of each step cautiously.

'I thought this sort of thing was finished with,' said Clohesy.

'It's still a proclaimed area up ahead.'

'But the strikes are squashed. There's been no trouble around here for months now.'

'There's always trouble,' said the police officer. 'Underneath nothing's healed.'

They reached the bridge. It spanned a dry riverbed — a mosaic of cracked mud. The native police were ordered to continue searching the bridge structure. They swarmed over it. They climbed its every pillar and peered at its every stanchion. No explosive device, no weakening of the supports. Nothing untoward was found, except an old boot which a native constable carried gingerly to the bank for his superior to view. Everbody looked down at the boot. 'Is there anything inside it?' the officer asked.

'Dunno, sir.'

'Well, find out, man.'

The constable picked up the boot and shook it. They all leapt backwards.

'Not like that,' yelled the police officer. 'Put your bloody hand into it — *gently* — and see if there's anything there.'

The constable was not pleased with the order. He crept his hand inside the boot, his face greying. Mutterings of sympathy came from his dark comrades. They had gathered to watch, at what they thought might be a safe distance.

'Anything, damn you?' yelled the officer.

A look of absolute horror came to the face of the constable. He froze there, his arm submerged beyond the wrist inside the tattered gape of the boot. The sun lashed down on him in the dry riverbed. His face went blank. All his concentration was centred at his hand. His hand had touched something. No one moved. 'Throw it,' said Niall under his breath. 'Get rid of it.'

Then a sickly smile spread over the constable's big black face. He moved the boot a little. His hand scratched around inside it. The boot began to jerk. The constable's hand jerked with it. Then he began to withdraw his hand carefully, dramatically. Like a conjurer producing a silk handkerchief from a hat, he held up a nervous, squinting lizard for all to see.

'All right. Bugger you,' the officer yelled, annoyed and relieved. 'Get on with the search. Work along the line now.'

The constable threw the boot down where it skittered on the hard-baked riverbed. Then he went off into the scrub to vomit, still gripping the lizard by its neck.

They found nothing unusual on or near the bridge. There was no explosive agent, no obstacle, no tampering. Just hoof and foot tracks, and the still-warm embers of a camp-fire by the base of one of the bridge's pillars. The engine was brought forward, but the driver refused to take it across. He wanted a train of empty wagons pushed across from the other side first, to insure the safety of the way. The police officer assured him that the search had been thorough. Still the driver wanted a more tangible guarantee. Finally he suggested that if the engine and his own life were to be risked on the bridge, then the police should take the risk too. The police officer agreed. The engine was uncoupled and the native troops ordered to climb onto it. They sat on any part they found not too hot. 'Get a move on,' the officer shouted from beside the line. The driver would not proceed. The officer himself must climb aboard. He did so, resentfully. He pushed past the native police so that he was standing above the cow-catcher right at the engine's front. 'Now are you satisfied?' he called. His face was very pink. The driver eased the machine across the bridge with a lot of wheezing, steam-spurting fuss.

Back in their seats, Niall and Paterson waited for the engine to be rehooked and the train to continue its journey.

'They not only have explosive devices with triggers sensitive to weight these days,' Paterson observed, 'but they also have clock

29

systems to set an explosion for a particular time. One could blow up a bridge and be miles away all at once.'

'Not a particularly comforting piece of knowledge for us to digest at this moment,' commented Clohesy as the carriage jerked and moved forward slowly.

'I expect you know that the strike camps still exist, even now. There are a few strikers who never went back to work. The hard core. God knows what antics they can still get up to, or what destructive devices they have at their disposal.'

The carriage inched its way across the bridge. The heat inside had increased with the train's stationary wait in the morning sun. Most passengers were quiet, listening for unfavourable sounds. There was sweat on Paterson's forehead. 'They'll spoil the bush, the Unionists,' he said quietly, under the pressure of the moment.

Beyond the bridge the train picked up speed. It rushed now, putting the bridge far behind it. Paterson laughed at last, with relief. 'You're not a Unionist supporter, are you, old man?' he asked.

'I can hardly afford to be. I am a police inspector.'

'So they said on the *Lucinda*. I can't help mentioning it, but you don't always act like a police inspector. Rather too likeable, I should say.'

'There are eccentrics in the police force, too, you know.'

'Mind if I ask what brings you out here?' said Paterson.

'Mind if I ask you the same question?'

The carriage rattled urgently. They sat on in its extraordinary rocking, hurtling westward, neither wishing to respond. Out the window, the landscape spun by, headlong and dizzying. The pace of the engine was insistent. Each was considering the marvel of their sitting still while moving so quickly. Then their eyes met—two gazes levelled across their lurching progress.

'Love,' said Paterson.

'War,' said Clohesy.

They had truly entered onto the flatness of the plains now. There was little vegetation, hardly any grass. The year had been bad. The earth had dried to grey and pink. There were regular scatterings of liver-coloured stones, sharp looking, scoured to the surface by the winds. They stained and blotched the ground. Only rarely the excited wave of dry grass patches; then dust, or larger stones, tan and pink and shiny-smooth as leather.

Niall saw a dead sheep hurtle by. It looked like a woolly rug tossed on the ground. Just a woolly pile in the dust. He closed his eyes.

'It's the sky that affects one out here,' said Paterson. 'Look at that great dome. There's more sky than anything else. In this land where only the need for water prevents you travelling exactly as the crow flies, you can get to know the sky extremely well. There are some surprising things in it too. Waterfowl, for instance. What a symbol of the vulnerability and genius of the pioneers — the water-bird in this landscape! There are plenty of them, too. Winton was originally called Pelican Waterholes. Five hundred miles inland! They'll be thinned out somewhat this year, undoubtedly. The drought's just too severe.'

Niall opened his eyes. All he saw in the sky was the pink obscenity of a flapping galah.

The train slowed to travel through a fettlers' camp. It was a row of grubby tents and bush structures baking in the sun beside the line. The only thing moving in the camp was a small child disturbing an ants' nest. Hitting it with a stick, and stepping back to watch the ants get angry. It was a girl. She looked up at the train without interest. The plain extended beyond her to the flat horizon. When the train went she would be the only child in the world again.

Not far beyond their camp the fettlers stood back from the line to let the train pass slowly. They were snorting Irishmen with shiny, sweating faces. They had gaps between their teeth. They pushed their hats back and smiled, leaning on their shovels and picks. 'Paper, paper,' they shouted. Niall leant from the window and passed out a newspaper he had bought in Rockhampton. Looking along the train he saw the conductor leaning out, too, proffering a paper which was accepted with some fumbling by a member of the work gang. An exchange, Niall realised. He would have to be on the alert. He sat back in his seat, glad to have seen the network in operation.

'They don't have much, the fettlers,' Clohesy said. 'Out here in the middle of nowhere. Insuring the progress of trains they'll never ride on — except if they're lucky enough to be transported out in a box.'

Paterson disagreed. 'Where's your romance, old man? It's a

hard job, but it has a certain glamour. The spirit of progress, the achievement of the railway's outreach —'

The conductor lurched into the compartment. Not only his nose, but his entire face was red now. His uniform was unbuttoned. There were damp patches on his chest. His cap was lost under a seat somewhere, but he seemed to care little about that. The stubble of his beard had grown ferociously in the past few hours. Its russet added to the demonic flush of his face. He appeared to have emerged from the boiler of the engine itself, so inflamed were his eyes and the hot red hole of his mouth.

His breath was powerful. 'Have to see your ticket again, sir,' he said to Clohesy in far fewer syllables than the statement deserved.

Clohesy searched his pockets. 'But you took it, didn't you?'

The conductor looked pathetically confused. 'Well. So I did, sir. I'd better give it back, then.' His hand poked a pink square of cardboard into Niall's palm. 'Sorry for the confusion,' he added unsteadily.

Niall got up and guided the groping conductor back down the corridor to his little compartment. Inside it, the night's bedding was strewn around, some of it on the floor where it had been trampled by dirty boots. There were sundry official-looking papers crumpled here and there. The conductor picked up his unlabelled bottle from the bed. With each mile west he could get drunker. He would sober up progressively with each mile of the return trip to the coast. Niall eased him down onto the devastated bunk. The conductor winked. 'Good on you, sir,' he said. He was not referring to Niall's immediate act of kindness.

On the way back to his seat Niall slipped into the toilet cubicle. He made sure he locked the door securely. There he stood for a moment trying to drain the unwanted excitement from his body. The ticket in his hand represented the first indication that he had been admitted into the web of the workers' network. His entry was acknowledged; they knew he was here. He studied the ticket. There was no obvious message, but it did have a row of holes punched in it. When he turned it over, he found an advertisement for Railway Refreshment Rooms on the reverse side. The row of punched holes underlined 'Refreshment Room' perfectly. He turned the ticket back over. A departure time had been written in: '9.00 p.m.'. Niall tossed the ticket down the clattering toilet bowl and it fell to the track below.

Longreach was the end of the line. Those wishing to travel farther west had to take the coach. The town jutted out of the dead flatness of the plain. Its sparse buildings seemed to Niall just a collection of sticks poking from the dust. 'This is what men have achieved out here,' he thought. 'They have poked sticks into the dusty air and linked some of them up. Fences, telegraph lines, houses, windmills, a grandstand — just jutting sticks joined up against the wind which regularly unjoins them.' And it was the wind that provided the strangeness of the town, for it kept the dusty streets deserted and it stained everything with drifting dust patterns and it made everything in the landscape sway. The whole town, from an old bucket hanging off a post to the Shakespeare Hotel itself, creaked and groaned, straining against the wind. For Niall, the most remarkable aspect of the town's structures was the obviousness of their divorce one from the other. Each was an entity separated by a stretch of the plain. Like the rare trees, each was a fortress besieged. Each was an island in a sea of dust. And in this endless flatness everything broken was left where it broke — half a chair on the hotel veranda, the carcass of a stage coach at the end of the main street, a collapsed wheelbarrow half-way to the horizon.

Clohesy and Paterson walked across the piece of plain separating the station and the hotel. Two dusty Aboriginal boys, who had been waiting when the train arrived, struggled with the visitors' bags. In the windowed cubicle called the hotel office, a tall woman with a pair of fists twice the size of Clohesy's wrote their names in the book. Some time during her career her nose had been broken. 'No nonsense in this pub,' she said, warning them. 'Trouble-makers get the boot. All right?' Paterson was piqued. He looked down at himself as if an item of his clothing might be missing. Verbally he assured her of their respectability. She took them up the stairs. The little Aboriginal boys followed, hauling and pushing the bags up, one at a time. The floor of the upper storey bounced as they walked on it. 'The rooms were all named for characters in Shakespeare's plays,' the woman said. 'You know Shakespeare? Wrote a lot for the theatre. Used to be in the theatre myself, once upon a time. The Romeo and Juliet Suite is my favourite room.'

Clohesy was put in the Hamlet Room. It was a bare wooden cube. The Aboriginal boy put the bag on the bed and smiled upwards. When he was given threepence he scuttled from the room like a happy lizard. Down the hallway Paterson was complaining: 'You can't put me in the Lady Macbeth Room. I hardly think that's appropriate.' 'Don't be silly,' the woman answered. 'They're all exactly the same.'

Clohesy and Paterson went down to the Falstaff Dining Hall at six o'clock. It was the advertised hour for dinner. The decor of the room owed nothing to Elizabethan elegance or exuberance. It was, like the rooms upstairs, an unlined wooden box, its proportions, though not its size, little removed from those of the simplest coffin. They were the only diners. The same woman came to take their orders.

Clohesy ordered a plate of vegetables. 'No meat?' she asked. 'Do you want gravy on the vegetables?' she asked. 'Are you feeling ill?' she asked. Then aggresively: 'You don't want *Chinese* vegetables, do you?' Clohesy said he didn't mind. 'Oh dear,' the woman said. She licked her pencil and made notes on the back of her hand. 'Just remember what I said about trouble-makers. All right?'

Paterson managed to please the proprietress by ordering spare ribs. 'Vegetables too?' she asked threateningly. Paterson declined.

Paterson's spare ribs arrived quickly, the hot grease swilling in the plate, spilling in gobbets on the table as the woman put it down. Clohesy's meal took much longer. When it did arrive it was a mass of boiled purslane.

'Only got purslane, I'm sorry,' said the woman. 'That's pigweed, you know. Still plenty of spare ribs though.' She went away.

'They probably gathered this lot in the backyard,' Clohesy said, 'or the main street. I notice it grows in the dust around here in spite of the drought. Kept most of the early explorers alive, I understand. Combats scurvy. But see how red it is. Scorched from the sun. It's supposed to be a green.'

Paterson was not impressed. 'Like some gravy on it?' He laughed. Clohesy was tempted, but declined.

Their voices echoed in the Falstaff Dining Hall. The rows of vacant tables, each draped with a white cloth, surrounded them. A light dust haze was hanging in the room. Splintery sounds of laughter came through the walls from the bar out front. The woman brought in a paraffin lamp and set it near them. Clohesy ordered a beer to finish the meal. Paterson watched him drink it down. 'Excuse me. I think I'll take a stroll,' said Clohesy. He wanted to be free of Paterson.

'I'll come too,' Paterson said.

They walked in the lampless stretch of plain the town called its main street. There was no need for lights. The stars provided more than sufficient to see by. Niall noted that they hung down from the sky as if suspended at the ends of strings. 'I've never really *seen* the stars before,' he said, his eyes swimming in the night. 'It's like a cosmic jeweller's window. All black plush and diamonds.'

Paterson was bathing in the starlight, too. He walked along with his eyes alternately open and closed for yards at a time. 'There are stars in the heart, you realise,' he said. 'Stars to guide on the troubled wastes of love.'

Niall watched him as they walked. Paterson's face, turned up to the laving starlight, took on a classic, sculptured appearance. The high polished forehead, the shadowy eye sockets, the handsome, bluff nose and generous lips, all seemed made of marble. Yet a marble that might be warm to the touch, not cold. And beneath the tilted head, the body moved with a springing step, for Paterson walked only on the balls of his feet, and the athleticism of his body was accentuated, rather than contradicted, by the slightly cramped way he held his left arm, as if it would not fully straighten. It was in the firewash of those stars, those weighty, pendulous stars, that Niall first conceived his acceptance of the idea of Paterson as a poet. 'They burn and re-burn, the stars in the heart,' said Paterson. He was in his thoughts a hundred miles away. Niall could only guess at his companion's problems.

They came back down the street and veered towards the station where Clohesy said he would use the railway W.C. 'See you back at the hotel,' he added, pointedly. But Paterson stayed with him, professing a similar need.

According to Clohesy's watch it was four minutes past nine. It was too late now to shake Paterson off. They went into the station's refreshment room together. It was crowded with shearers. They were spitting and yelling and telling loud jokes. When Clohesy and Paterson ordered drinks they realised the barman was upset by the large crowd. 'Don't usually have a mob like this. They won't let me close up. Should of closed up at eight.' He leant forward over the counter towards Clohesy and Paterson. 'All Unionists,' he confided, 'but they're behavin' themselves.'

Niall looked around. There was one drinker at the end of the bar who was not part of the general hubbub. He leant on the bar and steadily watched his own reflection in the mirrored wall in front of him. Beside his hand on the counter was a pink railway ticket. While Niall ran his eyes round the rest of the room, the lone drinker came up to Paterson and slapped him on the back. 'Hey! Aren't you The Banjo?' he said.

Paterson looked down at his drink.

'Hey, mate. I said aren't you The Banjo?'

'I think you're mistaken,' Paterson answered him.

'No, I'm not.' He grabbed Paterson's hands. 'Look at those hands. Writer's hands. Gotta be. You're The Banjo all right. Gotta be.'

Paterson was upset. He tried to wrench his hands from the drinker's grasp, without success.

'It's The Banjo for sure. It's gotta be.' He called across the room: 'Hey-whack! It's The Banjo himself. All the way from Sydney.' The news set the room astir. The men crowded over to the bar. They grabbed Paterson. They manhandled him to the centre of the room. He struggled until they forced glasses of beer into both his hands. They began to sing wildly, all at once, loud choruses from twenty different shearing songs. One of them chanted in a high-pitched, accusatory Scottish brogue: 'So you're back from up the country, Mister Townsman.' Paterson stood wide-eyed, gripping the beer glasses for support. He was in a state akin to terror.

Meanwhile the lone drinker who had started it all moved up beside Niall at the bar. In a whispered shout just loud enough to travel between them over the pandemonium, he began a rapid series of communications:

'One. Watch Withers,' he said. 'He's the Winton copper.

36

Opposition network, of course. Been sending queries re your arrival to his Brisbane HQ. We're having to intercept his telegraphs, but as you know — unreliable. Only seventy per cent loyalty in Post and Telegraph. Two. Bright's your contact in Winton. He'll say: "You could spend all day in the bath-house in this district." Got it? Three. Trades Hall doesn't like your travelling companion. He could be an agent —'

'Rubbish,' Niall broke in.

'He's a lawyer. Has squatter connections. His poetry has pastoralist sympathies.'

'It has worker sympathies, too.'

'He's not a worker. He's opposition. He will be delayed tomorrow. Don't wait for him.'

'What do you mean, "delayed"?'

'He'll miss the coach. That's all. He'll sleep in.'

'I don't want him to miss the coach. He is useful to me.'

'He's a celebrity. He attracts too much attention.'

'That's useful. I can hide in it.'

'I have my orders.'

'And I have my contract. It states that I have freedom to act independently. I don't want orders from Brisbane, just support. The Banjo is useful to me. I don't want him touched.'

'I'll relay your viewpoint. But my orders stand.'

'Bugger your orders,' said Niall. He made to move away. The man grabbed him by the shoulder.

'Four. Keep your doors and windows locked. And five. Don't write any more letters. We don't want you or your letters falling into the wrong hands. You should know that, Mr Niall.'

Clohesy pushed the drinker's arm from its drunkenly familiar embrace across his shoulders. He barged to the centre of the raucous group where Paterson still clung to the glasses of beer as if they were saving his life. 'All right,' shouted Clohesy, 'I'll take him home now.' They cleared a way for him out onto the platform. The drinkers kept cheering in the refreshment room.

'Got to get an early night,' said Paterson, walking like a drunken man. They had fixed him already. They had bent his elbows and the spiked beer had sloshed into his protesting mouth.

'You'll be right,' said Clohesy. He led him across the dusty street to the hotel through a dizzying wash of starlight.

As he climbed the stairs, Niall's thoughts were bitter. He imagined his clients sitting in Trades Hall in Brisbane. Sitting with the lights out, to save on the gas bill. Congratulating themselves on the cheapness of their contract with him. Six hundred miles away from Niall, saying, 'This is 'ow 'e'll do it.' Niall wondered where was the grandeur, generousness, delicacy, in their rock-hard fists, their dropped aitches.

In the crackling bed in the hot hotel room, Niall tossed violently. He was imagining the woman there with him, pouring her hot body onto his, massaging his limbs into fiery wings. She was building him into something tall—a tower, a spire. He rose up, a growth of ancient stones, of hot steels. He looked down from his height and he was a cathedral, a network of girders and filigree. Through him the winds streamed playing a chord like light, and in his lattice, in the singing grid of his body, the birds were nesting. He looked down from his soaring height on the trains moving along his body's network, and the armies marching, and the drovers whipping the wool-teams across the patterned geography of the plains of his body. And as he lay there, stretched as the motley skin of the earth, he saw the woman's image grow out of the wheeling stars, and she leant down from the sky and grabbed him by the lapels of his chest skin, and she turned him inside out and rolled him up in a wave and left him castaway, a soggy bundle washed on the narrow beach of the bed.

Niall had risen well before dawn. He had all but dragged Paterson from his bed and down the stairs. Now they stood close together on the hotel veranda. Their bags were beside them. There was no sign of the coach. A goat wandered along the pale darkness of the street, nosing at the darker shadows. The boards of the hotel clicked in the pre-dawn coolness. Presently they were joined by a nun in a white habit and large straw hat, and a squat man with a satchel clutched at his barrel chest. Paterson began to sing in a slurring, reeling voice:

> 'Sarah is m' darling,
> M' darling, m' darling—'

With the firm grasp he held on Paterson's upper arm, Niall gave
him a shake. The nun smiled understandingly. The squat man
ignored them pointedly.

The coach arrived out of the shadows. It drew up in front of
them. A depot clerk helped the driver load their baggage onto
the roof. There the mail baskets were already lashed securely.
The driver called down to them. They gathered themselves
together. The nun was handed up through the narrow space of
the coach door. She set the vehicle rocking on its springs. The
squat man went next, gripping his hat and his satchel. Then
Paterson struggled up. His hands and legs were almost useless.
Niall pushed him from behind and felt the heavy weight of a
body normally athletically light. He fell onto the seat and
appeared to drop immediately to sleep.

The driver checked the wheels and the chains. Then he
hauled himself to his seat. The depot clerk, the sole well-wisher,
gave a perfunctory wave. Niall smiled at Paterson. The nun
blessed them all. Then they moved off.

It was a tradition of Cobb's company that their coaches
entered and departed from towns at a breakneck gallop. The
idea was to advertise in the most populated areas the swiftness
and efficiency of the company's vehicles. This policy had caused
some spectacular accidents at the corners of main streets in the
past. It was continued nevertheless, even in the pre-dawn streets
of Longreach on this occasion when the only spectator was a
solitary roadside billygoat. Once beyond the town, the driver
calmed the horses to a practical trot. Only then was the nun able
to unclasp her hands, open her eyes, and think about reading
the tiny book lurking in the folds of her habit—a miniature
Bible. Paterson was soundly sleeping, but the others, no longer
so uncomfortably shaken, were able to appreciate the world
beyond the flapping coach blinds. That world was by now being
lit with the blue and orange of the dawn light.

His travelling companions were too considerate to begin
talking while Paterson slept. Had he snored, perhaps they
would have felt less well-disposed towards him. But he slept
gently, like an infant, and they were kind. When eventually his
eyes opened and he gave a sheepish smile the nun was the first to
speak:

'I find in this bush a certain pared-down elegance,' she said.

She had re-hidden her book in the white folds on her lap. The deserts of Jordan had given way to those of Queensland. 'Yes. The elegance of French ballerinas in a quietly bizarre ballet where all is asymmetry and minimal motion. Look at that tragic arabesque there.' She pointed past the flapping canvas curtain. A stand of scrub moved by. They all looked. The squat man with the satchel sniffed. The coach staggered in a pot-hole.

'I rather think of the bush as a too easy place in which to die,' said Clohesy. 'Just sit down under one of those mean trees and die. Nothing to it.'

'They're not mean,' said Paterson. 'They're accepting. They may be subdued by their environment, but they are not beaten. There is a twinkle in the lowered eye of the Australian bush. It's a generous environment if you know how to approach it.'

'But that's just the point,' said Clohesy. 'I don't know how. If I came to it with a problem — like hunger, or thirst, or jealousy — it wouldn't reach out to me. It would just droop there and I would droop with it.'

'If one was weak enough to do that,' said the nun, 'at least a death so tranquil would be more dignified than a city death — the ranting against time, the desperation, all invading your ears until the last moment.' She put her hands together in her lap. She was enjoying the conversation. The squat man looked at her with bulging eyes. He hugged his bulging satchel to his bulging chest. The coach blundered on.

'Those stunted trees may look as though they have died,' said Paterson, 'but of course they've not. They'll try again. There's a wonderful sense of the phoenix's spirit in the Australian bush.'

'The insane phoenix,' said Clohesy. 'It doesn't know when to give up. Such mean, sordid, crazy resurrections — those trees should just lie down and turn to dust graciously.'

The nun smiled with appreciation. Few people spoke their minds honestly with her. She had not for years so enjoyed a conversation she had started. The squat man opened his satchel and pulled out a bag of mustard sandwiches. He held one at his mouth with an oddly elegant manoeuvre. The movement of his jaws on the sandwich seemed to stimulate his vocal chords. As he spoke, little crumbs fell onto his chest and elsewhere.

'While you've been admiring the scenery,' he said, 'I've been counting the number of swagmen on the road.' He stopped. No one spoke. He continued: '"How many?" you ask. Three al-

40

ready. They're putting a few miles behind them before it really stokes up.' Everybody waited while he took three good bites to fill his mouth. Then he went on: 'And the fact of the matter is that the first swagman we passed was a dentist, the second was an insurance and real estate agent, and the third has a degree in English Literature. Now what do you reckon, eh?'

The others in the coach were surprised, not so much by the information as by its source. The squat man — with his trickle of grey hair from under his felt hat, with his rat's nose and whiskers, with his tendency to have his short arms always clutched round himself — had seemed to the others to be more in the nature of a travelling household pet than a fully capable human being. His physique seemed to disqualify him from the bush. His dependence on his satchel, from which they had already seen him extract and replace a newspaper, a pair of gloves, several bottles of pills, and the bag of sandwiches, seemed to suggest that his survival capability was entirely ruled by the satchel's contents. For them to find that he had any mental or physical existence beyond the confines of the satchel was a surprise. The nun, herself a surprising survivor, became immediately interested in him. She asked him his name. It was Wanless, he said. Then she asked him his occupation. He was the timekeeper on a property outside Winton. He took another stacked mouthful of sandwich.

'I know these characters,' he said, 'because they've all been given work on Gloucestershire Downs. It's a policy of the place. Any swagman walks on gets three days' work. No matter how hard the times. It's not charity — they get tough going. They can't shear for peanuts, usually, so they get ring-barking. Ring-barking in the desert it is these droughty days. But it's food and money for those men. The owner wouldn't have it any other way.' He had finished his sandwiches and his conversation seemed to be over.

'What pay does your excellent employer provide these men for their three days' work?' asked Clohesy.

The squat man cleared his throat — and in the process re-gurgitated a little of his last mouthful — just enough to say: 'One and threepence. Plus tucker and shelter. Very generous in these hard times.' Niall was not greatly impressed. A good worker should earn a pound a day. 'That's anyone who walks onto the place, you understand,' added the squat man, who had discovered a morsel between two of his teeth.

The coach stopped for a change of horses at a staging point serviced by a large property. The driver suggested the passengers stretch their legs. They had been excessively cramped by the ridiculous smallness of the coach interior. While the horses were being attended to, the driver led the passengers on a brief tour of the gully in which they had stopped. It included an area of smooth rock with indentations which the driver said were the footprints of prehistoric monsters. It also included a small heap of sticks which he said was a bowerbird's nest. But he was most keen to show them a system of two cleared circles, the size of cricket fields, joined by a path, which he said were Aboriginal bora-grounds. The passengers were fascinated, except for the squat man who belched impatiently. 'Hadn't we better be getting back to the coach,' he suggested. They all turned at the urgency in his voice. He led the way back amongst the gully's straggling scrub roots. His squat, shuffling agitation caused them all to realise how well-hidden the bird's bower was, how long-dead the dinosaurs were, how over-dressed and vulnerable they themselves were. They sank and flapped, up to their ankles in the gully's blistering sand.

Back in the coach the squat man whispered in Clohesy's ear: 'Love will do strange things to a man. What do you reckon? I'll wager our driver's got a gin back home. See his eyes light up in that Myall clearing back there? We're lucky we didn't get a spear through each of us. And him pleased as Punch to show the place off.'

Farther along, on a scrubby section of plain, the driver made another stop, to show the passengers a dead sheep lying on the road. They pushed back the canvas curtains. They leant out for a better view. The sheep's body was mauled and maggoty. Its eyes had been pecked out by crows.

'Wonderful dogs, in their proper place,' Paterson said. He squinted down at the torn flesh.

'Dingoes?' said Clohesy.

'You'd think so, wouldn't you?' replied the squat man, chewing on a ragged coolibah leaf, yet another satchel-surprise. 'But look at the slicing there, and behind the shoulder. That's the cut of a knife. Dingoes don't use knives. At least round here they don't.' His eyesight was remarkable. Of all the passengers he was the one with the worst view, the only one not craning forward keenly. 'This is the work of a human, I reckon. Probably one of those swagmen we saw back there. They rip the carcass up a bit to make it look like a dingo job. But you can tell the difference. Some bludging swagman did this. What do you reckon, eh?'

'Poor, poor man,' said the nun. 'His hunger must have been extreme.'

'Not hungry enough,' the squat man insisted. He spat arrogantly out the other side of the coach. 'Look at the size of the portion taken. Just a couple of days' meat. He'll kill another one further down the road rather than carry a bit more weight. Sheer bludging laziness. What do you reckon, eh?'

They peered on at the carcass in silence. They were like an impromptu funeral party. The dead sheep seemed vaguely related to each of them, some old friend of the family perhaps. The plains wind, hot and steady, shuffled the lank grey leaves of the battling gidgee scrub by the road. To fill the silence, the nun spoke: 'We find the sheep like this today. We'll find the swagman like this tomorrow.'

The driver cracked his whip. The passengers resettled themselves on the thin cushions. They arranged their knees to avoid touching. They secured the canvas curtains against the hot wind. The coach lurched on. Its wheels shirred through the sand and dust-drifts, then whined on the polished clay.

What is the time?

What is the time? By my own watch, which I wear pinned above my left breast (the face is surrounded by an exquisite diamond setting; it hangs by a little white-gold chain from a clasp fashioned as a peacock-shaped brooch) the time shown is three minutes past twelve. I know that is probably incorrect.

I have never been able to wear a watch on my wrists. The electricity in my body plays havoc with the mechanism. Even my breast-watch suffers slightly.

If I turn on the radio and wait . . . there! The announcer says it is three minutes to one. But if I turn the dial a little . . . what is it? . . . eleven fifty-eight and a half. My goodness!

And if I look through the binoculars (which will show me the suntanned nipples of the girls on Main Beach; no breast-watches there) I may read the digital clock atop the Perpetual

43

Life Building. . . let me see. . . 11.59. . . no, it's changed: 12.00.

Farther down the coast, I can see Coolangatta Beach. Just behind it, in the main street of Twin Towns shopping centre, it is midday for the cars travelling eastward, and 1 p.m. for those moving westward. The pedestrians crossing the street's centre line don't bother to adjust their watches. Though, strictly speaking, they should, stepping as they do over the border from one state to another.

So, what is the time? It hardly seems to matter.

When I took the bus to the John Oxley Library it left Surfers a minute and a half early, according to my watch. Naturally I had made allowances, leaving the unit in good time.

But those dreadful microfilm readers! I had expected to enjoy a pleasant day with the fragile crackle of old newspapers in my hands.

Instead I had the devil of a time pressing buttons, twirling knobs, and peering into an obscurely lit screen. What a disappointment it was! And what a crashing ache in the temples and the back of the neck I developed before the whole unnatural experience was over.

Luckily, the library staff took pity on me. They got the horrible machine to take a picture of what I wanted. Just a single column from an old newspaper. And here it is, not on gracefully ageing newsprint browning and gently wrinkling at the edges, but on a greasy photographic paper that issued from a slot in the machine like an overgrown sheet of disposable restroom towel.

(Footnote: *I believe the academics would write '[sic]' after several of the words printed here: e.g. poor Hoffmeister's name, which the paper spelt wrongly.*)

THE SHEARING DISPUTE

ANOTHER WOOLSHED BURNED

ATTACK BY ARMED MEN

A SHARP ENGAGEMENT

FORTY SHOTS FIRED

ESCAPE OF THE INCENDIARIES

A UNIONIST FOUND DEAD

ACTION OF THE GOVERNMENT

Affairs in the west have taken a serious turn — so serious in fact to justify the statement recently made in the House by the Colonial Secretary that the strike had developed into an insurrection. At about 8 o'clock on Sunday night Mr Tozer received a wire from the Police Magistrate at Winton stating that Dagworth shed had been burnt down by about sixteen armed men. Forty shots were fired. One constable was present at the time, as well as the three brothers Macpherson (owners) and three station hands.

Later information was received by Mr Tozer at 9.30 the same night giving some details of the affair. This wire stated that at about 12.30 a.m. on Sunday the constable and a station hand named Tomlin were on duty guarding the shed. The first intimation they had of any attack was about a dozen shots fired through the shed. This awoke the Macphersons and the others. The firing then continued, both sides engaging in it for about twenty minutes. While this was going on one of the unionists sneaked up under cover of the fire of his comrades and set fire to the shed. The constable and the station hands kept firing at the party, and when this ceased it was not known whether anyone was wounded. About forty shots were exchanged. Three bullets were fired through the cottage where the Macphersons were sleeping.

The unionists had taken up a position in the bed of a creek at the rear of the shed, and were almost wholly protected from the fire of the defending party.

Rain fell again shortly after the men left. It was raining, too, from the time the shed was fired until 2 p.m., but when the wire was sent the weather was fine.

Scarcely any doubt is entertained that this was the same gang who have burned the other sheds.

Information has been received at Winton that a man named Haffmeister, a prominent unionist, was found dead about two miles from Kynuna. The local impression is that he was one of the attacking mob at Dagworth and was wounded there. There were seven unionists with Haffmeister when he died. These assert that he committed suicide.

In consequence of the seriousness of this last event the Government are taking active steps to deal with persons found armed.

Every effort is being made to trace the insurrectionists by the police in the district. We understand that instructions have been given the troopers not to separate, and that the seven men who were with Haffmeister when he died have been detained pending enquiries.

[Dagworth Station is about seventy miles north-west from Winton, on the Upper Diamantina and adjoins Ayrshire Downs, where the woolshed was burnt down some time ago. Dagworth has about 80,000 sheep, and the shed which has been destroyed had stands for forty shearers. Shearing was to have commenced at the station on the 14th August, but was delayed owing to the strike. The station is owned by the Messrs. Macpherson Bros.]

BURNING OF DAGWORTH WOOLSHED

[BY ELECTRIC TELEGRAPH]

(FROM OUR OWN CORRESPONDENT)

AYRSHIRE DOWNS, September 3.
At about 12.30 a.m. yesterday (Sunday) the Dagworth woolshed was burnt by armed men, in spite of the efforts of Mr Macpherson, the station hands, and one constable, who were present. About forty shots were exchanged and one of the gang set fire to the shed under cover of the firing. The night was very dark, and it is not known whether any of the shots took effect.

A unionist is reported by his mates to have committed suicide about midday on Sunday with a revolver in a camp about twelve miles from the scene of the outrage.

WINTON, September 3.
A gang of men set fire to one end of the Dagworth woolshed on Saturday night, at the same time firing a volley into the shed. The fire was returned by the station hands camped at the shed.

A man was found dead at the union camp, twenty-five miles from Dagworth, yesterday, death having been caused by a bullet wound. The unionists stated that he committed suicide. The Police Magistrate and a doctor have gone to Kynuna to investigate the matter and Inspector Dillon and the police have also gone out. Mr R. Macpherson and others are endeavouring to track the men. The shed was only partially burnt.

— *The Brisbane Courier,* Tuesday, September 4, 1894, page 5.

CHAPTER

3

Inspector Clohesy sat at a small round table on the balcony of the North Gregory Hotel. The table was made of cane. So was the chair he sat in. He was breakfasting alone, with a view of the town.

In Vindex Street, the Rowley household was still quiet. The maid tip-trod round the kitchen, her big flat feet whispering on the wooden floor. She stirred the porridge conscientiously.

At the eastern end of Elderslie Street, beyond the post and telegraph office, a youth made gun-shot sounds with a stock-whip outside the Miners' Rest Bath House. The proprietor stood in the doorway watching the youth, concocting ways to get rid of him.

A maid brought Clohesy's breakfast on a tray. It was a bowl of hot salty porridge with a lump of butter melting on top. He asked about fruit. She said there was none.

In the police station Sub-Inspector Withers ground away at the telephone handle as if he were mincing meat. Still he couldn't raise anyone. 'Working? Working?' he shouted into the mouthpiece.

The clerk at Corfield and Fitzmaurice's sat on his raised platform in the middle of the store. He opened the book in front of him. He heard one of the overhead wires creaking and made a note on his blotter. It was the third time this week that the first business of the morning was coming in from the haberdashery department. It was the Christmas rush beginning, he decided. The little cannister approached him on the wire. When it arrived he unplugged it and took out the docket. Then he wrote

47

the first figures at the top of the column on the new day's fresh page.

Clohesy decided that the porridge was not too salty. From time to time he looked up from the bowl across the grid of streets of the town. Pimples on the skin of the plain, he thought, surveying the town's buildings.

Sarah Rowley sat up in bed and immediately put her spectacles to her nose, as she did every morning. She took her diary from the side table and recorded her dreams. Then she added a note to the effect that she would give Bartie another chance.

The day's work began for the Aboriginal boy who swatted the flies from Jacob Horan's meat. The carcasses were already hanging in the shade in front of Horan's butchery. The boy had armed himself with a long-leafed coolibah switch. He swiped at the first fly and it turned into two. He swiped at the two and they became four.

At the southern end of Oondooroo Street a bandy-legged drover had his team hitched up. He looked at the sag of his dray under fifty bales of wool. He looked at the ribs of some of his twenty-three horses. He looked at the six bags of flour on top of the wool. Riding gently, smothered in the flour, were six packs of dynamite to be delivered at the diggings along the way. He took off his hat and wiped his sweating old head. He had done everything except kiss his wife. She waited under the bull-nosed roof of the cottage veranda. She waited for his tobaccoey kiss.

At the bore site beyond the eastern end of the town the engineer sat in his corrugated-iron shed. He looked at his watch. It was never too early to get a start on, he thought. He opened the draw of the filing cabinet and took out a bottle. He uncorked it and poured himself a drink. It won't be long now, he said to himself. He listened for the hiss of the engine turning the drill.

A patient was wheeled onto the veranda of the hospital. He had one of his legs swaddled with bandages. He had cuts on his face and bruised ribs. The horse had come back after throwing him, and given him a stamp on the stomach for good measure, the blighter.

The maid smiled at Inspector Clohesy. He had eaten every skerrick of his porridge. She took the bowl away. He poured himself a cup of tea and watched the hawks wheeling above the town. They were a constant feature, hanging and sliding on the plains wind. Sometimes they came close to the ground, hovering at roof height, jerking and flinching to keep balance on the wind. They trained their eyes manically on the ground, but Clohesy did not see them dive to catch anything.

Behind the barbed-wire and the warning signs and the pad-way where the guard dogs ran, Gum Wah tended the vegetable garden. He and his sons had planted it in a dry channel of the river beyond the town. He tipped the watering-can so that a silver trickle ran along the new green line of radishes and carrots. The water sank rapidly into the earth. He went along the line again. Behind him the Chinese cabbages were doing well, and the bitter-melon vines had reached the tops of their poles.

Old Major Jarvis, PM, half woke in his bed and yelled 'Heremai lasi' twice into the stale air of his mosquito-net before he realised that (*a*) he was no longer in British New Guinea; (*b*) it had not been raining for the past four months; and (*c*) the Aboriginal servant who stood in front of him bearing his morning porridge was the Rowleys' housemaid, not Bamahuta, the village woman whose body had given him merry hell during the rainy seasons.

Clohesy scanned the gidgee scrub to the south, well beyond the lattice of the town streets. He searched for evidence of the shearers' strike camp. There was none. No sign of movement, no smoke or dust. Perhaps the wind was too strong. He looked back at the town. He looked at its wide bare streets, its torn trees struggling in their protective palisades. He looked at the buildings — new, gawky, angular. No gardens. Nothing to soften the bald facts of civilisation. Yet the town was not so much an imposition on the landscape as an irrelevance to it. Huge sky, huge plain, and the mosquito bite of a town rising. Dogs sprawled in the wide streets, an Aboriginal pranced on bare feet from a shop, a policeman sauntered towards the post and telegraph office, growing smaller in the wideness of the street. Whatever litter the wind could lift it tumbled amongst the buildings. The hawks wheeled, watchful and slow. The policeman came back along the middle of the street.

'No need to be nervous,' said Clohesy. 'This is purely routine.'

'I'm not nervous,' said Withers. Clohesy slid back the drawer of the filing cabinet. It did not run truly. There was a crack across the face of the drawer where the wood had been split by the heat. 'There's no reason for me to be nervous,' said Withers.

'Of course not.' Clohesy pulled out another drawer. He riffled through folders of paper. 'What's this?' he asked.

'Don't blame me. Brisbane wouldn't send the forms. I had to make my own.' Sub-Inspector Withers was not a patient man by nature, only by profession. He had long ago learnt that time itself was the best policeman, the best revealer and judge of the facts. But occasionally Withers's orders were to speed up the process. When commands allowed it, he gladly indulged his impetuosity. His favourite piece of departmental-issue equipment was the sabre, wrongly interpreted by many of his fellow officers as a purely ceremonial weapon. He delighted in baring it in public. But he was just as fond of it inside its scabbard where it was a secret and a threat, with an edge as sharp as the whetstones of fear and imagination could fashion.

Clohesy slid the drawer shut. 'Where are the reports on the shearers' strikes?'

'Under "S"...for scum.'

Clohesy opened the relevant drawer. He hauled out the fattest file. He laid it on a desk and went through it, paper by paper. Withers sat on the railing of one of the balustrades partitioning the office. His arms were crossed on his chest, his legs outstretched. He rocked back and forth, watching Clohesy from behind.

'I have an old friend at Headquarters,' said Withers. 'We were at Charters Towers together. Name of Armbuster. Rupert Armbuster. I think he's got his staff promotion now. You know him?'

Clohesy continued to inspect the file. 'What branch?' he asked. He could feel the wideness of his back towards Withers.

'With the Water Squad last I heard.'

Clohesy turned a page and kept reading. 'Never heard of him,' he said.

'You must have. Great reputation.'

'No such person so far as I can recall.'

Withers kept rocking. 'Must have left the force.'

'Must have.' Clohesy closed the file. 'Anything on the District Committee?'

'Only what's there. We don't keep a separate report. There's

50

the Special Commissioners' file, of course.'

Withers's office work only rarely came under scrutiny from Headquarters. On those occasions when Brisbane deemed it necessary to send a bureaucratic superior, Withers was invariably amused at the horror of the city theorists confronted with outback practices. All Withers's postings had been in the bush, and it was as a bush officer that he excelled. He considered it a minor personal challenge to send each city inspector back to Headquarters slightly better educated and somewhat humbled. He left the business of flattery and ingratiation to old Jarvis, the Magistrate.

Clohesy returned the papers to their drawer. 'Where's the equipment room?' he asked. Withers led him out the back and across the yard where the Aboriginal troop was drawn up in a crumpled parade. 'Tin...John!' yelled the Sergeant. The parade snapped upright.

'They look good,' said Clohesy. 'A credit.'

'Very kind of you,' said Withers. He unlocked the door of a shed. They went in. Spears of light came through the nail-holes in the corrugated iron. It was already as hot as a furnace inside the shed. Clohesy peered amongst the clutter of equipment.

'You've got a boat?'

'Up the back there. Haven't used it since the last flood. No call. Not much water around since then.'

'Condition?'

'Not the best.'

'Have it fixed, will you?'

Outside, the troop continued to stand fiercely at attention. The sun buzzed around them in the yard. One of the troop was a small Aboriginal boy wearing nothing but a cap. It kept falling down over his eyes. He kept pushing it back. The two men came out of the shed and walked along the line. 'The mascot,' said Withers, crushing the cap hard onto the boy's head.

'Will you have it ready by tomorrow?' asked Clohesy.

'If you like.'

'And don't forget the oars.'

After Clohesy had stepped out of the police station into the street, Withers took up the phone. He gave the handle a hesitant twirl. 'Goonda,' he said, and waited. A voice came at the other

51

end. 'He wants the boat,' said Withers. 'Wants to go rowing in the desert.'

'What is happening in Sydney?' asked Mrs Rowley.

'I don't think Bartie wants to talk about Sydney,' said Sarah. 'That's what he's come here for. To get away from Sydney.'

Mrs Rowley took up a teacup and pecked at it. She was being charming. 'Nobody who comes here from Sydney has any right to refuse to speak about it. I insist, Bartie. I have the argument of distance on my side.'

'Sydney is lively as ever,' said Paterson. 'They are digging a tunnel for a very large sewer pipe.'

'That's not the kind of news one wishes to hear,' said Mrs Rowley, tickled.

'Oh, but this is an engineering masterpiece. All the way from Martin Place to the sea.'

'To Bondi Beach,' said Sarah. 'Isn't it a shame?'

'It's natural,' said Mrs Rowley. 'What else is the sea good for? I certainly don't like looking at it. It's all muscles.'

'Mussels?' asked Sarah.

'Yes, muscles. As in bodies, my dear. Don't you find all those rolling waves terribly muscular, Bartie?'

'They are these days,' said Paterson. 'People are swimming amongst them, you know.'

'Oh, Lord,' said Mrs Rowley. 'Whatever for?'

'For pleasure, I suspect,' said Paterson.

'And what do they wear for such doubtful pleasure, I wonder?'

'There's a special costume. All arms and legs sticking out.'

'Oh, Lord.'

'Some of the bathing's not segregated.'

'Oh, Lord,' said Mrs Rowley. She swept air to her bosom with a Japanese fan. 'What will they be doing next?'

'Do you really want to know?'

'I think we need more tea.' Mrs Rowley was swimming delightedly in the conversation. She found city talk so clever and dangerous. And whenever she wished she could retire from the tingling pleasure of this particular conversation to sit and bask in the knowledge that she had performed a coup. Bartie wasn't just her sister-in-law's fiancé, nor just a visitor all the way from civilisation. He was a celebrity. He was a live piece of what was really happening in the real world.

Paterson lay back on the cane chaise longue. He held out his cup in front of him for the Aboriginal maid to refill. 'I love this house,' he said. 'So safe. So calm.'

'I hope you don't mind some arrangements we've made for you,' said Sarah.

'If they include sleeping and sleeping, I'll not complain.'

'They include riding, in fact.'

'Just for you, my dear,' he said, 'I'll drag myself into a saddle. But only as a very special personal favour, you understand.'

'We thought you might,' said Sarah.

The maid stood over Paterson to pour cream into his cup. He wriggled with delight, causing a slop of the cream to land on his trouser-fronts. He laughed. The maid was aghast. He saw the spectacular blues in the skin of her face, like opal surprised in a dark rock.

'My fault, my fault,' said Paterson, juggling his cup and saucer. The maid rushed out for a cloth. 'Don't worry. I have a handkerchief here.' Mrs Rowley bustled to his assistance. 'No, no. It's quite all right,' he said.

'She's normally so good,' said Mrs Rowley. 'Far more reliable than a white girl.'

'You did that on purpose, Bartie,' said Sarah. 'You moved your cup.'

'No, I didn't,' he said.

'You know I don't like it when you are perverse.'

'I wasn't being perverse,' he protested, 'just happy.'

Clohesy walked towards the Miners' Rest Bath House. Overhead the hawks kept wheeling. He supposed he would get used to them after a while. No one else seemed to notice their constant gliding and dipping. He half closed his eyes against the glare. Already, after a single morning in the place, they were sore, his eyes.

He walked on. Elderslie Street was busy now, mainly with men, but it was not the kind of crowd a stranger could become anonymous in. They all seemed to know each other, but they did not know Clohesy. The itinerants — the pastoral workers, the carriers, the miners from the nearby opal fields — lounged in every spot of shade and leant at every available post. The busier individuals were the town workers and the men on errands from the properties. Elastic-sided boots, cabbage-tree hats and coloured silk scarves were the fashion. Spitting in the dust was the custom. Waiting for the six pubs to open was the occupation.

Clohesy walked on, reading the signs: Winton Steam Aerated Water Works; Wolfgang Reitz — Practical Shoemaker; Nigel ('Bob') Mills, Blacksmith; Queensland National Bank; Commercial Hotel — Good Paddocks — Airy Horse-boxes — Every attention paid to Racehorses — Bathrooms up-to-date; C. Phillips — Tailors of Distinction; Reliable Tank-Sinking Co.; Yee Hap Bakery; Thring's Horse Bazaar. Clohesy walked on, treading the spaces in a motley carpet of dusty, flattened horse-shit.

After casually looking in at the Union Office, which seemed to be closed, he walked on to the bath-house. He stood outside it, turning the possibilities over in his mind. The Chinese proprietor sat at a cane table inside the doorway. 'You wouldn't expect so, but it is clean,' came a voice at Clohesy's shoulder.

'I'm not sure I need a bath yet,' said Clohesy quickly.

'Of course you do,' was the reply. 'You could spend all day in the bath-house in this climate — '

'In this what?'

'In this district.'

That was it. Word perfect. The melodramatic rituals of undercover work amused Niall. He followed Bright's narrow back through the bath-house door. The Chinaman stood up to greet them. He introduced himself: 'Arthur Young, at your service, gentlemen.'

'Arthur Young, be buggered,' said Bright. 'Your bloody name's Ah Foo Yong, so why don't you use it.' It was all part of the act, Niall hoped. 'We'll have the usual and we won't let you overcharge us.' The proprietor apologised profusely. There was no vacant tub at this very moment. Would they mind returning in half an hour? 'We'll have it now,' said Bright. He leant down to the shorter man's height, splaying his big hands over the Chinese characters on the papers on the cane table. 'We'll have it right now,' said Bright, shaking the shovel-shape of his full beard in the Chinese face. The proprietor was distraught. He moved against his will to the shelves where the neat rows of folded towels lay. He handed them each a prepared pile made up of a towel, a flannel washer, and a tiny cake of sandalwood soap shaped like a peach seed. To Clohesy's he added a moustache holder. 'Don't I get one of them?' said Bright. The proprietor gave him one. They turned and pushed through the calico curtain into the steaming, dark interior.

Niall had to remove the instantly fogged spectacles immediately upon entering. Once his eyes had adjusted to the dimness, he had the impression that he was inside one of the ghoulish fun-houses of an amusement park. Strangely animated faces and ghostly pale bodies emerged and retreated in the welters of moving steam. High-pitched laughter spilled from toothless mouths, gargoyle-like heads exchanged spouts of water. Sounds were distorted: those close at hand were inordinately loud; those a little farther away were muffled, seemingly distant. A Chinese attendant came and went in the dimness, carrying a bucket of bubbling grey water.

The steamy heat wrapped Niall's body and pressed at his eyeballs as he hung his clothes on one of the rusty nails provided. Bright was beside him, throwing his clothes down in a pile on the form along the wall. 'Hang on to your soap,' advised Bright. 'Once your soap's down, it's gone.' With his clothes off, Bright had become a milk-white spectre, sun-blackened at the extremities. There were three distinct lines, one each on his forearms and neck, beyond which the fierce suntanning gave way to virgin paleness. Bright looked as though he had been caught up by the feet and had his arms and head dangled in a pot of dye. When he moved off into the dimness, out of which the paleness of his body glowed, he seemed to be a headless, handless wraith, the victim of some terrible, infidel execution. Niall tied the loops of the moustache holder behind his ears. Then he moved after Bright into the swirling steam. He stepped off the wood-slat floor of the dressing area as if off the edge of the world itself. He navigated amongst bodies and tubs. He gripped the peach-seed of soap firmly in his hand. He stumbled on the unevenness of the river-rock floor. There was the glow of a furnace far off in one corner. The smell of embers mixed with the steam. He found Bright standing in a large round tub soaping himself. The water was up to his knees.

They stood in the tub together. Bright's beard was Santa-

55

Claus thick with soap froth. He leant it close to Niall and whispered: 'He's one of the opposition, the proprietor. This place is a link in their network. Very clever.' Niall wiped the moisture from his stinging eyes with the back of his hand. 'It's a useful ritual,' Bright continued, 'this washing business. It draws all the outlying areas of activity together at this one place, anonymously. It beats the pubs for secrecy. I'm quite envious about it. It's unassailable.'

'Do you keep a spy in here?'

'We've given up on that. What's the use? Things can even happen underwater. We couldn't beat it so we joined it. We use it ourselves now. Side by side the battle plans pass on. Very ironic and annoying.'

A missile hit Niall in the middle of the back. It was one of the seed-shaped soap cakes. There was a rumpus somewhere in the steam-clouds, a jocular fight. 'Good place for a murder,' he said.

'I bet they know it,' Bright answered. 'Luckily there's been no more than a bit of Chinese torture here. But the place has its possibilities, undoubtedly.' Bright sank down into the tub. The soapy water foamed over the edges and ran to the gutter by the wall. Niall sat in the tub, too. He dipped his head under. The hot water filled his nostrils and ears. The attendant loomed from the mist to pour a bucket of scalding water into the tub with them. 'It's quite a luxury, isn't it?' said Bright. 'Water is a shilling a bucket these days. But you know the Chinese. It's the same water going round and round. With the impurities boiled off in between, I suppose.'

Bright wrung out his long beard. It turned from a Santa-Claus snowiness to Oriental rat-tails. He peered amongst the swirling vapours. 'Bowditch's man,' he whispered. 'Looks like they've got a drop on.'

Niall peered round. 'Where?' he asked.

'Shhh. Nowhere. I can hear his voice.'

Niall listened, too. All he heard was a chaos of water-wash and soap-squelch and the demonic jocularity of the unseen crowd.

'There,' said Bright.

Niall caught a glimpse of a be-capped monkey's scamper through a steam-cloud.

'That's Withers's boy,' said Bright.

Niall erupted in a turmoil of waves from the tub. He was out and dashing for the exit in pursuit of the boy, slipping on the wet stone floor and glancing off soap-shiny, protesting bodies.

'Hey!' shouted Bright. 'Your clothes!'

But Niall was crouched and running. His hands were at the ready to deal with the mistakes of his slippery feet. His neck was thrust forward and his thighs strained. He almost reproduced the pursuit gait of the hunting-dog.

The Chinese proprietor stood in front of the swinging calico curtain. He took a stinging grip on Niall's arm, throwing him off balance into a sprawling heap in the doorway. 'You must complete your dress before entering the street, sir,' the proprietor said. He looked down Niall's nakedness. Niall's hand went up to the moustache. It was still there, held firmly by the cotton holder. A fully clothed man wearing a felt hat and a large grin pushed past them. He stepped over Niall's naked legs. 'Please, sir,' repeated the proprietor, wringing Niall's wrist, 'you must complete your dress.'

Niall went back to his clothes. Bright was there, one leg in his trousers. Bright was far from impressed with Niall's performance. 'Take it easy,' he said. 'You'll give the game away.'

Niall was furious both with himself and with the situation. 'Right under our noses,' he said.

'And where else?' countered Bright. 'You're in the middle of it now, Niall.'

Niall did not reply. He held Clohesy's pants in front of him.

'Breaking one strand won't bring down the web,' said Bright. He laughed. 'You would have been a treat, Inspector Clohesy, chasing that young monkey down Elderslie Street with all your knobs swinging.'

Niall replaced Clohesy's clothes with annoyance. He pulled the belt severely tight. The trousers were clammy. They stuck to his legs. Bright was already dressed. He shoved his hat over his wet hair. 'I'm going,' he said. He gave Niall a reassuring pat on the shoulder. 'Come out to the strike camp some time,' he said. 'We can show you a thing or two there as well.' Then he made his way to the exit.

Clohesy's clothes were drooping with the bath-house moisture. He had to work on them, primping and flattening them until they sat well. He commandeered the foggy mirror that hung from one of the nails along the wall. He gave it several unsuccessful wipes with his handkerchief. Insects had nibbled away much of the mirror's silver backing. The best reflection Clohesy could get was a speckled, moist image. He flattened his hair back and removed the moustache holder. The moustache appeared lop-sided, so he straightened it with his comb. He was not pleased with himself. He would have to sharpen himself up.

Clohesy paid the proprietor at the table by the entrance. 'Your friend forgot to pay,' the proprietor said, picking at his teeth with a toothpick.

'He's no friend of mine,' Clohesy said.

'I'm sorry to say he has a habit of refusing to pay his debts here.'

'I suggest you get the police onto him then.'

'That's a good idea,' said the proprietor, shaking the toothpick for emphasis.

'I am still a Special Commissioner of the Peace,' said Rowley, shaking clouds of pepper over his plate. 'The district is still proclaimed by an Act of Parliament as being "disturbed".' The Act of Parliament spiced Rowley's midday meal as much as did the pepper.

'Disturbed, all right,' said old Jarvis. He was the Police Magistrate and the Rowleys' lodger. 'I see the signs of chaos pass before me each day. Men who think they have power because they in fact have the cowardice sufficient to ignore the law.'

'But the strikes are over, are they not?' said Sarah.

'The fact that the full-scale operations are squashed doesn't mean the underground connections are severed.' Jarvis, PM, made the point with several sweeping arcs of his white-bearded chin. In spite of his aggressive manner of oratory, his speech was often unclear owing to his tendency to push his whiskers out of his mouth with thumb and forefinger while speaking. 'We've lanced the boil, so to speak, but we've not eliminated the germ. Most of the matters in the courts now are simply mopping up the dregs. We got some of the real leaders, and they've been made examples of. But there's much of the hard core still at large.'

'I've heard that the hard core is going into Parliament,' said Sarah. Her knowledge of the events was, like her knowledge of most things, considerable.

58

'Fat lot of good that'll do them,' said Jarvis. 'They tried to start a war here. Couldn't even do that successfully. They'll have no chance in politics, let alone in government. They'll have to get elected first, won't they, eh?' Rowley and Jarvis exchanged knowing, muddy-eyed glances.

'I have always considered it gravely unfair,' said Sarah, feeling that her spectacles might begin to mist up soon, 'that the shearers and other bush workers don't have the right to vote.'

'They have the right to vote,' said Rowley. 'The same right everyone else has.'

'But they cannot meet the requirements of the law,' Sarah said. 'It discriminates against them. The fact that the law requires a person's permanent residence in one place for six months before he can vote means that all itinerant pastoral workers are discriminated against.'

'The law discriminates,' stated Jarvis, PM, 'only against those who deserve it. That's what law is, my dear . . . the instrument of necessary discrimination. Society has the law so that it can discriminate against felons and conspirators. Discrimination is the major means of survival. We discriminate against poisonous fruits, for example. They will kill us if we eat them. I hear no complaints against that matter of discrimination.'

'Why discriminate against shearers, then?'

'My dear, you are talking about opening the floodgates. You'll have every kanaka and Chinaman and vagrant wandering the country with the right to elect a voice in government. Where will that leave us? It's hardly what we mean by civilisation.'

Sarah had laid her knife and fork down. The piece of corned beef in her mouth was taking an inordinately long time to get to the point of being swallowable. Paterson and her sister-in-law watched her struggle. Jarvis and Rowley munched on, their jaws creaking confidently.

'I agree,' said Sarah at last, 'that the type of man involved in the recent strikes was not society's most admirable individual. I was horrified by the burning and the raiding and the shooting. I was shocked that men could so willingly injure and destroy their own country, and could so cruelly treat their fellow men. And animals, too. That business of the strikers tying firebrands to kangaroos' tails and sending them jumping across pastoral lands to set the grass alight was the ultimate in cruelty. So if these are the effects, the causes must be equally inhuman. I believe I can understand a man's sense of dispossession when he sees himself sweating on his country's land while having no say in how it is governed. He feels like an animal, so he acts like one.'

Old Jarvis gave the red ring of his mouth a vigorous swipe with his serviette and sniffed like a bloodhound. 'My dear, my dear! Your thesis is perfectly sound for rational beings such as ourselves, but it has no application to the lower orders of mankind. Now, take the Papuans, for example. When I was Resident Magistrate at Kikori, that's deep in the Gulf of Papua, I made every endeavour to cater to the material and emotional welfare of my villagers. I was bringing them peace, health and some knowledge of themselves as a part of the whole system of things. What did I get in return? The habit of sleeping in full dress — boots and all, mind you — with a gun under my pillow. Now, what was true of the Papuan is true of the nomadic class of white man around her. His mentality obeys no laws of cause and effect. Treat him well and he treats you with disdain. Treat him harshly and he resents it. Ignore him and he undermines you. Call him an equal and he wants to be the master. If we turn our back on him he is too much a coward to miss the opportunity. We simply have to meet him face on and put him down. To teach him the lesson. And keep putting him down until he gets up, once and for all, sharing the knowledge that we have. No country can progress while simply restraining wildness and ignorance. We must not pen it up, we must eradicate it.' The old Police Magistrate sat back, not at all exhausted by the vigorousness of his speech.

'There will be dessert,' said Mrs Rowley, noticing that Jarvis had rolled up his serviette and replaced it in its ring while talking.

'Excellent,' said Jarvis. 'The corned leg was an unexpected delight.'

'What about you, Bartie?' said Rowley. 'Give us the Sydney lawyer's view of the disturbances.'

Paterson was cautious. He had noted Sarah's passion. He worked at choosing his words. 'I am never shocked by law-breaking,' he said. 'It seems to be a natural human occupation. Certainly a solicitor is pleased, from his career's point of view, that law-breakers continue to operate and be successful.

At the same time, I am an admirer of vitality and humour in human activities, and it is an observation not solely my own that many of the most vital and humorous enterprises are undertaken on the wrong side of the law. I don't wish to glamorise the criminal, but he does often have a jolly good time. Sometimes I think it's a better time than I have sitting rooted to a heavy desk in a law office patching up the messes he makes.'

'Ah, yes,' said Jarvis. 'I've felt that way myself. It's youth speaking. Pity we can't live our lives backwards, establish ourselves in our quieter years and retire in our primes. But it's the way of things. You're over the worst of it by now, even if you can't see so yourself, young sir. Wait until you're settled down and that old desk has retreated into context instead of looming large and foreign. You'll be in the saddle more often than behind the desk, I'll wager. There's a great legal future in Sydney.'

Paterson was restrained. He looked down at his empty plate. 'I shall have to be patient, then,' he said.

'Mr Immediacy,' muttered Sarah, spearing with her fork at a piece of fat on her plate.

'But you still haven't told us what you think of the handling of the uprisings here,' Rowley said to Paterson. 'For my own part, I was shot at on two occasions by incendiarists, and I had to quell a town brawl between strikers and free labourers on another. The forces for peace in Winton were completely outnumbered, but that did not prevent their prevailing.'

'An admirable job,' said Paterson, remembering that Rowley was his host and Sarah's brother. 'And it seems to me a job only performed so successfully because of the local knowledge of the law-enforcers.'

'Quite so. We did have some help from the military, but they were more a show of force than anything else. It was the special commissioners and deputies, the loyal town and station men, who really made the peace stick. It was a matter of their ability to adapt the law to the conditions which prevailed here. The Act of Parliament was a help, but Brisbane never really knew what was going on. It was a war and we won it.'

The dessert was served. Each diner received a narrow wedge of pawpaw in a champagne glass. Mrs Rowley had been looking forward to this moment since the meal started. Indeed, it was her only consolation during the 'serious' talk her husband and old Jarvis insisted on conducting. How she hated men's talk! Their boring interest in by-laws, agendas, mechanical contrivances, sports. Worst of all she hated the way their fists twitched when they spoke of boxing matches, or horseraces, or wars. The quality of the conversation in her household grieved her, dominated as it was by her husband and old Jarvis. The Police Magistrate never left his bench, no matter where he was. His adjudicatory tone was incurable. Her husband was the Town Clerk even in bed. She dared not break the by-laws. These men were such black and white creatures! They missed out on the colours in life. They were always too busy with the Acts of Parliament, the units of force, the potential for profit, the numbers of casualties. She ran her eyes sadly over the pale yellow crescents of pawpaw. They might have been larger, and redder, she thought.

'Congratulations, my pet,' said Rowley. 'Here we have one of the outback triumphs: honest labour prevailing over the desert.'

'It was rather small, I'm afraid.'

'Nonsense, my dear. A magnificent achievement. Geographically we are in the tropics but horticulturally we are in hell.'

'Three years that tree has been struggling,' Mrs Rowley said to Paterson, 'and this is its first fruit.'

'Watered by hand all that time,' said her husband. 'At a shilling a bucket for water this pawpaw is probably worth more than its weight in gold.'

They picked up their spoons and forks and attacked the fruit. The anaemic wedges were dreadfully sour. Mrs Rowley was greatly disappointed.

'The first fruit is never a success,' said Jarvis. 'That was my experience in New Guinea. Wait for the next ripenings. You'll see.'

'There are no more coming on yet,' said Mrs Rowley sadly. 'This was the lone fruit. Perhaps I picked it too early.'

'It's the season,' said Rowley. 'Nothing's growing that isn't hand-watered, and none of that's growing richly. Everything's sour here. Everything that isn't dead is sour. All we need is rain.'

'For sweetness,' said Sarah. 'Rain is for sweetness in pawpaw.'

Mrs Rowley set her dessert aside, with just the one round spoonful scooped from it. The others finished theirs out of politeness, though old Jarvis's tastebuds were worn to the point where taste was hardly a consideration when eating. 'Excellent,' he said. 'An unexpected delight.'

Mrs Rowley had the dessert glasses cleared away quickly, and the coffee brought round. She was plagued with the thought that Bartie's solemnity since morning-tea time was caused by flaws in her hospitality. Now that the pawpaw had gone wrong, where it might have been such a triumph, she was herself feeling depressed, and imagined she might have looked as despondent as did her guest. She did not discount the possibility that exhaustion, following his recent weeks of celebration and travel, was the cause of his short energy span, as he claimed it was. But she suffered from the hostess's insecurity, and therefore wanted to blame herself for his quietness. The other thing she noticed was that neither Bartie nor Sarah had smiled once during the meal.

'Shall we walk?' asked Sarah.

Paterson had no objection. He lifted the latch on the veranda gate. 'Where to?' he asked.

'Does it matter?'

'I suppose not.'

They started off down Vindex Street. From inside the house Mrs Rowley sent the Aboriginal maid who tagged along twenty yards behind them. They walked away from the town. Sarah held her parasol so that its outstretched spines did not bump his shoulder.

'What are you here for, Bartie?' she asked.

'For you.'

'And what does that mean?'

He fumbled with an answer.

She slid the ring from the finger of the hand in which she held the parasol. 'Is this what you came for?' she asked.

She held the ring up. She appeared to be about to drop it. As a reflex action, his hand shot out. In his palm the ring burned, reflecting blades of light from the shrieking sun.

She kept walking. She looked down at her dustless shoes. Then she looked up, towards the dust-stricken horizon. He shambled along beside her, cupping the ring foolishly in his hand.

'Please take it back,' he said.

She allowed him to slip the ring back onto her finger. She did not speak.

Vindex Street, which was little more than a track at any point along its length, now petered to nothing. Paterson and Sarah kept walking, but the Aboriginal maid sat down under a tree. She intended to go no farther. The couple traversed a ploughed section of paddock. They were two neat figures, one in blue, the other in white, stumbling a little amongst the dusty clods. They came to a fence. There were horses in the paddock beyond it. Paterson put his hands on the fence's top rail. With a sudden spring he vaulted it, his legs stretched out to the right, his coat-tail flapping. The straw hat fell from his head. He laughed. He turned to help her across, but she remained motionless. She stood and looked at him. Then she spoke.

'I shall be honest with you, Bartie. I don't believe we are a perfect match. Good, yes. But not perfect. I came to Winton to give myself space to think this over. I have been watching marriages, especially my brother's. But others, too. The Bowditches, the Connors, the Shipleys. Though few would agree with me, I think Mr and Mrs Bowditch have by far the best amongst those I have observed. There is an electricity which runs between them. I have seen it. They might be sitting on either side of the room, but it is there nevertheless. It is like a beam of light. More than that. If you walk through it you feel it. A sort of warm, intimate tingle striking against you, like touch itself extending through the air. That is what I want, Bartie. That is marriage. That is love.'

He stood with his hands on the fence. He was sad and annoyed and embarrassed. 'And I don't give you that, then? I don't send out a beam of love-electricity?'

'No, you don't.' She put out her hand for him to take to help her across the fence. She smiled. 'But that is not to say you couldn't.'

She climbed to the fence's middle rail. He steadied her as she gathered the lacy hem of her dress together. He held the hand holding the lace. The horses came across the paddock to watch. She climbed to the top rail. There she stood with the parasol held aloft above her. His hands were on her ankle and wrist. The two figures looked as though they were about to attempt some primitive experiment in aviation. She shook his hands off and for a moment she was balanced on the top rail, ready for flight. Her eyes sought the horizon. Her body felt the merest hint of uplift from a breath of wind.

She jumped. The dress ballooned upwards and exploded in a happy chaos of lace about her face. The parasol gave a surprised jerk and slanted sideways. One of the shoes dislodged itself from her heel. She slid down on the air and landed firmly in his arms.

The horses were startled into a propping gallop. They fled, tails raised, nostrils flared. At a safer distance they slowed to a canter, their bodies all liquid movement.

'Wonderful beasts,' said Paterson.

'Wonderful animals,' Sarah replied. They laughed.

They walked arm in arm. The sun was hot. Paterson removed his coat. They crossed another fence. Beyond it was the road leading to the bore site. They walked on the cream ribbon of road. Two figures on a plain. They had walked like this, arm in arm, along the promenade at Bondi Beach, a year ago.

They reached the bore site. Among the earthworks and machinery was a corrugated-iron shed. A man leant in the doorway watching them. He spat onto the ground and his spittle, like a blob of mercury, ran along gathering a coat of dust. When it stopped it sat, bold as a child's marble, discrete from the plain. The man invited them into the shade of what he called his office. They went in, as invited, and soon realised their mistake. Inside the tiny shed it was hotter than outside.

The man introduced himself, spitting into a wet corner behind him. He was Hanley, the Colonial Boring Company's site engineer. In fact (he spat again) the fifth site engineer on the project so far. There had been a Canadian, a Norwegian, and two Germans. At last, it was a Queenslander's turn. The bore was past the 2,400 foot level. He brought out a bottle from a drawer beside his desk and offered them a drink. They took it in chipped glasses. Sarah was surprised to find, when the clear liquid was at her nose and lips, that it was not water. She put the glass on the desk. The engineer tossed down half his glassful and continued his optimistic spiel. There would be a strike any time now. He was certain. The company's best water-diviners had said so. The artesian basin came up to 2,500 feet here. It could not possibly be any deeper. There would be gangs of water soon.

The town would be swimming in it. He spat comprehensively into the corner. There would be gangs of good water.

Sarah looked down at her shoes. She noticed the film of dust they carried was spotted and pocked. She wondered at this for a while. The spotting was droplets of moisture. She stood up, saying she must leave. The atmosphere was too close for her inside the shed.

They retraced their steps along the road. Paterson was in high spirits. He had drunk more of the engineer's hot liquor than Sarah realised.

'What a character!' Paterson said.

'He spat on me.'

'Pardon?'

'That man spat on me. Look.'

Paterson did not think. There was a rare hot liquid churning in his stomach and a hot sun stabbing beneath his hat's brim. There was the lady of his choice on his arm and there was the whole wide plain untransformed by the pathetic town struggling up in front of them. There was something enduringly comic about the outback, in spite of its seasonal tragedies. That something was the human element. It was humans brought the humour to the saltbush and the dust. Paterson laughed.

She broke away from him. She ran ahead and turned and ranted at him. She was hysterical. He chased her, but he could not catch up to her. She kept losing things which he had to stop for and pick up. She threw down her parasol. She dropped her handkerchief. She kicked off her shoes. He barked his shins on the first fence. She seemed to have a wonderful speed across the ploughed field where he was all clumsy boots and tearing ankles. When he struggled up the steps of the Rowleys' house laden with a tangle of her dress accessories and pursued by the scuttling maid, Sarah had already slammed shut the door to her room inside. For Paterson, fighting to catch his breath, it seemed the veranda heaved with a crowd of inquiring eyes.

That afternoon Clohesy inspected the preparations for the expedition. He paid special attention to the resurrection of the dinghy which had warped and split in the heat of the storage shed since its last use. He personally supervised the caulking of its timbers by one of the Aboriginal troopers—a Gulf of Carpentaria man handy with boats. He checked the soundness of the oars and the rowlocks. He left nothing to chance or error. He annoyed Withers by not confiding either the destination or the purpose of the expedition. Nevertheless he had a reasonable suspicion that Withers knew exactly where they would be headed. He insisted on a supply of stores twice as large as was necessary for two nights away, and he overruled Withers's contention that the station would be dangerously undermanned in the hands of just two native policemen. Withers wanted to stay, to hold the fort as he put it, but Clohesy ordered him to come. Withers's presence was vitally important, he explained (without explaining at all), to the success of the expedition. Withers decided to sit in the office with his feet on the table in a defiant sulk. That pleased Clohesy because he at least knew where the man was.

On the shaded veranda Clohesy watched the black thumbs of the policeman push the tar along the cracks in the hull. The tar-streaked lightness of the undersides of the hands gleamed occasionally as they worked. Afterwards Clohesy saw to the loading of the tent and the drag net and the other equipment onto the cart, and the final lifting of the dinghy to the top of the load. Then he inspected the native police and appointed the three who looked him most directly in the eyes to guard the loaded cart overnight. It was the best he could do, and when he had done it he left the police station and returned to the hotel. There he sat at the cane table on the upstairs balcony, looking down on the street in the approaching dusk. He thought about writing a letter, but decided it would be more prudent to devote himself to observation. He could see the loaded cart in the yard behind the police station, and he could see the comings and goings from the station door. He could watch the bath-house emptying and the hotels filling. He could follow the innocent people — the chemist, the bootmaker, the children bowling old bicycle wheels — heading for their homes under the failing sky.

Then, as suddenly as an ambush, the sky was alight. A furious sunset licked up from the horizon with the awfulness of wool-sheds burning. He sipped from a glass of stout to steady himself, to settle the dust of the day still in his mouth. Then it was other expeditions Niall's mind journeyed on. Expeditions in the past when he and his wife drove to Ithaca Creek. There they had taken off their clothes to sit in the pure creek waters rushing around them or to stretch on the flattest rocks with the hot bush sweat in pools on their bodies and their ears full of the hot scream of cicadas. As quickly as the sunset had come, it went, with a final inflaming of the whole stretching sky. Then the dark toppled on the town and the lantern-light reached out from the doorways of the hotels and the drinkers glowed like embers in the dim furnaces of the bars.

Niall left the veranda. He moved down into the street. He walked as a ghost would, keen to avoid the spillage of light from doorways and windows, noticing what no others were noticing — the sculptured shadows, the breathing of quiet dogs, the softness of dust lying down on ledges. In the dim window of Corfield and Fitzmaurice's store was a display: a single wheelbarrow, static, lifeless, an image flattened by the night light, like an icon. Lying in the barrow was a twelve-pound hammer, a roll of heavy-gauge fencing wire, a set of butchering knives, a contraption that might have been a dingo trap, a creamy willow polo mallet, a paraffin lamp, and, sitting on top, a pair of boxing-gloves. There was no comment on the display by way of neatly lettered sign or price-tags. It simply stood there centrally placed in the window space, a product solely of its own mystical significance, framed by an unadorned window and backed by a blank partition. It was a sacred collection of brand-new relics ready for holy duty.

Farther down the street the police station burnt a light in a single window. Niall moved to it and peered through from the shadows of the veranda. Inside was Withers with one pillow tied to his chest and another to his rump. He had pushed the forms and desks of the courtroom back against the walls. He was moving along the walls from one item of furniture to another, clinging to each as he went. The roller-skates on his feet clacked on the floorboards. Then he pushed himself off and travelled tensely across the room, bent double in the act of insuring his balance. The skates shrilled on the floor. When he bumped against the trestle table which served as prisoner's dock when the court was sitting, he grabbed it, almost collapsing it, regaining his stance by putting a hand to the floor. Then he straightened and launched himself again towards the opposite side of the room. The skates stammered at the ends of his crooked legs.

Niall drew back from the window. He retreated into the shadows where the heat of the day still drummed.

There were sports beginning in the street as Niall returned slowly towards his hotel. Men were wagering on a long-jumper's ability in the dust outside the Commercial Hotel. 'Boots on or off?' yelled the athlete. There was a garbled shout from the punters. He left the boots on. Farther down the street, in a yard beside the Club Hotel, two candles had been set up on a fence. Between the fence and the hotel wall was a space no wider than the length of a coffin. A horseman drove his mount over the rail between the candles, then turned the horse on its heels, jerking its neck back, almost making it cartwheel, then he leapt it across the fence between the candles again. A great shout came from his circle of admirers.

Niall did not feel at all sleepy. He walked around the block, along Vindex Street, and back towards the hotel. He caught a glimpse of a small dark movement in the shadows beside the police station. He crossed the street and crept to the courtroom window where he could see once again into the impromptu skating rink. Withers was untying the pillows from his body. The little Aboriginal boy buckled the too-large roller-skates to his own feet. Withers laughed as the boy tried to stand on the slippery wheels. He bent over the boy, lifting him upright, talking and smiling, encouraging him perhaps, but Niall could not hear what was said. Then Withers held the boy on the skates and walked with him around the room, holding him. He pushed him along on the whirring, clicking wheels. The boy laughed with delight. Around in circles they went, the policeman's generous hands clasped on the thin black shoulders of the laughing boy.

Niall returned to his hotel room. He felt nothing in himself apart from an obscure sense of threat. What he had seen through the courtroom window had struck him as innocent and beautiful. Yet the players in that scene were of the opposition, and the embrace they shared may have also contained a communication of importance to Niall, something as fateful, even, as the promise of his own death. The notion came to him as the call of a ghost somewhere in the cellars of his being, indistinct, muffled, only felt as an unlikely curse might be felt, or as the foreknowledge of a dam about to burst in another land might be

69

experienced by one not previously acquainted with his own prescience.

Great-aunt Sarah's diaries are a pleasure to handle. They are large in size, almost foolscap, but remarkably light in spite of their thick board covers. Their pages are of soft-veined rice paper.

Japanese ships used to ascend the Brisbane River to dock at the wharves. There the Brisbanites would flock to buy at the stalls set up on deck.

Intricate parasols, elegant fans, papier-mâché boxes, scented-wood chests—all at ridiculously low prices. They were carried down the gangways by delighted Australian customers. A bargain was a bargain then as now. Until the Customs put an end to it.

They were festive occasions, those days when a Japanese ship was in port. I can see Great-aunt Sarah stepping delicately across fat ropes lying on the wharf, clutching the blank-paged books to her bosom, thinking: I will use these for diaries. Accompanying her were the gentle family with whom she stayed in Brisbane on her way through to Winton.

All the entries were penned with mauve ink, in that neat, back-slanted script that never wavered, no matter what delight or tragedy was being described.

10th of December, 1895

One more chance, Bartie. Can I ever forgive you for what you have done already? Probably. The trouble with a gentleman's word is the gentleman; the trouble with a woman's determination is the woman. I came here to escape you, and you have followed me. Foolishly, I am flattered. Yet my wiser mind tells me it is pride makes a man chase again what he once held and called his own. If you have come on a hunt to destroy me, I will escape from you once more, permanently. If you have come to reclaim me, it will be on my terms. Love is a sensitive plant, Bartie. It bears the mark of every change in the wind. I intend to be happy, all my life. So it is up to you, isn't it? One more chance, you monster. To show you care.

There is a pressed flower interleaved at that entry. It is a clover

70

flower, with a leaf attached. The blossom is intact, but the leaf has been chewed by a grub during the years. The leaf had four leaflets, once. Now one of them is separated from the stem. The grub drilled right through it.

When I opened the tissue in which the flower was folded, the grub's cocoon was there too. It was empty. The grub had gone on to better things.

CHAPTER

4

The red dust lay baking on Elderslie Street, waiting for the later morning wind to dance it into the fine cracks between windows and their jambs, into the fine spaces between cartwheels and their axles, into the corners of mouths and eyes. It lay waiting innocently, the dust, for its partner in the dance into pockets, into teacups, into ears, into new and mended and broken things. It waited in its dry red innocence, baking softly, crackling in the morning sun, a talcum layer of soft excitement on the limb of the wide street.

Clohesy mounted into the saddle of the horse they had prepared for him. He looked over the loaded wagon, seeing how the dust had stuck to the new caulking of the incongruous dinghy. It was tied upside down on top of the load. It caused laughter among the lounging miners and shearers. Like the dust, they too waited in the street for the day's later turbulence, waited for the pubs to open so they could blow away their money and get their heads dancing, and their feet and fists. The Aboriginal troopers moved off, their mounts none too eager. The horses recognised the elaborateness of the preparations and sensed the length of the journey ahead. They pounded the dust with annoyed hooves. Then the wagon followed, and Withers and Clohesy moved after it.

'We have the oars, don't we?' said Clohesy.

'You loaded them yourself, sir,' said Withers.

'I know I did. Just checking.'

They headed west, down the main street. They stirred the dust gently into premature eddies with hooves and wheels. They headed from the ragged fringe of the town towards the low, flat mountain which lay in the west, seemingly a mistake on the plain. With the dinghy rocking on the wagon like a sacred relic for an obsolete faith, they headed from the dusty street of the town towards the greater dustiness of the west. The wide red plain itched in the morning sun, waiting for the wind to come and move its top layer towards the town.

As they left the town behind, as the horses struck sparks from the liver-coloured gravel even at that slow pace, as the hawks wheeled over them, curious and aloof, Niall felt that the man riding beside him wanted, for the first time in their relationship, to talk at length, to avoid riding in silence. It brought Niall to his guard, for it seemed to him that Withers was no longer resentful and no longer suspicious. It brought Niall to his guard, for he could see in the friendly, uncautious expression on Withers's face that the man had received orders, had gained some secret knowledge and was plotting on it. As they rode at a trot with the sun on the backs of their necks, Niall was brought to his guard, for it seemed to him that Withers had become so amicable there could be no other reason for it than his intention to kill when the moment arrived.

They were well onto the claypan by mid-morning. They slowed to a walk. The wagon sliced through an unusually sandy stretch. Withers dropped the reins and began filling a pipe. 'Tobacco?' he asked. Clohesy declined. 'Very wise,' Withers said. 'Dreadful stuff. Sheep-dip, they call it. Sheep-shit would be closer. Same stuff the squatters give the shearers in their rations. Same stuff we give the troopers, too. Better than nothing, I suppose.' He filled the pipe and stuck it in his mouth, without lighting it. 'Tastes better when it's not lit,' he said, smiling. 'Lasts longer that way, too.'

A large goanna scuttled off the road ahead of the leading horse, swinging itself through the pink sand like a swimmer in a pink powder sea. It lumbered twenty yards beyond the plodding horse-hooves, then stopped, lifting and turning its head, looking back over its shoulder, curious to see this odd procession, this disturbance on the plain. It sniffed for the water in the waterbags, that water lolling and sloshing with the progress of the wagon slicing through the whining sand. And Niall watched it, watched the lizard head lifted and turned to catch the scent of the procession, watched it as it exploded and flew off the lizard body exposing the dark meat of the throat, flinging jets of dark lizard mince which rolled in the pink sand and were coated like little rissoles in pink flour.

Withers put his gun back into its holster. 'It's the only remedy,' he said. 'They steal eggs.'

Clohesy looked at the sunburnt face under the slouch hat. 'So do snakes, hawks, crows. . . .'

'We kill them all. It's what we call living with nature.'

The sun beat on the horses' glistening necks. Niall felt his own neck prickling with sweat. 'I don't expect any trouble on this expedition,' said Clohesy.

'Neither do I, sir.'

'You know where we are headed.'

'You never told me.'

'You've been there before.'

'Several times. It's a popular picnic spot.'

Clohesy licked the scum from his lips. 'I'm glad to see your gun in good firing order,' he said.

'Pride myself on it.'

The first gust of the morning wind lifted dust in front of them, and floated it gently towards them like a pink mirage. Clohesy closed his eyes momentarily to let it roll past. 'It wounds the eyes, the dust,' he said.

'It wounds everything,' his companion agreed.

Mrs Bowditch was usually the last to rise of a morning on Goonda Station. It was one of the luxuries she reserved for herself. Like her other luxuries, which included the lush garden surrounding the homestead, richly cushioning it from the desert beyond, it was a luxury which grew out of excellent good sense, for it was both a pampering and a practicality. Mrs Bowditch rose at the leisurely hour of nine o'clock each outback morning on principle, because it guarded her independence and nourished her reputation for eccentricity. A woman needed those, independence and eccentricity, if she was to operate in the desert world ruled over by men and hawks and lizards.

So when she heard the nine strokes of the rosewood clock sweating out the hours in the long room at the heart of Goonda homestead, she lifted the silk sheet from her body and took the first steps of the day, as always, to the altar of her rituals. It was set in the angle of the room where her repeated image looked back at her from multiple mirrors. They reflected on her the jasmine-filtered light from the desert beyond the verandas, beyond the garden of her nurturing, way beyond the dusty river road which led back to the hard, itching town of Winton.

There she sat with her crystal bottles and jars, and her crystal reflections, soaked in splinters of prismatic light leaping from the crystal edges of the mirrors. Her mother-of-pearl fingers with their long pearly nails revolved the smooth lid of a jar. Then they dipped like a sleep-walker's wandering into the smooth cream. They lifted a snowdrop-scented coolness to the face reflected over and over in the mirrors. And in the mirrors her skin drank the smoothness of the cream, the smoothness of the cream, the smoothness of the cream which the blasting sun would drink out again.

The sun was like a man, she thought, like a man always taking more than it gave. Like a man never knowing when to stop. Like a man resenting eclipse. Like a man never knowing when to lift its hand but going beyond until it made a woman sick in the skull and inside the sensitive bones. Like a man endlessly full of fever and heat and hot stroking and invasion of the places not guarded. Like a man full of plunder and irreverence for scrollworks of satin and lattices of lace. Like a man, explosive and desirable.

Mrs Bowditch burnt like this in front of her mirrors every morning of the year.

Out on the plain Clohesy squashed a fly at the back of his neck. His hand came away with specks of the fly's yellow innards and a spot of its blood. He wiped it on the horse's mane in front of him. They were sluggish out here, the clinging flies, accustomed to the easy pickings on dead things roasting in the sun. Clohesy wiped his hand, then wiped his brow.

'There's the Goonda gate,' said Withers. All the men in the procession turned their eyes, black-irised and blue. They looked towards a horizon uncertain with mirage. They followed with their eyes the road beyond the gate to the shimmering speck miles away which was the roof of the Goonda homestead quivering like silver ice in the hot pink plain.

'My eyes are sore,' said Clohesy.

'It's the wind and the dust,' said Withers. 'They give you the blight.'

It was for one hour that Mrs Bowditch sat with her fingers in cream. Then the sweating clock struck ten dull strokes through the heat of the house. It reminded her that the maid would bring the morning cup of camomile tea brewed of the leaves from the mistress's own garden. She tied the sash of her kimono in the usual loose knot. She took the tea from the maid whose footsteps in the hall were always a continuation of the clock's ten strokes. She moved through the bedroom's open French doors onto the veranda where each morning she inspected the fragile lushness of the foliage with which she had wrapped the house. She looked for the merest signs of wilting upon which she would direct the attention of the houseboy who stood, as expected at this time of morning, in the silent shade of one of the oleanders. He held the can of mud-pink water he had carried without spilling from the dam beyond the house.

Sipping her tea, she moved along the veranda, her pale bare feet on the hard, shiny timber. She peered into the secret coolnesses of her garden, the spangled shadowy depths of it, the private moistness of its pampered earth. The fountains of herb bushes bursting in small explosions at its base. The vines stretching in bold green strokes along the veranda rails and up the posts in hugging spirals. The jasmine, the antigonon and the grape. The trees shrugging higher to caress the house eaves. The frangipani, oleander and cumquat. The heavy blaze of the bougainvillea, the big-leafed droop of the mulberry, the surprising exuberances of tomato plants and pumpkin vines pushing through here and there like weeds. All of it washed like a green wave against the house, a green wave tossed from the desert paddocks, a lush littoral for the island of her house in the surrounding sea of desert dust.

It was the smaller plants that needed attention. She called the boy. He carried the watering-can in his sinewy black hand. 'Water these little ones,' she said. She pointed at the new herbs given her by the Chinese cook from the men's quarters—the promising slip of rosemary and the feathery shoot of a fennel plant. 'That's enough,' she said. 'Now pick me that flower. That one.' The boy bent and picked a single flower, a frail lavender

76

bloom from an earth-hugging plant which had sown itself. Some sort of desert violet, she supposed. He pinched it off and handed it up to her where she stood on the veranda. Then she sent him away. She raised her arms to set the flower in her hair. As she did so the kimono rose with the action of her arms and below its hem her knees were revealed to the billowing mirages on the far, uncertain horizon.

When they arrived at the billabong Clohesy ordered that the camp be set up at the end nearest the overshoot where the waterhole divided into three branching arms. One of those was suitable for the launching of the rowing-boat. He left Withers and the men to unload the wagon. He checked the stoutness of his cane, in case of snakes, then set off on a walk along the billabong's banks. He wanted to familiarise himself with the stretch of tree-lined water. It was much bigger than he had imagined, about thirty yards across, and of a length sufficient for it to disappear round a corner half a mile away as if it were a true flourishing arm of the Diamantina River. But it wasn't a true section of the river, it was just a motionless arm severed from the main system by the sloping rockwork of the overshoot built a few seasons back to dam up the water after floods. He walked along the thin green margin of fortunate grasses and drooping coolibahs. He crossed at the overshoot, noting the careful mosaic of stonework over which the wagon and horses had come. He also noted the dead dryness of the gravel channel on one side of the dam and the mud-coloured water riffled by the afternoon wind on the other. Looking back along the billabong from the middle of the overshoot he felt he might be standing at the end of one nave of a cathedral whose arches were formed by the overhanging boughs of the coolibahs on either bank. They leant their arthritic shadows on the brown surface of the water. And it was the brown surface of the water which was most striking. Everything leant towards it, the gidgee scrub and the coolibahs; and the sky, too, was drawn down to it — greys and greens and blues vividly reflected on an opaque brown canvas. Some of the trees stood in the brown water, while the roots of others on the bank were exposed like tangles of pipes running into a reservoir. But the water was absolutely opaque; all sight was stopped at its surface.

Niall walked towards the far end of the billabong, examining the abandoned machinery of nature on the banks: ruined clumps of grass, exploded dry boughs, scattered piles of sheep-shit. He kicked them over with his booted foot, picking up some for a closer look. Overhead there were clusters of dry sticks caught like nests in the forks of the trees. They showed the height of the floods when they came. Above them the hawks climbed and swung in the plains wind. At one point Niall scrambled down the steep hoof-broken bank to feel the water. It was delightfully cool and soft on his hand. But he could not stay there at the water's edge, for he was sinking in the slow soft mud, his boot uppers disappearing with a gentle brown sigh of the mud. So he disengaged himself from the slow sure suck of the mud and continued along the top of the bank, imagining that a body sucked down into the stomach of the billabong would be caught by the tangle of tree-roots and seduced by the mud so that, cool and soft, it would lie in the secret water for ever.

By the time Clohesy got back to camp the tent was erected. A fire of quick wood was chattering. A couple of the Aboriginal troopers had thrown hasty lines into the water to catch fish. Withers was sitting on a convoluted dead bough polishing his gun with a rag torn from an old serge uniform. 'Find anything?' Withers asked.

'Only these,' said Clohesy, showing him the two halves of an empty mussel shell he had noticed in a section of dried, crackling mud.

'Plenty of those around,' said Withers, unimpressed. But to Niall they were a surprise. He had not expected to find these signs of life in this incongruous stretch of dead outback river. He cradled the ribbed halves of green-black shell in his palm, turning them to allow the afternoon light to pick up the hints of pearliness on their undersides. He placed them one on top of the other. He felt how they fitted together perfectly, the two halves of a secret fragility saved from the burning mud, and fitted together once again as a god must have fitted them originally.

'There's plenty of life in the billabong,' said Withers, not lifting his eyes from the job in his own hands. 'Crabs, mussels, fish. Lots of yellowbelly, you know. Lots of them.' He sighted down the barrel of the clean gun. 'One of the best fishing spots around,' he said.

After dinner Mrs Bowditch was left alone again because her husband had to go out. To see to his horses. By the time he was back it was late and the first she heard of him, returned to the house, was his voice shouting to the servants that he wanted the lights out soon. Then he came to the bedroom where she sat at the mirrors, her fingers dipped in her night-creams.

She always loved this man as he tossed his work clothes down in a sticky pile each night, talking with her in that loud voice he was accustomed to use shouting towards horizons during the day; tossing his work clothes down in that violent, negligent way, something he never did with the town clothes he hung and folded neatly with his absolute sense of the fitness of things. All the while he recounted to her the events of his day: the horse that was lame, the missing sheep, the leaking dam, the new bearing on the windmill, the cloud he had seen momentarily in the west before it melted as fast as it had appeared, all the things she loved hearing him share with her, and then the tossing of his long stern body on the bed and his lying there listening for the nine strokes of the sweating clock, upon which he would shout through the house to the servants' quarters and the message would carry to all the outer huts: it was time to put out the lights. And their own light, too, in the fitness of things would be extinguished by her creamy-skinned hand so that in the dark she would find her way to the bed beside him where he lay like a thin stranded whale on the shore of the night. Then they would talk and touch in the dark if it had not been a bad day for him, and his voice in the dark was a different voice, a tender voice, which she knew came from that same stern cliff-edged face only because she had seen it happen in the light of day on special occasions such as the difficult birth-giving of a favourite mare or the tipping into the earth of a loyal fallen stockman.

Tonight he lay beside her with his hard hand resting on the softness of her upper arm and he said a word she knew he hated: 'Barret'. Then he said, 'They went to the waterhole today', and that was all he said. So she knew what he was thinking, and she knew he loved her beyond all his favourite horses and beyond all his stricken lands and beyond all his besieged visions of advancing nobly into their future. So she reached out her gleaming hand and ran it down the stern leanness of his spine and heard the grateful sigh escape between the thinness of his stern lips. It is worth it all, she thought, it is worth the labour and the using, worth the lending and the borrowing and the closing of the mind to the stink and unpleasantness and the cleaning up afterwards. Worth it all to be here together, touching in the uncluttered night, while outside in the garden the grasshoppers lie at the ragged edges of the fattest leaves and the grubs crawl to the newest, greenest shoots, and the goannas sleep around the largest eggs swelling their bellies.

They made an early start out at the billabong. The blue air of the sunrise still lingered amongst the trees. The Aboriginal troopers carried the boat to the water's edge at the most accessible of the little inlets. They stumbled amongst the tree-roots as they went. They dropped the boat on the pink mud then slid it into the water. There it rested, motionless on the dead water while they tossed in the oars and poles and grappling hooks and a net on a pole and lengths of rope, until the boat was loaded and ready. Then Clohesy insisted that Withers go in the boat with the Gulf man and another trooper. But Withers said he preferred the idea of staying on the bank because he would get seasick. Clohesy wouldn't listen to him, so that finally Withers got into the boat unsteadily, not placing his weight over the keel, and the boat lurched. And one of its gunwhales rose up, taking with it one of the troopers whose foot was caught in the mud so that he went down onto his knees in the muddy water and he laughed and all the troopers laughed. But Withers did not laugh. He yelled at them furiously as he clung to the rocking boat while from the bank Clohesy told them to get on with it and Withers renewed his suggestion that he was not the man for the job. But once again, Clohesy refused to listen to him.

Then the boat was steadied and pointed towards the broad length of the billabong. Once pushed away from the bank, it nosed out of the inlet bumping on tree-roots as it went. The Gulf man set the oars in the rowlocks and rowed gently across the land- and sky-scape painted on the rippling surface of the brown water. The other trooper stood in the bow like a figure-head. Withers sat furious in the sternsheets like a landlubbing Captain Bligh. Clohesy stood on the bank with laughter inside his stomach but not showing on his face.

When the boat reached a point midway between the two

banks Withers gave the order for the hook to be used. The trooper fixed a pole to the end of the hook because he found the bottom there in the centre too deep to reach otherwise. Withers ordered that the Gulf man row up the middle of the waterhole for several hundred yards then back again with Clohesy watching them, not countermanding Withers's orders. Around them the galahs and pigeons and peewits and smaller birds played in the trees and in the roots of the trees. Three black swans sheltered in an inlet. A pelican planed down from the large sky to land on the water then turned off, thinking better of it.

On the end of the hook there appeared muddy stumps and muddy bits of root and the mandatory muddy boot and even a muddy saddlebag in such good condition it wasn't thrown back. But there was nothing of interest to Clohesy until a heavy object dragged up to break the surface proved to be the muddy carcass of a sheep which must have fallen in and drowned, as Withers's shout suggested and Clohesy's returned shout seemed to agree. The muddy sheep was allowed to sink away and drown again. Then Clohesy called them back to the bank. The sun had raced half-way up the morning sky to tell them all it was time to have a cup of the tea smoking on the camp-fire.

After they had rested awhile, they saw one of the hawks circling overhead make a dive and in its claws take a fish plucked from below the water's surface. It made the black men shout in praise; it made Withers wonder how on earth a fish could be spied beyond that opaque pink skin of water surface; it made Clohesy stand up to announce that this time he would go himself in the boat to direct the search, but that Withers would come too in spite of his remonstrations because his shore leave was not yet due, a statement Withers found to be no joke at all.

Once on the water Clohesy ordered that the boat be kept much closer to the shore, as Withers should have done. It made the task more difficult for the trooper. He had to pole now, rather than row. Clohesy stood in the boat's bow probing amongst the tree-roots with the gaffing hook. Right along the billabong's edge they went, beyond the bend in the bank, to where they were out of sight of the camp. Beyond the point to which Niall had walked the evening before, almost to the far end of the waterhole, to where Clohesy caught hold of a part of the thing he was looking for.

81

It was yet another old boot. But not an ordinary old boot of the kind usually fished up in watery places, for it contained a foot, or what Clohesy knew to be a foot, even though it was just a muddy soup with odd bones swimming in it. Without saying a word, Clohesy placed the bootful of soup upright in Withers's reluctant hands and leapt over the side of the boat to be up to his belt-buckle in muddy water thrusting his arms downwards, the discoveries of his feeling fingers showing in the rapt concentration of the face bent close to the water's surface. Then he began bringing them up, the legs, the arms, in tangles of muddy shreds of clothing, what was left of the flesh hanging in streamers, or perhaps that was some kind of weed growing off them, the balloon of the heavy canvas pants a bag of bones alive with river crabs and leaping tiny fish and water worms all surging in a mucous pile on the bottom of the boat. 'Get the hook,' Clohesy shouted as the writhing ribs slithered in his hands and his hands came up furred with the jelly of decomposition while the bloated weights beneath the surface lolled and stundered drunkenly falling away and foundered invisibly bouncing the mud-dull bottom. Then with the shreds of flesh trailing in streamers from his hands Clohesy worked the gaffing hook until the exploded rib-cage rose and bobbed like a nausea at the surface and the trooper held it to the side of the boat with the pole stuck into it. But still the head rolled somewhere on the bottom and Clohesy's slime-rich fingers caressed the unseen mud, trembling to latch into an eye socket or to caress the hairless skull, but it came up eventually with its hair still on though muddy and ragged and matted like a close weed hugging poisonously, so that once he had hold of it Clohesy did not dare let it go and he held it up for Withers to see with its jaw bone hanging down by shreds of weed or flesh and only then did he realise that Withers was standing in the boat with his gun aimed down saying: 'Get into the boat, Clohesy or whatever your name is', and Clohesy had to do as he was told.

Yet he did it without upsetting the boat as he might easily have done rolling awkwardly over the gunwhale to a momentary jumbling with the soggy pile on the boat's bottom. Instead he joined the triumphant boatload with the most delicate manoeuvres possible because he did not intend to go diving again for what he had come so far to retrieve. He moved carefully to the bow where he sat, taking the muddy head drooling in his hands, refitting the undone jawbone, turning the ravaged face towards Withers, now seated, the gun swelling in his policeman's hand. So they sat there. The boat floating motionless on the dead water, buoyed up by its own reflection.

The trooper, who still wedged the waterlogged trunk against the boat's side with the pole, looked away from the contest between the two men. He scanned the green margin of growth kissing the waterhole, and beyond that the restless dust of the broken plains, thinking: These inexplicable white men, these complicated, incautious white men, fooling around with death.

Then Clohesy spoke, as if the gun wasn't there, holding the ragged skull up to the bruising sunlight, sliding his finger back from the head's temple. 'See this, Withers,' he said.

'What?'

'This fracture, Withers.'

'I don't think I see any fracture.'

'Assault, Withers, I would say.'

'I don't think so.'

'It could be, Withers.'

'Injuries received on diving into the waterhole, more likely.'

'No, Withers. Look at the extent of it. The lacerations, too. Look at the raggedness. Might even be the passage of a bullet, don't you think?'

'Hardly. That's natural decomposition. Or the fish. Don't forget the fish. The body's been in the water for a long time.'

'No matter, Withers. That won't prevent its revealing the cause of death. We can study these fractures, once we get back to town.'

'I'm not sure that we'll be going back to town. I know you're not a policeman. I am quite within my rights to deal summarily with you right now.'

Laver threw the skull. A lobbing, gentle throw, describing an arc through the still air between his hands and Withers's, the length of the boat. For Withers a gentle catch, not a threat. Rolling slowly in the air the head came towards Withers. He watched it turn over like a strange planet passing except that it wanted to land in his lap. And behind it in the thudding light between them came the man, Clohesy or some other name, hurtling the length of the boat; and although Withers had lost the gun somehow, preparing to catch the sudden head, he was ready for the man, and he caught his rush in the quaking boat and crushed the living head down on the gunwhale and held it there where it was inches from the collapsed head fallen a moment before, and it occurred to him to rip off the false moustache of the impostor so he began to do just that when the living head screamed, 'Blast you, Withers, that's my own hair, you fool', and the indignant Laver struggled under the policeman's hold until he found the badge in the sopping pocket of his own trousers and shoved it under Withers's gaze saying, 'For God's sake, man, get your filthy hands off me', while Withers, hypnotised by the mystery of the gold-plated badge burning in the hand before him, released his hold and Laver sat up, furious at the manhandling, rubbing the side of his face where the gunwhale had left an imprint, patting his stinging moustaches and looking for signs of bleeding on the tips of his fingers, while Withers held the worrying badge and said, 'What's this?' and Laver picked up the damaged skull and took it back to the prow of the boat, noticing there was still a crab in the jelly inside, noticing that the jawbone was adrift so that he had to work with his hands to fit it back together again.

Withers pushed the badge back at Laver, and resentfully took up his gun from the nauseous floor of the boat. He sat in silence picking the flecks of sogged flesh from the gun. Finally Laver spoke, giving an order which arranged things so that Withers changed places with the Aboriginal, taking over the pole which held the waterlogged bust where it rode beside the boat like a stricken porpoise. The faithful trooper took the oars and rowed silently down the billabong. Then in answer to Withers's perplexed silence Laver said: 'My name is Laver. Lycaenidae Pseudodipsas Laver. As engraved on the badge. My father collected butterflies. He never had a butterfly named after himself so he named me after a butterfly. But that is by the way. I am on the staff of the Colonial Office, though I rarely have cause to say so. You have forced me to show my hand, Withers, but it is imperative that you now maintain my cover. There is an Act of Parliament to threaten you in this matter so I need say no more about it. However, in the need that I have to depend upon you in the near future, I can tell you that the Pastoralists' Association has asked the Colonial Office to patch this mess up and that I am here to dispose of such impediments as there may still be to the maintenance of the peace. The Unionists must not know who I am. They would thwart me in my brief. My presence here is inflammatory. If they knew my exact intentions hostilities would restart on a scale undoubtedly identifiable as civil war. I hope you understand me, Mr Withers. My identity must be kept secret. Your own role in this matter will not go without recognition.'

Withers sulked. Although he was relieved on a variety of counts, he was determined not to show it. The executioner's role had been lifted from him—a double release because he now found he would have been making a gross mistake. He had seen the network at fault before. He despised receipt of muddled orders. Aside from that, he had never shot a white man at such close range, not even a Unionist, and he now fancied that the job was more difficult than he had previously supposed. It wasn't like potting goannas or dingoes or Myalls, it wasn't blasting wildness back to pure dust. This aiming into the living, watery eyes of another human wasn't like sport or survival or war or police work at all. It was more like one's reflection aiming at one from a mirror, causing the hot thought of the reality of both gun and target to travel and disturb the quiet back-roads of the brain.

'What are your intentions, then?' Withers asked.

'To patch up the mess. To dispose of the evidence. To make sure there's nothing left to be found.'

'Like Barret.'

'Exactly.'

'How do you propose to dispose of him?'

'The most innocent and permanent way possible.'

'And that is. . .?'

'A large public funeral. Lots of pomp, lots of noise, lots of interest. It will work, you'll see. Providing we don't admit it's Barret. Providing no one else does, either.'

'Why shouldn't they? It's inflammatory.' There was a sly mixture of doubt and excitement in Withers's pursed expression.

Laver answered quickly. 'No one dares keep the dead from the grave, Mr Withers. Not even the hell-bent.'

The troopers were in no way pleased about the unloading of

the boat's cargo, nor its arrangement on a canvas under the shade of a coolibah-tree, in accordance with Laver's orders. They considered the whole fearful process to be absurdly dangerous. They closed their eyes when lifting the pieces; they skittered carrying them. When the jigsaw puzzle was as good as complete, and Laver went crawling on all fours round and round it, turning items over, poking at others, gathering up bits that rolled away, saying things like 'I am fascinated by death, Withers, aren't you?', the troopers averted their eyes fearing the worst sort of cosmic reprisal. Then Laver began toying with the head, rocking the skull back and forth so that the jawbone seemed to move alive. The troopers were panic-stricken. Laver said: 'Look, Withers, it's going to talk.' And the resentful Withers looked at Laver and wondered if the man was mad. And in a voice rich with truthfulness Withers said, 'You know I led the detachment against the Goonda raiders but I did not kill this man.' Yet Laver kept the jawbone working, saying, 'Isn't this a bullet wound, Withers?' And Withers had to say again with the helplessness of one being exorcised, 'I did not kill this man, Mr Laver. I identify him as William Rose Barret, but I did not kill him.' Yet the jaw gaped and stammered and would not let up. And it said, 'In that case, who did kill me, Withers?' But the question was not life or death to Withers and the spell was broken. He turned away, only answering, 'It's a crazy game, Laver. Why don't you quit it?'

So they wrapped the pieces of the corpse into a bundle, they tore down the tent, they piled the wagon up with the camp equipment, they put the bundle on top of the load covered by the boat. They left the billabong with the afternoon sun pounding in fists and the mirages waltzing on the horizon.

They rode fast, but Niall hardly knew it. His mind was moving faster. Now that he was Laver as well as Clohesy his performance must be twice as capable. And twice as difficult. The box of Barret's bits was dynamite. He wanted to run it down Winton's main street to see what would happen. To see how the pieces fused and rose up in the minds of the onlookers. But to convince as Laver, Niall knew he must not appear to upset the Pastoralists. He had already decided to conspire with Withers to give the tangled corpse a false identity, for the feigned sake of the peace, for the real sake of his performance's survival. It would be a politic distraction, Niall calculated. Anyone who refused to subscribe to the charade risked civil war. By the same token, the guilty could be pleased with the deception. It was not the name on the box that mattered. The hooves of Niall's horse hammered on the unconsecrated ground.

It was midnight by the time Clohesy and Withers appeared along the star-struck river road into Winton. Their arrival provided a momentary distraction for the desultory sports and brawls that glimmered in the long arena of the town's main street, the participants being those miners and shearers still not drunk enough to fall down and sleep. The two sweating police horses passed amongst them at an inconsiderate gallop, like a pair of nightmares in pursuit of an innocent sleeper. They hauled up at the darkened police station and went inside.

When the lamps were lit, Laver and Withers went straight to work. From the jumble of the store out the back they retrieved an ancient unclaimed swag recovered from the flood waters years before, and a rusty pistol confiscated during a previous shearers' camp raid. Laver took a blank Labourers' Union ticket from his wallet and filled it in, holding the pen in his left hand, so that it showed the name James Turnbull, no person of that .identity having ever been known to either Laver or Withers in all their lives. They considered writing letters from a sweetheart or mother but decided against it. It wasn't necessary, and there wasn't time. The fewer details the better, they reasoned. Then they took the ticket out the back and folded it several ways and threw it down in the dust of the yard and poured water from the waterbag over it and walked back and forth over it until it had all but ripped in half and its edges were torn ragged and its inscription was muddy and virtually unreadable. Then they put it between two sheets of blotting paper and hung it up to dry a little in the dry night air of the police station office. Then Withers went out into the yard again, carrying the swag. He unrolled it and poured water into it, and he pressed the rusty pistol into it so that there was an imprint of rust in its centre. Then he rolled it back up again, good and soggy, and the job was done. Thus they were able to lie back in the government-issue chairs and feel united one with the other, Laver and

Withers, loyal network agents, and wait for the arrival of the troopers with the wagon still struggling in the star-struck sand on the road miles out of town, passing the Goonda gate.

I have made another trip to the Golden Casket Newsagency (I think you may have suspected it). I dislike the woman who runs the shop. She stands at the cash register with a cigarette hanging from her mouth, always making pen-marks on a TAB form guide.

Because the drawer of the register is constantly open, and because the woman never bothers to ash her perpetual cigarette, one always receives a scattering of ash with one's change. I'm afraid I can't help resenting it.

Also I resent the open drawer. When I pay for something I like it to be rung up. I feel I am being robbed when those little tabs don't pop up, accompanied by the reassuring ring of the register bell. Why should I pay tax and she not?

Thus I feel no guilt whatsoever when I stand at the fiction shelves in her shop thumbing through her stock. I believe she dislikes me as much as I do her.

But she has a good range of paperbacks there (obviously not her own selection). I found one marvellous book, a Penguin Classic, recommended price $4.85. At first I thought the entire novel was written in a single paragraph, 383 pages long. But I was wrong. It was several paragraphs, in fact.

I began reading and my head began to swim. The style! It was marvellous. It flowed, on and on, with dizzying eddies and a gripping undertow, like a drunkenness, or an epidemic, and it made me feel quite faint, so I had to lean against the fiction shelves for support.

It was too much, that style on its own, but I could see how something similar might serve my own purposes, at times.

Then I selected another modern classic. It was just the opposite. Its style was prickly, clipped. It moved in jerks. In sharp, single flashes. Yet each of those flashes, like the frames of a movie film, blended together in the reading.

It sobered me, that style. It was the antidote to the style of the other book. I thought about that for a while.

88

*Then I heard the annoyed bell of the cash register closing,
and the woman was at my side. She took the paperback from my
hands, and shoved it back on the shelf, tearing the cover as she
did so. 'No pay no read, luv,' she said.*

It's not an easy business, this writing.

*On that same day when I wrestled with the microfilm ma-
chine in the John Oxley Library, I also caused trouble at the
Registrar-General's Office.*

*Luckily the two buildings are almost adjacent. I had only to
walk across the intervening park where Queen Victoria stares
down blind-eyed (poor woman) in the shadow of the Treasury
Building, flanked by two spoke-wheeled cannon on which
children played. The walk took fifteen minutes.*

*At the Registrar-General's counter the young man explained
that a search would cost $2.50 for the past two years and $4.50
for each five years before that.*

*I thought it preposterous. $79 the bill would have come to.
$79 to see a piece of paper. And only a photostat of it, after all.
The queue was lengthening behind me.*

*This is a project in the national interest, I protested. No
matter, madam. But I am a pensioner, I said. There are no
concessions, madam. I have paid taxes for more than sixty
years. I'm sorry, madam.*

*Somebody was being rude in the queue behind me. I hit my
walking-stick on the counter.*

*Pretty soon I was sitting with the officer-in-charge (a most
accommodating middle-aged woman) in the vault of the building. Between two alarming motor-driven bookshelves (a whole
bank of them swayed and clashed together on rails), I copied
down the details of the following:*

District: Flinders
Registration No.: (Blank)
To the Registrar of Deaths, BRISBANE
      Form C
      STATE OF QUEENSLAND
      Certificate of Death
First names (in full): William Rose
Surname: BARRET
Occupation: Shearer
Sex: Male

Age: Not Known
Date of Death: —/—/95
Place of Death: Combo Waterhole
Usual Residence of Deceased: Itinerant
Father of Deceased: Not Known
Mother of Deceased: Not Known
Spouse of Deceased: Not Known
Children of Deceased: Not Known
Cause of Death: See attached
Name of Undertaker: N.B. Mills

I certify that the above information is correct for the purpose of insertion in the Register of Deaths.
    Initials and surname of Informant: R.d'A.
      JARVIS
Relationship (if any) to Deceased: None
Residence: Court House, Winton
Witness: C.C. Withers
Date: 11/12/95

And attached to this, a document handwritten in the style of the official form:

CAUSE OF DEATH

    In the Matter of the Death of <u>WILLIAM ROSE BAR-RET</u>, on the<u>   </u>day of<u>   </u>, 1895, at <u>COMBO WATER-HOLE</u>, Queensland, I, <u>REGINALD D'ALGHIERI JARVIS</u>, <u>POLICE MAGISTRATE</u>, hereby Certify that <u>DROWNING</u> was the Condition or Disease leading to Death, and that <u>AN ACT OF GOD</u> was the Morbid Condition or Antecedent Cause giving rise to the above Cause. Approximate interval between Onset and Death was <u>IMMEDIATE</u>.
    Signed by my own hand, this <u>ELEVENTH</u> day of <u>DECEMBER</u>, 1895, at <u>WINTON</u>.

The documents were scorched at the edges, and stained in patches. They had survived flood and fire.

CHAPTER

5

Although the strike camp had now deteriorated, there were still signs of the military precision of its heyday. At what had once been the street corners, the flags still fluttered, though now they were ragged and faded. Hardly legible on them were the old street names: Liberty, Republic, Freedom of Contract. There was little to denote the strict order of the streets and rows of tents which had flourished previously, except for the vague outlines of water trenches here and there and the litter of an occasional broken ridge pole or a torn square of stained canvas part-buried in the sand. Most of those tents now standing formed a defiant knot beside one of the dry river channels, but a few unhappy survivors still retained their original places scattered in the once large grid of streets. No one had bothered to move those isolates into the main cluster after the majority of strikers had picked up and gone back to work. So now it was a ghost tent town in which the flies outnumbered the humans by a million to one, in which the broken bottles burnt where the eager boots once marched, in which the liver-coloured gravel lay in crowds so that the whole empty flat looked like a ravaged and abandoned ants' nest. Those who stumbled here these days, singly, in the shuddering heat, perhaps in search of something to roast — a dying river crab or a smug goanna or an incautious galah — they were the dregs of a revolution which had boiled and brewed and poured itself into the hot sand leaving only this discoloration, this stain on the landscape, this clearing where nothing grew but despair and defiance, with at its centre a blue flag drooping on a hardwood pole much taller than any of the trees between it and the horizon.

The dust-crazy arrival of the police troop could no longer stir a swarm of activity as before. Withers sat on his horse pushing buzzing things from his face and calling for a full minute before Bright appeared from the bushes beyond the tents doing up his trouser buttons and buckling his belt with the resentment of a man interrupted in his day's single pleasure. Bright glared at the native troopers, as was the custom.

'Something for you,' said Withers. He took a swag from the nearest trooper and tossed it down onto the gravel. 'Funeral this afternoon, in case you're interested.'

Bright did not touch the swag. 'We know all about it,' he said. He shielded his eyes to look up at the man on the horse.

'You do, do you?'

'Dredged up from Combo Waterhole. My spies told me.'

'Do they know about this, then?'

Bright read the ragged union ticket handed down to him. 'Never heard of him,' he said.

'Check your records. He's one of yours all right.'

'We'll be there,' Bright said, handing back the ticket. 'Any excuse for a booze-up.'

'The spirit of Unionism,' Withers scoffed.

More Unionists had silently appeared. They glared at the native troopers, as was the custom.

'Is that all you came here for, Mr Withers, to tell us what we already know?'

'I don't think so. We could run a weapons search while we're here, couldn't we?'

'That's an original idea, Mr Withers. God, but you must bore your report readers.'

'On the contrary, Mr Bright. They never tire of a good episode of harassment for the likes of you.'

Withers kicked his horse towards the mess shelter. The hooves sprayed fountains of sand. The calico wall tore down. The shelter exploded like a grenade. Pots and pans flew as Withers bent from the saddle to grab a handful of the utensils that spewed around as the sapling mess table clattered over.

Withers catapulted his horse back out of the ruin. Its front hooves reared at Bright's chest. 'Weapons, Mr Bright,' Withers yelled. 'I could confiscate these.' He brandished the handful of cutlery in Bright's stony face.

'Go ahead. We'll eat with our hands.'

'I don't advise it. You'll get a disease.' He slammed the cutlery down around Bright's boots.

'We have diseases already,' said Bright, catching the blue of Withers's eyeballs. 'They come and go.'

The police galloped away, sending sand and gravel stinging through the camp. The men watched them go, smiling. Then they melted back into the bush beyond the tents.

Standing in the dimness of her pantry, Mrs Rowley had a dreadful thought. She thought of turning into a snail. She passed a hand across her shoulder and a little way down her back, feeling for a swelling; hesitating, imagining the shock of discovering a bony shell there, heavy between her shoulder-blades. As a snail she might have curled up under the lowest shelf in the pantry and avoided the afternoon, but as a snail in the pantry she would probably be trodden on, by accident or intention, and the shards of her broken shell would slice through her poor flesh.

The clatter of chairs scraping on the veranda boards told her that Mrs Bowditch had arrived. She heard the men's voices, grave and excited, welcoming, worshipping. She imagined her household rolling back like Red Sea waves on either side of Mrs Bowditch's entrance. She wondered had Mrs Bowditch brought with her, as she sometimes did on visits to town, the entourage of her five Aboriginal maids, all dressed in gleaming white lace. Privately Mrs Rowley admired and detested Mrs Bowditch for her extravagance and wisdom, but especially for her ability to subdue and intimidate men, to make them all fall in love with her.

If she were a snail Mrs Rowley would crawl secretly to the veranda, then onto Mrs Bowditch's white shoe, then under that dress of froth until she emerged from the cleft between Mrs Bowditch's breasts. There she would sit until the men's flattery sank in their throats, until she felt, near at hand through the perfumed skin, Mrs Bowditch's strong heart falter.

Old Jarvis flung back the French doors. Rowley repeated something he had already said. Paterson grasped hold of the hand floated towards him. Thus buoyed up by considerations and compliments, the squatter's wife entered Mrs Rowley's house.

'I've been looking forward to meeting you, Mr Paterson.'

93

'Very kind, Mrs Bowditch.'

'Call him Bartie.'

'Yes, please call me Bartie.'

'He likes being called Bartie.'

'Special friends call me Bartie. And family, of course.'

'We do so need you out here, Bartie. I mean, we need poets. Our souls thirst for poetry. In all this barrenness.'

'A glass of sherry?'

'It soothes the savage spirit. Poetry does.'

'Don't you think so, Sarah? In all this wilderness poetry breaks the soul's drought. It irrigates the senses.'

'The less suicidal forms of poetry, undoubtedly.'

'Perhaps a brandy?'

'I don't find prose nearly so thirst-quenching. Just the look of it on the page. It reminds me of plains extending from one horizon to the other. Great blank slabs. But poetry comes at you like a river, with whirls and eddies, and little waterfalls.'

'I saw a cloud in the west yesterday.'

'I think I know what you mean. The rhythms. The music.'

'It didn't last long, the cloud. It just melted.'

'Prose has its rhythms too.'

'But they are so subterranean, don't you think, Sarah? You need a diviner to show you how they run. I like the flow to be on the surface, where I can see it. And touch it.'

'I wonder where Mrs Rowley has got to?'

'One can't dive into a subterranean river for refreshment.'

'I never thought of reading poetry as a sort of bathing.'

'Oh, but it is. It envelops you. It makes you tingle. It refreshes. Like an immersion in another element. The men on Goonda prefer reciting poetry to washing themselves. They'll come in after a hard muster and just lie down and lave themselves in a rollicking ballad. It's extraordinary.'

'Unhygenic, I'd call it. No wonder they contract boils and ringworm.'

'Mrs Rowley should be out with the luncheon soon.'

'A case came up before me just the other day. A shearer.'

'By all means, take your coat off, Bartie. You don't mind, do you, Mrs Bowditch?'

'The police could hardly identify him, his face was so distorted with carbuncles.'

'I won't accept that poetry causes carbuncles.'

'Bad diet causes carbuncles. It also causes revolutions. I have a theory that the future of Australia lies in the balance of the outback diet.'

'Oh, Sarah. Really?'

'The New Guinea natives eat very poorly. All roots and shoots. Hardly any meat.'

'Most bush Australians have a positively injurious diet. Far from keeping body and soul together, it prises the two apart. The black and white diet, I call it. Black tea, black salt meat, white sugar and flour. Under their suntans Australians are developing a distinctly grey pallor.'

'The New Guinean's idea of a gourmet banquet is to stuff himself full of bananas.'

'Compare the Chinese in the Australian bush. They value a proper range of foods. They even take their lives in their hands to insure that they get their green and yellow vegetables. They have to fortify and guard their plots, not because the swagmen want to raid them, but because Australians treat good diet as a heathen outrage and mount crusades against it. There have been cases recently of swagmen preferring to starve rather than accept food offered by the Chinese. And the attitude of the Australian towards the Aboriginal diet is equally ignorant.'

'The Myalls certainly enjoy Chinese cuisine. They say the yellow meat has an oily sweetness.'

'Oh, Bartie. Don't be naughty. Sarah is serious. And absolutely correct. On Goonda the men get good greens. At least pigweed stew, and pumpkin when possible. We've not had a case of scurvy in seven years.'

'The New Guineans' first agricultural project was the fattening of a boatload of Chinese in pens. We put a stop to that sort of thing.'

'Exactly, Mr Jarvis. Diet is politics and culture and art and religion, and that is why I make the point that Australia's future is dependent upon the pumpkin on the plate of the rural worker.'

'My dear Sarah, your argument is positively Darwinian. You will have us all turned into cows because our staples are wheat and sugar, which are grasses after all. Or perhaps you will have us as slugs because we fancy lettuce. I must confess my impatience with this notion. "We are what we eat" (as the philosopher said) only in the sense that we develop according to our spiritual and intellectual diets. Of course the brain deteriorates as an organ with lack of food, but its contents, the ideas, concepts and memories, are not products of one's literal digestion. The only time a nation's future is dependent on its diet is in time of war.'

'Napoleon's army marched on croissants and coq au vin.'

'They were defeated by the wind at Waterloo.'

'If Australia is to advance it must do so on a full and varied diet. How can you get a superior performance from a racehorse running on inferior feed?'

'It is minds that count most. Minds feed on ideas.'

'On feelings, I think. Through the senses.'

'On food. It's simple chemistry.'

'Luncheon is served,' said Mrs Rowley, sliding into the room bearing a silver platter on which rode a rich pink corned leg. Her guest, Mrs Bowditch, greeted her lavishly, inquired urgently after her health, insisted that she abandon the role of maid, sat the poor woman in her chair, and took over command of the table herself. The men were well pleased with the arrangement, for Mrs Bowditch dealt to the household chunks of corned meat in proportions unaccustomedly generous. As she did so she leant forward in such a way that each male felt favourably blessed with the aspect of solid pink mountains of flesh approaching them by the plateful across the table. Then there were beans and white radish and a spinach salad to earn little Mrs Rowley the praise of all. There was a sweet French wine which had not perished too greatly in the heat or the travel and which Old Jarvis proclaimed to be a colonial miracle. So they sat at table in the angry heat that dried the sweat on them before it even had a chance to show, eating and drinking because it was the custom, and watching the food pass into each other's mouths before the serviettes came up to dab at the moistures glittering in lip corners. Thus the luncheon might have progressed normally, with Mrs Bowditch bountiful, and Old Jarvis ravenous, with Bartie champing at the bit and Sarah vocal but restrained, with Rowley beaming through his nonentity and his wife tied in a psychological knot, except that there came to them, like the smashing of many bottles and plates and glasses, a great shout in the main street not more than a block away, at which the ladies blanched and the men went rigid. Nevertheless, they all ate on, subdued, no longer tasting the food, no longer listening to each other's conversation, while their awarenesses stumbled between the crème caramel and the main street of town a block away. Then suddenly they realised, with worry's concern for irrelevancy, that the cutlery was hot with the heat and even the wood of the chairs and the table were hot with the heat and the house was vibrating with the heat that bludgeoned the rooftop. Then with the second wild shouting, longer and more accusatory than the first, they each knew that the town was in trouble, but none felt the shout piercing as did Mrs Bowditch, from whom the air seemed to drain as from a balloon. She collapsed back into her chair and did not object when Mrs Rowley, like a newly animated stick insect, saw to the fetching of damp flannels and Japanese fans and a glass of her husband's precious brandy. Then Old Jarvis took charge, acting the part of the fort commandant he wished he had been. He ordered the fastening of all blinds and shutters, because in a riot it's best to appear to be not at home. He ordered the ladies into the pantry, because that was the part of the house safest from flying missiles. And he ordered Paterson to go to the main street to see what was happening, because he certainly wasn't going to do it himself.

Thus, once the orders had been carried out, once they had seen Paterson plummet down the front steps with an almost impolite eagerness, once Jarvis and Rowley had fussed about with their guns and stationed themselves in lonely vigils on front and back verandas, once Mrs Bowditch had been comfortably seetled, if somewhat cramped, with her two friends on chairs beside her in the pantry, then Mrs Rowley was able to sit and muse on the ironies of fate and how she never expected, two hours earlier, that the course of the afternoon's events would return her to the dimness of her pantry with, within foot's reach, Mrs Bowditch as the snail with its shell already broken.

The aftenoon was drunken and lurching in Elderslie Street. The blasting sun staggered in the sky, the roadway sprawled, the uncertain buildings swayed towards each other's shoulders and leant there seeking support. An air of anticipation weighed on the street thick and nauseous; only the hawks ignored it, persisting in their giddy circles. The town is about to vomit, Niall thought.

From where he sat on the veranda of the North Gregory Hotel, Niall saw the two mules start up with the flat cart outside the blacksmith's shop. The blacksmith himself, scrubbed immaculate and wearing the only top-hat in town, led the off-side mule in a shambling processional gait. As the cart came along the street, the men joined the cortege in twos and threes, holding their hats to the sides of their heads, suffering the blows of the sun on their foreheads, all in the good cause of making seemly the haste with which the box on the cart demanded delivery to the hot earth. Onwards it came. The blue flag draped over the coffin hardly stirring with the progress. Onwards it came, gathering its own dusty momentum, bisecting the heavy heat of the street. Past the post office, past the police station, looming onwards in the gorge of Elderslie Street, welling and swelling as more men joined in, their shuffling become a ragged march, their faces red and proud, littered with hair, their eyes scoffing. The town is about to vomit its guts, thought Niall.

Beneath where Niall sat on the North Gregory's upstairs veranda, the members of the United Pastoralists' Association (Winton Branch) spilled out the door from their meeting in the billiards-room. They stood along the hotel's front wall as spectators to the procession, but they looked as though they might be lining up for a photograph. Gaunt, healthy men; they had something akin to smiles on their faces, as if they shared a joke between themselves but not with the rest of the town. Their eyes remained squinting and slitted, as usual, against the sun, wind and insects. They wore coats, vests and ties, in spite of the heat. They had boots of excellent leather, scarred and unpolished. Their hair and beards were neatly trimmed. Their necks were strong, their mouths shut and sardonic. They kept their dusty hats in their hands as the procession drew along the street.

One of them was Squatter Bowditch. He was taller than the rest. His dark striped coat had dark leather buttons and a dark kerchief blossomed from his vest pocket. Above his high collar and large-knotted satin tie was his Gothic head — thin-lipped, eyes set close together and countersunk, forehead cliff-high. Although he was middle-aged he had lost little of the lanky stallion look of his youth. The hair that had been blown from the top of his head had found its way back to the jutting pile of beard sharp-pointing from his chin. While the other squatters stood against the shaded wall, just managing to be respectful towards the burning progress of the coffin, Bowditch moved forward from amongst them. He stepped onto the roadway.

From where he sat above, Niall saw the sun-struck dome of Bowditch's head emerge into the street below. There Bowditch stood, expressionless, waiting for the procession to reach him, not giving the impression that he wished to confront the funeral march, but rather that he was motivated by an ineluctable deep passion the importance of which he had only just realised. As if someone in the crowd had just told him that the body in the box belonged to his own father, or brother, or even to himself. Bowditch's stepping forward into the sun-bashed arena of the street seemed almost unconscious, almost a sleepwalker's act, as if the man stepped intimately in his own dream. Onwards the cart came. The town is about to vomit its entire guts onto the plate of the plain, thought Niall.

When the mules reached level with Bowditch they stopped, seemingly held back by the will of the marchers behind. The blacksmith did not attempt to encourage his charges onwards. He waited, expecting Bowditch to speak. The pastoralists muttered together and stepped out from the shade of the hotel veranda to grip Bowditch and draw him back from the street. But their moving forward sparked a flinty voice in the halted ranks of the cortege: Bright's voice it might have been. 'Murderers,' it called. And the sound of the word leapt like a flame in the tinder-dry street, causing a shout to blaze from the throats of the cortege, a shout that passed through wood and rock and bone like a nausea. Now the town is vomiting its poisons onto its own chest, thought Niall.

The shout tore Bowditch from the bridle of his dream. He shook off those who held him, and strode away. The mules walked again, with no order given. The blacksmith stepped off beside them. The men continued behind the warping wood of the box. A new veneer of unity, like an ash from their shout, settled on their eccentric gaits and uneven shoulders.

But they had not progressed far before Bowditch was upon them from behind, the stabbing hoof-fall of his stallion agitating the road dust, its frontal thrust scattering the marchers, until Bowditch was there beside the coffin, his horse rearing, his whip hand rising in the arc above his head and falling so that the whip lashed the coffin once, scorching the flag, then twice again, cutting it to blue streamers. And as the plaited hide snaked round the coffin the sound was not one of awful hollowness, but of awful solidity, as if the box were packed tight with an earth or a metal, as if the pieces of the corpse inside had rearranged themselves into a man much larger than the original, who in a soggy and bloated tumescence pressed against the inside of the boards of the coffin, threatening the nails of the coffin with a lively new strength. Then, after the last lash had fallen, Bowditch turned, with a smile on his face, well-pleased with a revenge he seemed to claim as his right, and then was surprised at the headlong rush of the marchers at him and their furious clotted shout and their tearing at his legs and his horse. But even though he raised his whip he did not use it on them, and even though one of them sank a mouthful of teeth into his leg and hung on like a bulldog, he was more concerned about controlling his horse and saving it from damage. Then it was that Sub-Inspector Withers ploughed amongst them on his horse and somehow managed to quiet things down so that the blacksmith could rearrange the tattered flag and straighten the adrift coffin, so that the mules could calm down and get on with the job, so that the marchers could proceed with the hot thumping of their hearts in their chests gradually waning.

From where he sat on the upstairs veranda of the North Gregory Hotel, with the afternoon sun beating back the line of shade on the table before him, Niall saw the procession recede down the length of Elderslie Street then turn off across the baked plain for the cemetery. He saw the pastoralists go their several ways on horseback and in traps. He saw the townspeople return inside their buildings. He saw the hotels' doors close and he saw the drinkers left outside lie down in the shady dust. And apart from the echo of the shouting still ringing in his own head, he felt nothing of the incident just passed. The street of the town had fallen down into a dead drunk sleep.

When Paterson came up the steps of the hotel veranda, Clohesy said to him: 'The town lies in the puddle of its own hot vomit. Can you see it?'

Paterson looked across the dazzling street and nodded: 'It's almost evaporated already,' he said.

Among her papers, Great-aunt Sarah had kept the following. She recorded that it was cut from page 3 of the Winton Mercury, *November 19, 1893. In fact it was reprinted from the* Spectator, *June 10 of the same year, pages 767-8.*

THE VEGETARIAN TRIUMPH

We do not quite understand why vegetarians are so triumphant at the result of the pedestrian contest just completed between Berlin and Vienna. They have established a point, but it is one which, to all who knew the facts, was well established before. Provoked, it is said, by the example of the horsemen who recently performed the same feat, a number of pedestrians agreed on a walking-match between Berlin and Vienna, a distance of a hundred and fifty miles. About seventy competitors presented themselves, and although they were forbidden to walk at night, the first two covered the ground at the rate of more than fifty miles a day. They were both vegetarians; and all vegetarians point to the achievement as proof that their system of diet in no way interferes with health or physical endurance. It is no proof of health whatever; and as to endurance, who that knew anything of the subject ever put forward any serious doubt? If there is one thing certain about the races which eat no meat, it is that they can march. . . . A regular Hindostanee carrier, with a weight of 80 lb. on his shoulders will, if properly paid, lope along over a hundred miles in twenty-four hours, a feat which would exhaust any but the best-trained English runners. We feel, indeed, some doubt whether the relation between the power of walking and what is properly called 'physical strength' is at all a close one. Many classes of Bengalees, who are a feeble folk, seem in walking tireless; and it is within the knowledge of us all that many comparatively feeble Englishmen can walk all day, and sit down at the end far less fatigued than men who, in a struggle, would throw them in five minutes on their backs.

Nor is the strength derived from a vegetable diet confined to any particular race. Highlanders fed on milk and porridge are the most active gamekeepers in the world.... Men can live and grow strong when fed only on vegetarian food; but they do not prove that Providence or Evolution, in providing us with flesh-tearing teeth, made a wasteful blunder. The health of the vegetarian races is not equal to that of the races which eat both flesh and farinaceous food. They live, on the average, at least ten years less. They die of disease much more readily, — so readily, that in the face of some diseases, small-pox especially, they seem to have no resisting power at all.... The flesh-eating races have mastered the world, and the Northern Asiatics, who eat meat, have, with their comparatively insignificant numbers, conquered the innumerable vegetarians of India whenever they have invaded them. Economy is the unquestionable 'pull' of vegetarianism.... The mass of mankind never can, or will, get anything but the cereals and other vegetables to eat. To abandon flesh-diet is not to advance, but only to go back to the involuntary practice of the majority of the uncivilised.

As to the moral advantage of vegetarianism, it rests, so far as we can see, on no evidence at all. Meat-eating is said to develop brutality, but, as a matter of fact, it is the civilised and self-controlled classes who are the greatest eaters of meat. The English gentleman is the largest and most habitual eater of flesh, and is on the whole the best man extant.... There is not the slightest moral difference perceptible among the poor who get meat and the poor who avoid it, nor will any honest and sensible man aver that he finds a distinct moral difference in himself — we exclude, of course, the question of alcohol, although it is strictly vegetarian food — because he has changed his diet.... Hunger is a foe to morality; but the method of relieving hunger, provided the food is honestly acquired, matters nothing to morality. The vegetarian races are as cruel, as lustful, and as wilful as the flesh-eating peoples, and incline, we should say, to be decidedly more vindictive. Certainly, we would rather offend a prosperous English artisan with two flesh-meals a day, than a Sicilian sawyer fed on macaroni and melons. There is nothing to be made of that argument, or of its relative, the brutality of killing animals for food. It is awfully brutal *not* to kill them. We wonder if the people who repeat this argument so glibly, and who are really more shocked by the ugly look of shambles than by any destruction of life, have ever reflected for a moment how animals die when they are not killed by human beings. They die either of bites or kicks from other animals, or of disease usually painful and protracted, or of starvation, the latter being, so to speak, the regular course of death arranged by Nature. The horse, in particular, dies in this way with his teeth fast locked together; while the bullock pines away to a ghastly skeleton. There is much to be done which ought to be done to make the death of the edible animals painless, and especially to avoid the agony of fright frequently inflicted on them; but the death itself is a mercy, and would be one even if they did not obtain such compensation in good food and good treatment, and the removal of the perpetual fear which torments all animals left in their natural condition. They are always watching for expected enemies. Of course, to those who deny to man the right to take life, . . . this argument is worthless; but then they should, for the sake of logic, go a step further, —refuse to eat fish because it has life, eggs because they have potential life, and animalcules because life cannot be measured by size. Indeed, we are not sure that they should stop even there. In these days of hyper-sensitive faddists, we are almost afraid to suggest it lest some man with a conscience should be moved not to eat at all; but it is not yet proved beyond possibility of doubt that plants are devoid of life. A nasturtium will creep along a trellice as if it liked the support, and suppose the liking is conscious, as conscious, say, as a hen's fear of a chalk-line, or a parrot's amusement when it has said something funny, what would an unhappy 'vegetarian' on principle resolve to do? He would have to live upon sand, or depart, as a tiger would if it were suddenly afflicted with a moral sense, from a world so badly organised that nothing within it could exist without destroying life.

CHAPTER

6

For the Aboriginal maid it was both a treat and an honour. She sat high in the sulky with Miss Sarah and Mr Paterson, on her face a look that suggested she was a black princess accompanied by her white retainers. In fact she was the chaperon—the customary insurance that people needed not think about Sarah and Bartie getting up to mischief. The Rowleys called her Stella, a name which had nothing to do with her real tribal name. She sat on the sulky's cushioned seat, her narrow buttocks taking up little room. She looked straight ahead over the horse's ears. She waited for the roadway to begin to move underneath and push itself back behind them. 'Good-bye, Stella,' the Rowleys sang from their low station down on the ground. 'Enjoy yourself, dear,' said Mrs Rowley. And Stella thought of the biggest moments of her life—as the ground began to rumble and turn the wheels—the two biggest moments. The first time she realised why she had been circumcised; and the first time she knew the taste of person-meat. 'Good-bye, Stella,' they called to her, and she waved back like a white woman.

In the early morning the drive along the river road was a pleasant one, though the river, which ran alongside all the way, was nothing but a winding dry gravel bed, more like a road than the road itself. They stopped just once because, owing to the excitement, Stella wished to relieve herself, and the excitement gave her the courage to say so. She ran behind the trees on the river bank, lifted her new skirt (specially selected for the trip from Mrs Rowley's cupboard full of cast-offs) and urinated like a man, sending a strong jet out onto the glittering riverbed.

Then she ran back and took her place in the sulky. The next time Stella climbed down was to open the Goonda gate. She regretted doing it, for it meant the ride was almost at an end. Looking ahead Sarah could see the Goonda homestead with its surrounding garden as a fertile spot painted in jest on a vast canvas of desolation. With the river trees receding behind them, there was now so little to remind of life that it seemed possible the drought-cramped plain would extend beyond the horizon for ever. Even the hawks had gone. The sky here was as dead as the land.

'It's hard to believe,' said Paterson, encouraging the horse through the gateway, 'a drop of rain and this will be covered with Mitchell grass.'

It was not in Sarah's nature to feel any confidence in the countless millions of seeds that were supposedly there in the blind dust. But resurrections of that sort were amongst Paterson's stock in trade. With a limited faith, he believed in seeds and seasons, just as he believed in men. Nature and men seemed equally dependable, and equally foolish. They endured in spite of themselves. (Not a little of his optimism was based on his own life. He felt he had overridden fate on several occasions. The best example was literally at hand. The carriage of the withered arm which he always held crooked at his waist had become for others a mark of his transcendent athleticism and respectability. In spite of the unvoiced questions he often saw in people's eyes, he had no intention of ever telling how the deformity had been caused. He had overheard whispers to the effect that he had been dropped by an Aboriginal maid when he was an infant, and that he had fallen from a racehorse while in the lead then been trampled by the followers. He was pleased to allow both versions to circulate.) But the drought was nature's foolishness. To be caught by it was man's foolishness. He knew the disastrous consequences for those whose money lay there, along with the dormant grass-seeds, in the dust. His father had been a grazier broken by poor seasons, and the son knew how a property's dust ached in the owner's heart and in the hearts of the family. But he was now a beneficiary of the city's mild seasons. With a city man's faith, he believed in the miracles performed by insurance companies, those whose job it was to raise from the dead, bring back from disaster, and turn the water of failure into the wine of success. The wide open spaces, parched though they may have been, were still escape from the bars of the city for him. He relished the thought of riding wildly over them, in a gallop faster than galloping, careless of control because there was nothing you could run into. You didn't have to keep to the track when there was nothing at all to collide with between you and the horizon. All you needed was gravity—the spinning globe's gratis insurance cover—to stick you to the earth's gentle roundness.

His vision of wild riding was interrupted by Sarah. 'The Greeks were wrong,' she said. She was watching the drought. 'There's no action in true tragedy. No action at all.'

As they completed the approach to the homestead they saw it grew up out of the plain like a green bush slashed with silver. Paterson directed the sulky round to the back of the house where the true entrance was. Mrs Bowditch came down the steps in a whirling great sun-hat. Under her instructions, the five Aboriginal maids whisked Stella off to the giggling servants' quarters.

'Come on out of the sun. Get those bags, Billy. What a lovely horse! Come on inside, this sun just ruins the skin.' Mrs Bowditch was flushed and energetic. She was building up to great festivities. Sarah and Bartie were the first guests. Mrs Bowditch intended that the Goonda weekend would be remembered long after by those she had invited. Long after the drought, long after the century's end—Mrs Bowditch would make them remember that Goonda was the hub of the world, the heart and home of pleasure, and the epitome of Australian living.

In the afternoon Mrs Bowditch shooed the couple off on a walk around the dam. With the station children at their heels and circling round them, they passed through the brief Eden of the garden and took the path by the sheds towards the windmill standing at the dam's edge. The children fussed around them, showing off their knowledge, eager to hear the sounds of strangers' voices, keen to show the wonders of their world to visitors who had come from the unknown city and seaside.

'There are crabs in the dam.'
'And mussels.'
'I can catch them easily.'
'There are thunder-stones in the bank.'

'You crack them open and there's an opal inside.'
'Sometimes there is.'
'Not often.'
'Can you braid stones on the water, Mr—Um?'
'You mean *skip* stones.'
'They have to be flat ones.'
The children's prattle went on. The trees surrounding the dam were a kind of tea-tree, each with an elaborate network of boughs fanning out from a low trunk. Sarah stood in the fine lace shade beside one of them. She placed a hand on a textured branch. It was in flower, she saw. Tiny brownish flowers hardly noticeable.
'You'll get a tick,' said the children.
'A tick wouldn't like me.'
'Why not?' they asked, surprise in their eyes.
'I'm too old. They only like children.'
'They like everybody,' said the wisest boy.
Paterson was induced to search for stones and skip them on the brown water surface. He was shown how by a group of demonstrators more eager than successful as their stones took one or two desultory hops or sank ignominiously on hitting the water. When he flung a perfect lilting throw which launched and re-launched itself on the water right across the dam until it made a stuttering end on the far shallows and finally came to rest on the opposite bank, Paterson earned the respect of the circle of children.
'He's done it before.'
'Have you done it before, Mr Paterson?'
'Where did you learn?'
'I was a boy once,' said Paterson. The children were amazed.
Sarah did not wish to go too close to the water's edge. Some of the children already had muddy shoes. Sarah walked amongst the trees, where the ground was firmer.
'Let us catch you a crab, Miss Sarah.'
'It's easy. You can see the bubbles.'
One eager boy, the timekeeper's son, wet his shoes and socks splashing in the water. He thrust his hands down. He brought up a small, languid crab, not at all a fierce creature. He spread it out in his two hands, holding it by the nippers. The crab struggled a little. One of its nippers fell off. The boy juggled

tenderly, trying to help the crab, trying to retain the triumph of catching it. Then the other nipper came away.

'You've hurt that crab,' said one of the girls.

'It did it to itself,' said the boy, disappointed.

'You can't pick up crabs, because you hurt them.'

The boy tossed the crab and its nippers onto the ground. The creature scuttled back into the water. 'See? It's all right,' he said. He wiped his hands on the sides of his pants.

They left the children. They walked among the lacy trees. 'I'm pleased you're speaking to me again,' said Paterson.

'You're on probation, Bartie. There's no point in my not speaking with you.'

'I shall not disappoint you.'

'You've taken me to the edge, Bartie. Several times.'

'I know. It's my manners.'

'It's not just your manners. More just your...being a man.'

He dipped his hand into his blazer pocket. She watched him warily. 'I've written you a poem,' he said. He brought out a folded paper. 'Will you read it?'

She took the paper and unfolded it. She read the poem, taking her time. When her eyes reached the bottom of the page he saw they returned to the top. She read it again.

'What do you think?' he asked.

'It's not your best work. Love lyrics are not your forte.'

She handed the paper back. He wanted her to keep it, but she wasn't interested. 'I'll remember it if I see it again,' she said.

'I have no intentions of publishing it,' he said. He folded the paper roughly and jammed it back into his pocket.

They walked back on the path by the tennis court. In front of the house station hands were erecting stalls for the gala day. The spidery frameworks were covered with brightly striped canvas. The children were on the lawns where the turkeys strutted. The birds were not pleased when their chicks ran in waves to the children. The parent birds called to their unsuspicious progeny with *tic-tic-tic* noises. The chicks swarmed about the kneeling children, pecking for promises in the young hands. Sarah wanted the chicks to come to her, but they wouldn't. Paterson laughed. The chicks heeded the mother turkeys' calls when confronted with the adult humans. They swarmed back for protection. In the brindled turkey world children were tolerated but adults were not to be trusted.

There was more. The pair of pea-fowl nestled in the shade beneath the burning bougainvillea. The whole scene produced a feast of colour almost too rich for Sarah's eyes. 'What a splendid bird is the peacock,' said Paterson. 'Do you know it has to grow an entire new set of feathers each year? Sometimes the strain is too much. A peacock can die from the effort of renewing its plumage. And the Indians say the peacock is more than a match for the swift-striking cobra, yet he stands for execution to the leopard. Hypnotised by the spots, apparently.'

'And what of the pea-hen?'

'No such complex glory attaches to her, I'm afraid.'

'I don't believe you,' said Sarah.

The drink of fresh-pressed cumquats Mrs Bowditch sent out for them when she saw they had returned was cool and tart. It was just a little sweet from sugar, with the green scent of the mint leaf tingling as they drank. Then the Goonda afternoon provided the event that fascinated Paterson most. Bowditch came in in a trap with a bundle struggling on the tray behind him. Two men lifted the writhing sugar-bag and carried it to a cage beside one of the huts. 'For the hunt,' said Bowditch, as the bag was cut open. Inside was a trussed-up dog, its legs and jaws bound with strong rope. It was a dingo. Its heart thumped visibly inside its rib-cage. 'Gave us the hell of a run-around,' said Bowditch. 'Should be good for a quarry, eh?' They put it in the cage and cut its ropes, the jaw rope last. They left it there. Paterson and Sarah watched as it paced around the cage. It was handsome, skinny, light-footed. The ground of the cage seemed not to hold it quite, the dog's feet seemed to tread just a little above the ground, on their own elastic invisible footing. It lifted its head and sniffed, not for anything close at hand. Its nose, like its eyes, had a concern only for the distant horizon.

'The poor thing,' Sarah said.

'It's all right,' said Paterson. 'It's the lucky one. Probably get a good feed tonight. And tomorrow as well.'

Bowditch came back with the children in tow. Among them was a small Aboriginal boy. He was skinny and graceful. His largest parts were his head and feet. 'Watch this,' Bowditch said. Bowditch opened the gate and the boy got into the cage. He talked to the dog all the while in a language the whites did not understand. The dog circled, but the boy caught it and leapt onto its back. He rode it around the cage, lying along its back with his feet pressed into its flanks, gripping the back of its neck with his hands and teeth. The dog bucked and pig-rooted, but the boy's teeth and toenails held firm. The children laughed. Paterson yelled 'Bravo!'

'All right,' said Bowditch. The boy got out of the cage, his smile glittering with the congratulations.

'All we need is money,' said Bright. 'We've got everything else. We've got the numbers and the expertise. We're prepared. But we need money. It takes money to make and maintain a war.'

Niall was sitting in the mess shelter at the strike camp hearing the staccato flap of tent canvas in the hot wind, hearing Bright's voice fighting against the surge of the wind through the shelter.

'You don't look healthy,' Niall said. 'None of you blokes looks healthy.'

'We're all right,' said Bright.

'So when will the unions send more money?'

'When they can. When the southern unions get back on their feet.'

'And until then . . . ?'

'We'll be right.'

'You'll starve.'

'We'll be in reserve.'

'Why don't you give it up, Bright? They've elected to fight in Parliament now. There's no future in the bloody revolution theme.'

'We won't get anything with politics. We'll still be bossed and galloped over. We can't win that way. We wanted to do it peacefully, but we weren't allowed to. I wanted to do it peacefully. Now I don't care about peace, I care about my stomach. And I wonder what you care about, Niall. Because if you're not here to help start the war again, I don't know why you're here at all.'

Niall looked quickly round the shelter. There were two other men there, both of them yellow-faced. One was asleep with his head on the rough table, the other stared vacantly, having no energy to swat at the flies writhing about his head.

Niall said, 'You have no need to question my loyalty.'

110

'It's all right for you. Freelance adventurer. Got a handsome contract. I don't know why they spent money on you when they knew we needed it here.'

'They spent precious little money on me. Don't worry about that. And my totally inadequate contract runs out in less than a week.'

'Well, you better make some moves, then, hadn't you?'

'I wonder did they get me to do this job, Bright, because they see in you a personality somewhat lacking in subtlety. It's useful in time of war, you know. Subtlety is. The Trojan horse was subtle. You don't get something as big as that into the enemy's camp without subtlety. You be the soldier, Bright; I'll be the Trojan horse.'

Bright looked beyond the shelter at the dust blowing through the scattered skeletons of gidgee bush on the hopeless plain. 'Just testing you,' he said. 'Just trying you out. Want to go for a walk?'

They pushed their way through the dry stubble of bushes behind the tents until they came to a gravel channel. They followed it for several hundred yards. Then they turned off, pushing through more spike scrub. Suddenly they were out of the wind. They had dropped down into a scrub-lined depression which seemed to Niall to be a silted, dried-up billabong. At the end of it there stood a rough shed, and along the banks of the depression were gibbet-like structures, some of them with bulging, heavy sandbags hanging down on ropes.

'There it is,' said Bright.

'There *what* is?'

'The arsenal and training ground.'

'Wonderful,' said Niall, dry-mouthed.

They went into the shed. There were poles stacked in the corners. Some of them had shear-blades attached to their ends. Bright opened boxes containing old Snider rifles and other veteran firearms. There were also storage lockers for explosives, but these were empty. The place stank from the empty paraffin cans stacked along the wall. Niall also thought he smelt urine.

'At least it's still here,' Bright said. 'That means something, doesn't it? The coppers have been all over this camp a hundred times but they never found this. We had six hundred men training here last year. Before the money ran out. They might be working Graziers' Contract now but they'll not have for-

111

gotten what they learnt. Sandy Hollow we called it. The coppers never found it out.'

They walked to one of the training gibbets. Niall pushed the hanging bag and let it swing. On each arc of its swinging, some of its stuffing — sand and bits of wool — spilled out through the slashed shear-blade holes. 'Tell me about Barret,' Niall said.

'Barret had my position. He was the branch secretary, and he was the camp secretary, too. He was a bit of a loner. Perhaps he had a special brief from Brisbane. I don't know about that, but I'm sure he was loyal. He was an intellectual. I think he'd been to university somewhere — overseas of course. But it wasn't his education the men disliked him for. They weren't jealous of education. It was something else. He led a fuller life than they did. He'd been in the theatre at some time, I think. Played Shakespeare and all that. He could quote pages of it. Anyway, he could dress up and act a part when he needed to. Like you say, he had subtlety. But it didn't go down too well with the men. They weren't sure who he was. And when the rumours started going round they had nothing they could say they knew about him for certain. He was an enigma. And when you're fighting for bread and butter you don't have much time for enigmas.'

'What were the rumours?'

'That he was up-ending the woman of Bowditch.'

'And was he?'

'Well, I was never there looking over his shoulder. But I think he was.'

'And the men didn't like it?'

'The rumours caused jealousy. There was some loss of confidence in his leadership. As you pointed out, the most subtle forms of loyalty don't look like loyalty at all. Barret was spying in the enemy's camp. But the men were too worked up to see it that way. Consorting with the enemy was bad enough. The fact that most of the men had starving wives back home made matters much worse. Barret just seemed to be having too good a time. There were a dozen or so women in the camp, but they were wives, even the black ones. There was a good moral sense amongst the men. But, God knows, we were like sailors who'd been at sea for years. Anyhow, most were too blind to see that Barret was often the source of the most important snippets of intelligence. He'd know of movements in the district before they happened. Our spies would later verify them. He'd know numbers — quite exact sometimes. Bales of wool in a shed, pastoralists at a meeting, scabs on a train, troopers on a station. God knows how he used to get her to talk. But he must've. Still the men were carrying their stalks around in wheelbarrows and couldn't see past them to the fact that even if he was enjoying himself Barret was our key agent.'

'And how did he and the Bowditch woman arrange their meetings?'

'He used to hump a swag over on Goonda now and then and meet her in the woolshed at night. That's how the rumour went, and it was probably true. The men took particular delight in burning down the Goonda woolshed. They would have loved to have found the two charred skeletons locked together there in the ashes. That's why they surrounded it and stayed, fending off the troopers, hoping for Barret and Mrs B. to come running out with their bums burning. But they didn't.'

'Yet Barret failed to come back to camp that night.'

'That's right. That was the night he disappeared. He was missing for the rollcall next day, so we went looking for him. As you know, we never found him.'

'How hard did you try?'

'Look, we didn't have the equipment to drag the billabong. The money was well and truly running out then. Goonda was the last shed fired, wasn't it? We had the paraffin "on credit" — I mean, stolen — from Corfield's for that job. Besides, we thought the billabong was the last place to bother looking, seeing as the Pastoralists were spreading the notion that he'd been sprung for stealing and drowned himself there. "Upped and jumped into the billabong," Withers told us. We thought it was a load of horse-shit. We searched everywhere else, even down the abandoned mines at Opalton. The billabong story didn't ring true. Barret could swim like a snake.'

Niall looked down at his boots. Unconsciously he had been carving a series of grooves in the sand with his right toe. Bright looked down too. 'I wonder who did shoot Barret, then?' Niall said.

'I don't know,' Bright replied. Then he was silent for a moment. He looked up, at Niall's face. 'What do you mean "shoot"? He was drowned.'

'No, he wasn't,' Niall said. He took a bullet from his pocket and held it out in the palm of his hand. 'He was shot.'

'Where'd you get this?'

'It was lodged in Barret's skull behind the jaw. He was shot square in the face.'

'It was no one from the camp. Those who questioned his devotion to the cause still admired him as a man. Not a one of us wouldn't have waltzed Mrs B. rather than Matilda any day. If he was shot it must have been the troopers.'

'This isn't a trooper's bullet. It's a revolver bullet. Who's got a revolver around here?'

As he asked the question Niall smiled into Bright's face, and Bright smiled too as he answered.

'Almost everybody.'

When Laver came through the doorway of the police station he had the bullet in his hand. He found Withers untying the roller-skates from his boots. He had been filling in the time waiting for Laver's return with a series of figure-eights in the cleared courtroom. Laver tossed the bullet into the ashtray on Withers's desk.

'What did he say?' Withers asked.

'He said no one at the camp would have shot Barret.'

'Did he deny all knowledge of Barret's shooting?'

'Of course.'

'Then they're not changing their story.'

'And you say you saw Barret at the strike camp after the Goonda firing?'

'You're damn right I say it. It's all there in my report. Signed and dated, and Brisbane receipt acknowledged. It's in the files.'

'I know it's in the files. You say you investigated a shooting incident at the camp. A striker had been shot "by his own hand" according to witnesses. You had suspicions that he had in fact been shot in the Goonda raid and carried back to the camp, but you couldn't prove them.'

'I had other suspicions, too. The scum hadn't washed the blood off his face when I saw him. They gave his name as Hoffmeyer, but I knew it was Barret. I had talked with Barret often enough. There were eight hundred men would have said they knew him as Hoffmeyer and that they'd seen him shoot himself in the head with a rifle. It was a plausible story. They *were* going crazy out there, what with the heat and the starvation and the losses to their cause. Suicide was on the cards all right. But, of course, there was no bullet. I searched round a bit, got the boys to do a bit of sniffing. "Lost in the bush," the scum said. So I told them to bury him. He'd been a nuisance, anyway. It was a help to have him out of it. Brisbane told me to forget about him. Which I did. Seems they've changed their minds now.'

'You said you had other suspicions?'

'Well, hardly suspicions. He'd been shot as a traitor, hadn't he? The whole Goonda operation had been timed to spring him there at the woolshed. He was Mrs Bowditch's contact. Everybody knew that. He was double-crossing his own lot for all he was worth. I put money in his hand from time to time — you know... "discreet disbursement of government funds". He was one of the few who would take it. Thought he was safe because he had a cover — could always say he was insuring his credibility with us. Did you know they had an execution squad out there at the camp? Very effective, it was. Kept the strikers loyal to their cause. Most of them, anyway. Many's the time we tried bribes and found a lack of co-operation. Even when they were starving. They had the death squad hanging over their heads all right.'

'So how did the body get into the billabong?'

'They carried it there, I suppose.'

'Why didn't they just bury it, as you told them to?'

'Because it was Barret, eh? And they'd said it wasn't.'

Withers took the knife from his belt and began using it to clean the wheels of his roller-skates. Laver leant back in his chair and took off his spectacles. They needed cleaning too.

'Where do you live in Brisbane, Mr Laver? If you don't mind me asking.'

'West End. Overlooking the river.'

'Nice house?'

'Very pleasant.'

'You got a bathroom?'

'Yes, I have, as a matter of fact. What makes you ask?'

'I thought you'd be the kind of man would have a bathroom. No offence meant, mind you. It just struck me that way. You're the kind of man would get himself a bathroom, aren't you.'

'I'll take it as a compliment.'

'That's what it is, don't worry. And by the way. That problem you've got with your eyes. Best thing for it is to piss in an eye-glass and apply it before going to bed. Works wonders.'

Withers put his skates on the shelf behind him and stood up. He shouted for the Aboriginal Sergeant who was quickly at the door. He gave the order to saddle up. The Sergeant turned and left. Withers looked down at a note on his desk. 'Oh, a message. You're welcome to ride with us if you like. I understand Bowditch has extended an invitation to you, too. For his Gala Day. I think you should go.'

'So do I,' said Laver.

It was almost dark when the police detachment arrived at Goonda homestead. Niall had seen, as they rode up the track towards the house, that the sunset had reddened not just the western sky but the entire sky to the east. It had given him cause to imagine that the sun was in a slaughterhouse, its blood spattering the sky roof. He was hardly surprised when he walked through the yard gate to be greeted by a row of sheeps' heads, their eyes still bright and knowing in death, their noses bloody and fly-clotted, their jaws moving back and forth talking in high-pitched squeals and gruff growls. The children thought it a marvellous joke. They played in the near-darkness, using the heads for every kind of fancy from frightful masks to footballs. Their clothes were bloodied, and their limbs. One boy struggled under the weight of two heads, his arms thrust up through their throats. His hands worked away inside the jaws while his own mouth talked the two voices of a sheep conversation: 'Hullo, Mary'... 'Hullo, Bert'... 'I saw you getting shorn this morning, Mary'... 'Yes, Bert'... 'They took off all your clothes, Mary'... 'Yes, they did, Bert. Aren't they naughty'.... The children laughed and tumbled merrily in the gory dust. They were having a marvellous time. Their parents, like the clotted sun below the rim of the plain, were a million miles away.

On the precious strip of lawn between the tennis court and the house, the guests were gathered. Tall torches had been set around and lit; their streaming flames danced up the thickening darkness, starting shadow-plays on the lighter-coloured clothes and faces. There were Japanese lanterns strung amongst

116

the garden trees. There were punch-bowls and cut-glass de-canters on wickerwork tables attended by the nervous hands of stockmen. There were canvas chairs and tartan picnic rugs draped with the glowing forms of the guests. There was a shuttlecock soaring into the darkness beyond the torchlights accompanied by exclamations of glee and dread. There were dogs which needed chasing off, and a pair of pea-fowl which refused to come down from their obscure roost atop a garden shed. There was, somewhere in the garden, a shrub pumping out a heavy, dreaming fragrance, and there was the high-strung snapping of the gidgee-wood fire over which a splayed carcass was turned on a spit by a sweating, smiling Aboriginal station hand. Beside him, laid out on trays covered with gauze, were further cuts of meat, mainly sliced livers, brooding darkly as they waited for the sting of the fire. Amongst the guests the six Aboriginal maids (Mrs Bowditch's five plus Stella) slid like moths, winged forward by their trays of dainties and glittering cups of punch. The murmur of the guests rose and dispersed in the vast night; like the torchlight it climbed for a warm yellow moment then was lost, vanished towards the emergent stars in the great black hot stomach of the sky.

For Niall, moving forward across the lawn, the blurred guests were at first just anonymous portions bunched under the dark gauze of the sky. But as his awareness adjusted he picked out one he knew. Paterson was there. And as their features began to individualise beneath the constant painting of the torchlight, he was able to recognise others he had seen in the town. It was a gathering of the best and the best-dressed people of the area. It was the outback high society, talking and laughing smoothly on Mrs Bowditch's miraculous stretch of green lawn in the desert. They murmured and chuckled and played smoothly like a well-oiled, clean machine.

From the centre of one of the groups emerged Mrs Bowditch. She lifted a handful of the fire-licked lace of her long dress as she swept across the lawn towards him. Floating behind her, as if on a string, came one of the tray-borne maids.

'Good evening, Mrs Bowditch. Inspector Clohesy. I was pleased to receive your husband's invitation through Sub-Inspector Withers.'

The woman took him by the arm and steered him away from

the flickering party group. They veered towards the house. 'Careful of the steps, Mr Laver,' she whispered in the dark.

They stood on the veranda. The torchlight seeped through the foliage just sufficiently for them to see each other. Near at hand was a rosemary bush. They stood in the aura of its burning scent. As she spoke she gripped his arm, and looked up at him with childish large eyes.

'Pardon me, Mr Laver. I did not wish to draw attention to you on your arrival, but there is no other way to do this. You see, I have received no instructions on how you should be treated. I have simply heard from Withers that you are here to investigate. I sincerely hope that you will find my own activities to be of the requisite standard of devotion.'

'I have no doubts whatsoever concerning your loyalty, Mrs Bowditch.'

She was holding him by both hands now. 'But I must warn you of one thing, Mr Laver. I do not share any of our secrets with my husband. Perhaps you know this already, but I cannot afford for you to make a mistake. My husband shares our cause, but he is not part of the network. I manage to supply him with information, but he considers it my business how I come by that information. He is a fine man, and I love him devotedly. He is one of the reasons why the future Australia we work for is bound to be a success.'

In the torchlight her eyes glittered moistly. Niall felt her hand's pulse in his own. She was an exceptional woman, he realised. But through her acting he could feel she did not trust him. He wondered how comprehensively she was lying to him. He had presumed since the bath-house incident that Squatter Bowditch was central to the Pastoralist network. He had also presumed — from the start — that initially they would all lie to him, no matter which side they were on. They would all be wall-building. His job was to work out their mazes faster than they could extend them. Where was the country, he wondered, that was not the country of guilt and deceit?

She dropped his hands when they heard a noise in the house, a squeaking of floorboards. 'Who's that?' came a voice through the French doors.

'Only me, Eugene,' Mrs Bowditch replied, 'and Inspector Clohesy.'

118

Bowditch came out onto the veranda. Even in the inadequate torchlight Niall saw that the squatter's front was splashed with blood and the blood was spattered up his cheek too. The dark hand with which Bowditch gripped Clohesy's was wet; wet with that particular smooth wetness Niall knew was blood.

'Pleased to meet you, Inspector,' said Bowditch before their hands slid apart. 'Pardon my appearance. Kill Night, of course. But it took a little longer than anticipated. You are very welcome here, sir. I notice that Withers has installed a peace-keeping force for tomorrow's events, and I am indeed grateful about that. Now, if you'll excuse me, I'd better make myself decent. I'm looking forward to talking with you, Inspector.'

Mrs Bowditch hurried her husband off with an affectionate wave of her hand. Niall could not help noticing how strikingly white the hand was. 'He's such an honest man,' she confided, once Bowditch had gone. 'Sometimes I feel dreadful about my own reputation for intrigue. But he understands. He is wonderfully understanding.' Then she took Laver's arm with a sudden girlish jerk and said, 'Come on, Mr Laver. There are some lovely people here. I want you to meet them all.'

Back on the lawn the children had been called up for their share of the meat. They had successfully scandalised the adults by displaying the play-stains smeared on their limbs and clothes. So, with a chorus of motherly gasps — 'Look how you've ruined those new ribbons' and so on — the children's hands were subjected to the rigorous attentions of a maid, a flannel, and a bucket of water. Then they were allowed to scamper off with the Kill Night meat black and juicy on their plates.

Once the children were out of the way, the adults were invited to partake. Goonda's oldest and most faithful employee — an ancient stockman with a nose half wasted by a cancer — carved delicate thin slices of roasted meat direct from the carcass where it hung over the fire. He allowed the juices to drip off and hiss in the gidgee embers. He was the veteran of a thousand and one Kill Nights, and each of them, from the earliest he remembered in youth, was as magic as this. The magic of fresh red meat under the cathedral dome of the wide night sky.

Mrs Bowditch descended upon Paterson and Sarah's group with Laver in tow. 'This is Inspector Clohesy,' she said.

'We are old friends.' Paterson smiled. 'Sarah, may I in-

119

troduce Inspector Clohesy? Miss Sarah Rowley.'

'How do you do?'

Mrs Bowditch continued: 'These are my neighbours, Robert and Angus Macphee. And Miss Christina Macphee.'

The Macphee brothers were thin young men, almost identical, with close shorn haircuts. Set deep in their heads, each had those outback eyes which, damaged by the plains wind, looked like bowls of bloodshot porridge. Their sister Christina, on the other hand, showed nothing of their taut, scrubby look. She stood in the group with an easy, ironic stance, lifting a soft drink coolly to her lips. When she spoke, Niall noticed how the moist tip of her tongue advanced a little eagerly, giving her an attractive, slight lisp. 'Delighted to meet you,' she said.

'I was just telling Bartie here,' said Robert Macphee, 'about the Combo Waterhole — which I understand you had cause to visit recently, Inspector.'

'Yes, I did. A marvellous spot.'

'Indeed, very popular with picnickers. But also a treacherous stretch of water.'

'You are familiar with its dangers, Mr Macphee?'

'Naturally. I own it, you see. It is part of Dagworth. Though, of course, we allow free access to anyone who wishes to come and use it.'

'The police made excellent use of it, I assure you.'

'So I hear. But it occurred to me, on meeting Bartie here, what a wonderful story that waterhole might tell. I was just suggesting the idea to Bartie because he says he's a writer.'

Christina spoke: 'Oh, Robert. He's a very well-known writer.'

'Well, I don't read books. I'm sorry. But I'm sure a writer could make that billabong speak in an entertaining way. It's seen a few things, old Combo Waterhole.'

'Like what, Mr Macphee?' asked Clohesy.

Mrs Bowditch thought she should intervene at that point: 'No business, please gentlemen. I couldn't bear to think that my party was turning into a police investigation.'

Just then Bowditch came across the lawn. His tall figure was resplendent in a cream suit and maroon tie. He carried a brandy balloon like a lamp in front of him, and was followed by an Aboriginal boy who carried the decanter.

'Ah. Now here's a man who's heard me tell this story in detail,' said Macphee.

'What story's that?' Bowditch asked, smiling as he came up to them.

'The story of the jolly swagman.'

Bowditch's face changed. 'There's no such thing as a jolly swagman,' he said. 'All the swagmen I ever saw were starving, out of work, and had blisters the size of saucers on their feet.'

'Well, what about the one I scared off down at the Combo that time. He was jolly all right. Just scored himself one of my sheep, he had. Very jolly he was with his billy going and his slaughter knife flashing. Good Lord, the smoke from our woolshed was still hanging in the air! The insolent so-and-so (I *am* sorry, ladies). There's no end to the impudence of these Unionists, I reckon. So I rounded up the native troopers who were moping round in the woolshed ashes trying to look useful, and I took them back down to the waterhole where the republican was having his lordly banquet and I gave him a scare he won't forget till his royal funeral, that's for sure. I've never seen anyone jump so high from a sitting position. It was as though a dingo trap went off right under his—oh, I *am* sorry, ladies. Up he went into the air and over went the billy and in he went with a giant splash and the waterhole bore him away. Well, me and the troopers were laughing so much we just about fell off our horses. There was King Ned's table so nicely set out on the ground— fillet of shank, a couple of juicy kidneys, a pannikin of bush tea glowing like your French champagne—and there was King Ned himself thrashing across the waterhole getting tangled in his own clothes and yelling for help. Well, we thought we'd wait until he'd had a few draughts of good billabong water as a sort of aperitif to his feast, but somehow he got to the other side and ran off into the scrub. Good Lord, what an athlete he was. Well, we left his gear there, and the tucker, so he could come back for them if he was game, and we took the rest of the sheep home and put it to good use in the stomachs of its rightful owners. When I went back to the waterhole the next day to see if he'd picked up his bluey and so on, the lot was gone all right, but what I was really looking for wasn't there at all. Now don't you reckon he could have thanked me in some way—left me a message scratched in the dirt or spelled out with twigs or something of the like? Not on your life. The blighter just up and took his full stomach with him with never a hint of thanks. Unless you say the midden he deposited (oh, I *do* apologise—his calling-card, ladies) was a vote of his appreciation. I certainly didn't take it that way.'

They were all smiling in spite of themselves. Paterson laughed out loud. 'Yes, it's a marvellous story,' he said. 'I like it. I like it very much.'

'Why don't you write it?' suggested Mrs Bowditch. In spite of her happy wink directed at Paterson, Niall had the feeling that the story's delivery had been set up for his own, not Bartie's, benefit.

'But what about the treacherousness, Mr Macphee?' Clohesy asked. 'You said the waterhole was treacherous.'

'It is treacherous, too,' he answered. 'There's all sorts of snags under the surface. You can't dive in with any guarantee of safety. But worst of all is the double treachery of that old waterhole allowing the thief to dive in and get away. It's a rogue, Old Combo, a certified old rogue.'

They sat in the canvas chairs set out for them, and nibbled at the food brought to them. An elegant drinks waiter with perfect butler's English (who was the new smiling jackaroo) served them with exquisite charm. And the spirit of the waterhole story continued in various branches and metamorphoses in the group as they pursued their separate concurrent conversations. Christina suggested to Sarah that they should all have a picnic there; Paterson claimed to Macphee that Shakespeare's father had been fined twelve pence for depositing a large midden in the high street of Stratford; and Bowditch involved Clohesy in one of his own favourite topics, that of plumbing.

Bowditch. I would be a patron of the arts, Inspector, if there were any arts for me to patronise here —

Paterson. So if you charged twelve pence a midden, you might make a fortune.

Christina. Don't take any notice of Robert. It's a delightful place.

Bowditch. — but as it is, my spiritual and intellectual ambitions have been perverted into an obsession with physical achievements —

Macphee. Swagmen have a singular element in common, Bartie. Their pockets are always far emptier than their bowels.

Sarah. Do you swim there yourself?

Bowditch. —yet it is an obsession that I find appropriately contrary to the terrifying crudity of Australian manners and pursuits in general—

Paterson. I don't know that I could use all the aspects of your story. I might have to censor it here and there—

Christina. Heavens, no. I leave that sort of silliness to the men.

Bowditch. —I am designing a plumbing system for this site, to take in the house, the huts, even the stables. You can't have civilisation without plumbing—

Paterson. —make it a little less vivid unfortunately, a little less colourful.

Sarah. I know what you mean. They are such insecure creatures.

Bowditch. —I intend it as my masterpiece. It will put Goonda just a little closer to Utopia—

Macphee. I could tell you plenty more, Bartie—

Christina. Always showing off.

Bowditch. —I suppose it's perfect order in one form or another that inspires all of us, eh, Inspector?

Macphee. —Ghost stories? Do you like ghost stories?—

Sarah. So childish, so brutish. Egotists all of them, yet so insecure.

Clohesy. But one must be careful about the quest for perfection. It maddens, I have found.

Macphee. —The youngsters delight in 'em. Mad for 'em, they are. Good Lord, but they love a good scare—

Christina. They drive you mad. Yet where would we be without them?

Bowditch. On the contrary. It purifies.

Macphee. —So do the sheep, I reckon.

Sarah. I know very well where I would be—

Clohesy. Maddens and purifies, perhaps.

Paterson. You tell your sheep ghost stories?

Sarah. —I'd be in paradise.

Bowditch. I'm not saying it makes one happy. The pure state is beyond emotional vagaries—

Macphee. Of course I do. I've tried them all, in fact. Comical stories are no good: no sense of humour, sheep. Tragical

123

stories? They don't give a damn. But ghost stories —

Christina. Surely you can't mean that? There would be no love.

Bowditch. — but who among the great painters or writers, for example, ever went mad? I mean, the *great* —

Macphee. — Good Lord, sheep delight in 'em. You should see their teeth chatter with excitement —

Sarah. No love? Why do you suppose that?

Bowditch. — those who did achieve perfection. They weren't maddened. It is not the quest that maddens, it is the failure.

Macphee. — and they lick each other in delighted horror. Their little tongues go in and out, in and out.

Christina. I'm sorry. I don't think I quite understand you.

Clohesy. I can only disagree to the extent that I've always thought of the quest as interminable.

Paterson. I think you're pulling my leg.

Sarah. I mean, dear, don't you find solitude preferable to male company?

Bowditch. Then you have not eyes, nor ears, nor tongue, Inspector. But, worst of all, you have no faith.

Macphee. O' course I'm pulling your leg.

After it was all over, after the sleeping children were carried through the night to their beds, after the closest neighbours had set off in their traps in the moonlight, after the maids had flitted amongst the litter on the lawn, after the dogs had crept up for the bones, after the torches had been extinguished — after it was all over, Niall lay in one of Goonda's many beds in one of Goonda's many guest-rooms and dreamt of women, masses of them, thousands of them, crowds of them all dressed in huge sun-hats, each carrying a parasol, moving and milling in plazas and squares, rising and dropping on a lacework of stairways, standing and sitting on platforms and balconies and towers and gazebos, and from the centre of them all, from the very centre of the focus of their collective attention, there rose a statue, a heavy monument achingly solid which nevertheless rose, seemed to levitate, stood in the air, plinth and all, a statue of the Empire's Queen gripping all the instruments of her office, the mace, the sceptre, the crown, with at her feet the lion of Africa, the tiger of India, the wild dog of Australia, while beneath it all, straining on the wires keeping the statue aloft, were Niall and two other men whose bulging throats gave out a triad howl, a chord of desperation, pumped from strangling muscles and knotted tendons, so that Niall awoke with the howl still quivering in the moonlight in the room and he wondered, fearing, whether others in the house had heard him call out. But he need not have worried, for the howl came again, staining the air in the hot room, tearing and dripping along the moonlight in hot gouts of sound. It was the implacable howl of the creature outside the window, the dingo pacing the narrow perimeter of the cage, ablaze with moonlight, stopping again to ululate for the wild, fecund horizon beyond the cage bars.

Form RT — Classified
Government of Queensland
CONFIDENTIAL

Projects Bureau,
Colonial Secretariat.

Parliament House,
Brisbane.
In the wilderness
14th December

My Sweet Angel!
It has worked wonderfully! The letter you addressed to Bartie reached me today. Bartie (as all seem to call him here) was quite bewildered by its arrival. He handed it to me with the oddest of expressions on his face. I could see the works ticking furiously in his brain, but I don't believe they were providing him with any satisfactory solution to the puzzle. The idea seems to have worked so well, I shall 'borrow' some of his envelopes to use in the return post to you.
I don't believe you can imagine how excited I was to receive a tangible proof of your continued existence. I have had the most abominable and unworthy imaginings during this time of separation from you. I have had nightmares of you electrocuted amongst all that fizzing hydropathic equipment, and of you drowning at the seaside. Considering the advanced state of the drought out here, my dreams are ironic, to say the least. I must also admit that I suspected as much as you intimated regarding Harris's pestering of you in my

125

absence. Men will be men, I suppose, but I'm damned glad to know that you, as a woman, will always be an angel to me. If that seems either glib or convoluted, what I mean to say is that I trust you implicitly. I've had cause to observe several marriages and friendships out here and it gives me great heart to discover (once again) that you and I have a union unparalleled.

I shan't pretend to be elated at the way the project is progressing. Suffice it to say that all my contingency plans are being called upon and seem to be holding together fairly well. In spite of Harris's betrayal of me in the field of love, he seems to be doing a tolerably good job of support in the field of war. They still don't know who I am, in spite of their vigorous inquiries. When you see him (which you will undoubtedly — he is a persistent sod, I know) you may thank him for me.

By the way, my darling, there is a beautiful dingo in a cage here at Goonda. They plan to use it for a hunt tomorrow. I am certain you would appreciate its beauty. I've never viewed anything so wild. It's quite ethereal! It seems to have the wilderness dispersed amongst the molecules of its body. It paces the cage — there but not there! Perhaps it knows it is finished already. Perhaps it is rearranging itself so it can fade through the bars. If you were here, you would steal out and release it tonight, wouldn't you?

Good night for now, my astounding one. You are lodged in my heart.

Your True Mate,
H.

PROGRAMME
GALA DAY at GOONDA
15th December 1895

1. Official Opening by Mr Corfield, M.P.	9 a.m.	
2. Fire-Fighting Demonstration ('The Busby Fire Sweeper')	10 a.m.	
3. Ladies' Photography (on the lawn)	10.45 a.m.	
4. Flood-Fighting Demonstration (Mr Campbell's Winch)	11 a.m.	
5. Armaments Demonstration (Major-Gen. McIver, C. de G.)	12 noon	

126

6. Station Employees' Photography   12.45 p.m.
   (by the back huts)
7. Water-Diving Demonstration   1 p.m.
   ('Old Jack' Woolley)
8. Gentlemen's Photography (on the lawn)   1.45 p.m.
9. The Hunt   2 p.m.
10. Gala Ball   8 p.m.

Booths and Entertainments will operate during the day.
Mrs Bowditch's celebrated Cumquat Punch (free of alcohol) will be available.

'O God, we beseech thee,
in this our necessity, send
us moderate rain, to our
comfort and to thy
honour.
Amen.'

CHAPTER

7

The day's dance began in the false dawn. The smallest creatures looked out from their narrownesses; the larger took their first bowing steps. Shyly they rose to the light, primping and preening mock-secretly, extending a feeler, wing, paw, to the tentative stretch of the sun. Out they all came, standing firmer, stepping higher, intent on the weaving of the day's figure — its demands, the meetings and avoidances, growing in them. Then committed, the sun touched them surer, moved around them, held them with a growing keenness, so they swept the ground with trains of shadow, stepping across each other's fresh-lit trails. From the plains-turkey's plunging in the grasses by waterholes to the wallaby's weft through the skeletal scrub; from the brolga's low curtsy on the fringes of the claypan to the hawk's plaiting in the stunning high air; from the sway of the peacock on the precious narrowness of lawn to the gasp of the goanna at the fence-line: from these the day's figure was about to trip and reel. And when the sharp-eyed goanna was lifted from the lawn, scarecrowed on the air for a dawn moment by a bullet which smashed its spine to splinters, then the day at Goonda had begun in earnest.

'Ladies and gentlemen, I was kindly invited by Mr Bowditch to officially open today's gala proceedings, and I did not hesitate to accept the invitation, not because I saw the occasion as an opportunity for political speechifying, but because I recognised immediately the significance of the undertaking. I have no doubt that you all join me in applauding the boldness of gesture represented by this Gala Day at Goonda. We owe to Mr Bowditch and his gracious lady wife a vote of particular appreciation, not only because they have untiringly and imaginatively organised for us a day of varied pleasures, but also because they have made a statement for us all — a statement of confidence in our land, a statement of defiance towards our present afflictions, and, most importantly, a statement of faith in ourselves. Now, I have often heard Mr and Mrs Bowditch speak of their vision for Goonda's future, and I know you too have heard them speak of it: it is a private and grand thing for them, it is a personal thing; but it is shared by us all in the sense that we, each and every one of us, dream the best for our own families and properties and for our country. I believe that by calling us all together here today in an atmosphere of social harmony the Bowditches of Goonda have set an unparalleled example for our entire and troubled district. Though we be beset by drought at this time, by flood and fire at others, it is always and only ourselves on whom the blame rests if we fail to advance at all times. Now, I'm not going to take up your play time with matters of Parliament whose care you have entrusted to me, except to say that, as you know, there is an election next year. I will stand again for the honour of being your servant, and, if elected, will continue my present course of laying directly beneath the noses of the legislators the problems and achievements of our district. For example, the fire-bug problem has been addressed by special grass-fire legislation (I ushered that Bill through the house personally); construction of the railway line from Hughenden has been commenced (and I humbly take the credit for the initiative there, too); finally, artesian boring in the township is well advanced, and though there's no strike yet I will personally guarantee a flow of a million gallons a day in the very near future. My own confidence in the commercial and social future of our district is wonderfully bolstered by the grandness and promise of the festivities here at Goonda today. I know you all feel the same. It gives me undeniable pleasure to proclaim this Gala Day's proceedings *open.*'

'Ladies and gentlemen. The fire-fighting display, as promised, is about to take place here in the home paddock. As you can see, a few of the blokes are spreading round a tin or two of paraffin, but, Lord knows, the dryness of that crop of grass needs little encouragement. Anyway, there it goes, ladies and gentlemen, as vigorous a blaze as you'll ever want to see the last of in your own home paddock. Now, in the present dry conditions such a blaze is a menace both to property and lives. Look how it's moving along there at the sides — a man couldn't run that fast. Anyway, it's not only droughty conditions that put us at risk, ladies and gentlemen, it's also the incendiarist tendencies of some of our erstwhile friends, and though we pray to God that such practices are a thing of the past, nevertheless it is comforting to know that we now have the new invention — *which you can see entering by the far gate, ladies and gentlemen,* THE BUSBY FIRE SWEEPER, named after its inventor, Colonel Busby of Busby and Sons, Parramatta. Now, it is a noble-looking machine, I think you'll agree; it needs just one man as operator, and, of course, two steady horses of the draughting class. There you see the operator manoeuvring the machine into position before the face of the fire. The heavy steel mat stretching in advance of the team sweeps the burning grass towards the ground already burnt. In fact, this is the first time the team before you has actually faced a fire, ladies and gentlemen. Considering that, I'm sure you'll agree they are doing a remarkable job. The horses are kept protected from burns by leather leggings, and the operator, too, is clad in stout, woollen clothing which singes but does not catch aflame. Naturally, beaters are a necessity at the fringes of the fire, but I'm sure you can see the work performed by the Busby Sweeper has stemmed the main advance of today's blaze. There goes another head-on charge, and the fire is all but out. Ladies and gentlemen, your appreciation please for today's operator — it's Ben Dobbin from Oondooroo — and also for the Busby Fire Sweeper, *a marvel of science in the land's service.*'

'Step this way, ladies, for a cooling refreshment. Made to Mrs Bowditch's own recipe and supervised by her in the making. Cooling cumquat punch, ladies.'

'Novices specially catered for, my lad. There are no secrets, no magic. I have catalogues here with full instructions. Why, even a girl could succeed in the basics of photography. Take this Daumier Dry Plate Process Camera, the most rapid and reliable on the market: only four guineas will put you in proud possession, and I'll throw in the tripod for nothing. All the latest imports, all the quality equipments. Or perhaps you'd prefer the simpler job on the other side of the lens, ladies. Don't be shy or afraid. The photographic process has been thoroughly tested both overseas and in this country: there are no damaging effects. Enter the booth at your leisure. Marvellous choice of back-drops: the Catskill Mountains; Nordhoff Fjord; the Leaning Tower of Pisa; novelties too. Couples and groups a specialty.'

'As advertised, gentlemen, a flood-fighting device for pastoral use, specifically designed for these parts. I'm calling it the Goonda Winch, gentlemen, in honour of today's occasion because this is, in fact, the first time the device has been demonstrated before the general public. Now, before we start, if there are any who don't know me, please be informed that I intend to produce copies of the prototype on order over at Campbellton, that's on the Jundah Road. All right. Are you ready, Dick? Well, push off, then. Push them off, boys. There's not much to say really. Unless you're Blind Freddy you can see that the winch bolts onto the side of the boat in a simple manner. Yes, come round here a bit, Dick. We'll let the wether go in a minute. No, don't do anything yet. All right. You'll probably need two in the boat, one to row and one to work the winch. No, better keep away from the inlet pipe, Dick. Yes, that's better, that's well positioned. Now we'll toss the wether in. Go on, old boy. Blimey, you'd think he'd appreciate the swim. Go on, in you go. Give him a boot, Little. That's the one. Look, if we all move down to the water's edge, mind the mud. Perhaps he'll swim for the other side. There he goes. Now you catch him, Dick. Row man, for God's sake. Now you see, a sheep caught in a flood is easy enough to catch up to but the hard part comes getting it into the boat. Hey, you haven't got the harness round the right way, it's back to front, Bill. Back round the other way. No, the other way. The buckle should be towards you. Back towards you. That's it. No, the other way. Yes, that's it. Now, as I was saying — yes, stop him with the oar, for crikey's sake —

131

now, once you've got the blighter alongside—of course, a sheep in a flood for a few hours wouldn't be as frisky as Old Jumbuck there—that's right, slip the harness over and wind up slowly, *slowly—distribute the weight evenly—HEY!—Oh, lawky, fish them out, boys, I don't think Dick swims too good. Move your bloody arms and legs around, Dick.'*

'OK, the book's officially open on Mr Norton and Starlight here. On Mr Norton and Starlight here. Now, Mr Norton wagers he can match 'The Breaker' Mr Murrant's feat, 'The Breaker' Mr Murrant's feat, of a clean jump over this four-foot solid rail fence into the six-foot space, a clean turn and a clean jump back out again. Now who says he can't? Who says he can't? Come on, it's money in the bank. Into the trap and out again with never an inch to spare. He's got to be joking. Only Murrant can do it. What do you reckon, eh? What do you reckon? Double your drinking money. Here's Mr Norton and Starlight. Who ever heard of them before? Not likely. Not likely. Let's see your money.'

'Never fear, ladies. A soldier's not a danger; a gun's not a monster. Except to the adversary. You can move in closer there, dear; we would never load one of these items with ladies present. Nor would we fire one off so near to delicate female ears. Warfare is the sport and commerce of *men*; we try to keep women out of it. However, we can't say the same for the mean class of our adversary. You can come to the rope fence there; no closer, please, gents. Now, can you all hear me? The name's McIver, General (Retired). One of the Heroes of the Soudan. That's not a boast, it's a fact. We were all heroes, weren't we? Showed Mother Britain how we'd come of age in the colonies, by golly. But enough of history. We now have our own uprisings to quell. And we have the equipment to do it. Here on my right is the Gifford gun, gents. On my left, the Winchester rifle. Now, the Gifford is the superior firearm. It makes no report and leaves behind no smoke. "Why is that an advantage?" we ask. It's simply a matter of not giving away our position. If the adversary neither sees nor hears our weapon, how does he know where we are? And if he doesn't know where we are, how can he shoot us? Military logic. A devilish clever weapon, ladies, and one your protectors would do well to appraise. It is no joke to think of the advantage the rebels will derive from possession of this firearm. Dear God, forbid it. I will take your orders presently. Then, in the case of mass riot, a phenomenon we've seen too regularly in these parts in recent times, we can turn to the Gatling gun (on my right), or its improvement, the Nordenfelt gun (on my left). Here we have some of the benefits of invention spurred on by military necessity. Guns of this imaginative nature have kept the unruly peasants down in America, Europe and Africa, and we see no reason why they should not work equally effectively here. These are the weapons of the twentieth century, gentlemen, but they are available to us today. As protectors, you would do well to appraise them. My dream for this district is a Gifford gun beside every bed, and a Nordenfelt at every woolshed. Then we who own the land will feel secure in our possession of it once again. Are there any questions before I go on to the clockwork explosive and the rifle-grenade?'

'There's water everywhere under the earth. Rivers and lakes of it. And it don't dry up in droughty times: that's a God-ordained fact. It just lies and runs there in natural basins and channels, and you don't hear it or smell it, you just walk right over it, and that seems like a miracle, don't it, eh? But there's nothing miraculous or occultish about it, or about finding it. I believe I see you smiling already, sir. Let me say, there are more things in Heaven *and in earth* than are dreamt of in your philosophy: that's a God-ordained fact. Now the marvels of science are ruling your lives and you don't seem to mind it one bit, so let me give you a scientific explanation of the marvellous faculty of water-divining. And let me assure you that though many claim the power, few truly possess it, for it is, above all, a matter of universal physical properties in conjunction with uncommon body chemistries. Now, those of you who went to the university — are there any? — will probably recall that the world is a big electrical battery, with north and south poles, and that the electrical fluid between these poles usually passes through the watery outer layer of the atmosphere surrounding our earth, but sometimes it falls closer to the ground in the form of lightning when a storm brings the outer layer down around our ears.

Now, a lightning-rod, like that on the homestead there, is a powerful attractor of the electrical fluid and the diviner's rod is just the same. When the electricity is passing from the waters far above the earth to the waters far beneath the earth the diviner's rod frets and jumps with the rhythm of electricity. If you haven't seen it with your own eyes, I'll show you in a minute. So why isn't everyone a water-diviner, and why don't the rod jump for all? Well, the God-ordained fact is that we're all built different. The molecules of each man's and woman's substance are spaced different, so in some, only a few, whose molecules are tight-packed like the steel of the lightning-rod, like the twig of the water-diviner's tree, only in those few can the electric fluid flow. But otherwise, in those with loose-spaced molecules, whose bodies are like sieves, the fluid gets lost in the cracks between the molecules and it don't carry. So it's a simple God-ordained fact of science that when I hold this rod here in both hands, gripping it with the right scientific pressure, and it jumps around *thus*, I can safely tell you all there's water lying under this parched paddock, lying there *like liquid opal waiting to be mined*, and it's not far down, not far down at all — watch the jumping of the rod count out the rapidity of the electrical flow — *fifty feet, seventy feet, ninety feet* — and it points this way. You're standing on the middle of a river, ladies and gents, *if you only had eyes to see it.'*

They had come from all over the district, in contingents from the stations, from the town and the mines; they had come on horseback and in buggies, traps and wagons, and some had even come on foot; they had dressed themselves up, given themselves splashes of scarlet in neckerchiefs or emerald green in sashes, and they had dressed up their transport too, decorated their buggies with precious green boughs or picked scant bush flowers for their horses' manes; they had come for the dancing or the footraces or the hunt, or they had come for the secret talk of commerce or romance under cover of the crowd; they had come to show off and they had come to watch others, and they had come for the combat, especially that; they had come to immerse themselves in the constant themes of combat that gave their lives drama, meaning, and hope.

But one who had come for the money alone was the photographer. He was commissioned for three group portraits: the ladies, the workers, and the gentlemen. Beyond that he could trade as free as he pleased. His bustling eagerness brought out stains of sweat on his hound's-tooth suit, as he organised the ladies on the lawn, seating and standing them, raising and lowering them, straightening their backs, neatly curving the rows they formed, draping several of the youngest across the bottom of the group, insuring their spectacles were removed. There they stayed, silent, demure, motionless, eyes modestly lowered or gently disdainful of the poke of the camera: Mrs Bowditch, looking older on purpose, monumental at the centre of the group, beside her the older women, age flowing away to youth at the edges of the group through folds of sensible material and sprays of lace. And there they stayed, the draping flow of their dresses intermingling until they were just one fabric sea with mermaid heads bobbing amongst lace-spumed wavelets, and the photographer under his hot black cloth caught them like that.

Then it was the workers' turn to gather, to line up and squat down, even to lie down, on the wood-, wire-, wool-littered ground before one of the huts. They fooled and fidgeted with a humorous resentment of the cameraman's ordering; they refused to treat with awe the occasion of the photograph. Ragged boots, coat sleeves too long or too short, baggy shirts, horse-stained pants, all eclipsed by the dash of scarves knotted rakishly at necks. Larrikins, flat-skulled, broad-cheeked; others thin-headed and morose; some simmering behind big Ned Kelly beards; one, an oval face, a few days' growth, an intense, amused, calculating stare. They glare, scoff, frown, snigger slightly, or laugh to keep the sun out of their eyes; one blinks his eyes and doesn't seem to be able to unblink them again. For the photograph they impress as not a club, not a rebellion, not a unity, just a loose mob of individuals with only their individual pasts — a wide range of experiences — on their faces. They would make a stirring team, each a star out to score the glory; they would fight side by side, but not for shared, and therefore relinquished, power. The team trophy in the hotel hall meant nothing to them; they cared about experiences, not things; their favourite combat the one-to-one fist fight. Yet a few of them, slouch-shouldered, wary, careless, the unselfish intellectuals, one of their number wearing the picture's only watch-chain, these formed a close-knit, vulnerable sub-group to one side;

135

these were the fools who appreciated quality in enduring ideas and were bound to disappointment. Yet these shared with the rest of the group (except the blinker) one thing in common: each man looked straight at the camera.

The gentlemen were last. They were used to having their photographs taken. The venerable sat on bentwood chairs brought to the lawn; the younger stood behind or lounged in front; they held each other round the shoulders easily, or touched each other's arms or knees with broad hands, bonily sensual, sensitive beneath the calluses. The ancients had double-breasted coats, faithful dog faces, and long hair which splashed out around their ears. Most of the younger were dressed in scarlet riding-coats and tight tan breeches, ready for the hunt. They held their faces taut for the camera, ostentatiously ignoring its presence, looking towards the horizons, disdainful, good-humoured, careless of the impractical, appreciative of quality (for quality is that which is practical longer). When they unslitted their eyes for a sharp moment the junkety whites were there, vulnerable, almost visionary; they were used to looking to the future, they were great imaginers of the unbuilt building and the unborn prize ram; they dreamt a great deal, these slow, strong men; their minds were far cleaner than their dusty bodies; they did not work for luxury, but for quality; they fought the transient present to attain permanence; they had no time for maintenance, they wanted that which endures without maintenance. There is a time for this and a time for that, they believed: they were purposely wild in youth, purposely respectable and sturdy in middle age, purposely venerable nearing death. They always had something else to do, always something better to imagine, always some plan demanding to be made: except when there was a time for the family, the horse, the Association. They were not women's men: there was a time for women, and a time for leaving women alone; they did not touch women as they touched each other. They wanted heaven here on earth; and they would get it, these brains laved in dreams of quality, these eyes hard to get back from beyond the horizons, these clean-washed heads, these sappy, thinly sweating bodies, these sturdily shod feet that didn't care how dusty or muddy their exquisite leather got; they would trample this world till it was heaven.

136

'Thank you, gents,' said the photographer.

The cage was carried beyond the first paddock and the crowd followed. The men admired the warrigal's size, the women the sleekness of its coat. 'A prize, that one,' they said. 'Do for a mat, with the head and pads.' There paraded among the cattle-dogs two hounds specially imported for the event. Used to the scarlet and the horn, they were very smug dogs, strutting and haughty in the crowd. And the thoroughbreds, with cropped manes and tails and polished coats, sweated and fretted, nervous for the ride and the fences. And on the thoroughbreds the gentlemen, scarlet and scornful, and the women, side-saddled, feminine-grim. And in the sky, the exploding sun.

Then, after the warrigal was despised and admired sufficiently for its elusiveness to haunt each brain, and after the dogs were sufficiently frantic with the tangibility of its wild odour, the cage was carried ahead while the dogs were restrained and the thoroughbreds lined up, and the riff-raff were ordered to the sides of the hunt and instructed how to ride so as not to interfere. Then the cage was opened and the horns were sounded and the warrigal was away for the horizon without even a hint of hesitation and the pack and the scarlet and the larrikins on the sides followed and the whole mass hammered on the drought-pocked plain and swept up a cloud of dust never dreamt of in the English countryside.

They leapt the post-and-rail fences; they dashed in the brittle scrub; they exploded the rotten deadwood; they stained the plain with foam and spur-blood; they never checked or steadied; they never thought of their necks; they rode in the maelstrom of their own dust-cloud. The toffs got mixed with the riff-raff; the hounds got baulked by the station dogs; the ladies got jostled by the drunks. They collided and cursed; they whipped, they buffeted; they wailed and flailed; they opened wounds and closed eyes; they yelled and fell. And they came back in ones and twos drenched with sweat and dust, the scarlet stained and stinking, indistinguishable from the stockmen's coats. And they told how, amongst all the red splatter on the grey-dust plain, the dingo had disappeared.

Niall had the feeling he was riding in a cyclone. All about him the clatter and slaver raged. And it raged so constant it hardly clattered or mattered at all. He gulped the dust-blizzard till it filled his mouth and lungs and mind. He could not have told his direction, or his speed, or what obstacles lay in his way, or how high from the ground he rode. He simply left it to the horse, and hung on. If he was surrounded by other riders, he could not tell. Sometimes another joined his dust pocket momentarily, then was gone. Occasionally he thought of the dingo, but he could not think of it as being ahead. Rather it seemed somehow behind. It was not the dingo he rode for. It seemed to him, as the dust pressed in, that he rode for nothing but an end to riding. And it seemed to him, as he gulped for air in his cocoon of dust, that he had changed to something basic as an insect, something that fought a foe basic as a willy-willy. And he felt that none of it mattered much. It was simply light and wind and dust dancing. It was no more than a disturbance on the plain spinning itself out. Or a bright shimmer fading. It was a mirage hunt followed by mirage men and animals, all in a dizzy dance of dust. At the end of it there would be the eaves of Goonda and gallons of Mrs Bowditch's exquisite cumquat squash.

The hunt was abandoned. The dogs milled and whined. Some of the riders set off at tangents, but returned to the gathered, halted groups, disappointed. There was no sign of the warrigal. Bowditch laughed, high on his stallion. The hunt was finished. Paterson was annoyed. He wanted to be the one who redis-covered the quarry. He flung his horse through patches of scrub, wheeling and propping. He dropped into a dry channel and found Sarah.

She was off her horse. She was tangled in a thornbush. He rode up beside her. 'Are you all right?' he said.

'I think so.'

He saw bleeding on her arm. 'Did you fall?'

'Just slid off. I'm quite all right.'

She looked up at him, above her on his horse. She saw the sweat glistening on his neck and wrists. She saw the heaving of his chest where the fire of the hunt's exertions still pounded. She saw the strained, blood-shot eyes, and a little pulse jerking at his temple.

He came down from his horse. He grabbed her arm and examined the scratches. She was fiery-faced, as he was. She

panted from the hunt madness and from the shock of her fall.
'Are you fit to ride?' he asked.
'Of course I am.'
He held onto her arm. He looked again at the hot scratches
springing little bubbles of blood. His examination became a
caress.
They collapsed together into the dry channel bed. On their
way down the dark grey stuff of her dress showed itself to be still
enmeshed in the thornbush. He tugged it away. They lay down
on the hot liverish pebbles of the channel bed. They felt the
glide of each other's sweat.
In Paterson's mind he still rode the hunt. He saw the blasting,
weaving tail of the warrigal. He was right on it just before it
vanished.
He stood up. He helped her to her feet. He looked around for
their horses. She gripped him by the arm. She said his name.
She did not think he heard the desperation in her voice. He
turned on her a vacant look. 'Sarah,' he replied. But it was only
the ghost of a word.

The day's activities melted and darkened into the night's activities. Those who were staying the evening at Goonda took
their places on Bowditch's bathing roster and used an extra-
vagant amount of water preparing themselves for the ball.
New-washed, they emerged, shining and perfumed. The sweat
still sprang on them, but it smelt better.
The evening's celebrations started earliest on the homestead
lawn. There in the dusk the children indulged in a water-fight.
They splashed around the sculptured bird-bath until they were
herded off to supper and bed. The activity swelled in the
workers' mess hut where light and music and singing spurted
from windows and doors. The hut structures shook to the
dancing of a mass of men and a few ladies. Several of the latter,
black skins a-glitter, had been brought off the plain like island
beauties to a visiting ship. Finally, the violin and piano shud-
dered to a start in the homestead's long room. It was the size of a
small hall. Tonight it was the Ball Room. There the elegantly
groomed lined up along the tables of dainties like nervous
racehorses. All flushed from the day's exertions, all glossy from
the sun's insidious stroking, they were charged with the hope

that before the night was out some exceptional visitation would
have poured itself into their stomachs or hearts or wherever the
quenching-bed of their particular exquisite pleasure lay.

(In the dark they dismounted. There were only three of them.
Half a mile away the Goonda homestead was ablaze with lights.
Even at that distance they could hear the music radiating on the
flat plain.)

'This is civilisation,' said Bowditch, tilting the brandy decanter against Clohesy's glass. 'Liquids in the desert.'

'I've already had cause to be impressed by your wife's cumquat squash today. Saved me from sunstroke, I'm certain.'

'You rode like a devil, I noticed, Inspector.'

'More like the joker in the pack. I believe I will suffer for it
tomorrow.'

(One of them stayed with the horses by the gate. The other
two set off towards the homestead, walking at an easy, watchful
pace.)

'Isn't that Mozart they are playing now?' Sarah asked.

'I really don't know, dear,' said Christina.

'I thought you played the piano.'

'Not really. Not properly.'

'She plays it well enough over at Dagworth,' said Macphee.

'I play by ear,' Christina said.

'Yes. It's Mozart,' said Paterson.

(Climbing over fences in the dark, they felt the texture of the
rough-split wood more significantly than if they had been doing
it in the broad light of day.

'Blast. I've got a splinter.'

'Shhh.')

'Sheep's balls?' said Bowditch.

'Pardon?'

'Sheep's balls, Inspector. Would you like one?'

'No, thank you.'

'Not a vegetarian, are you?'

'I'm afraid so. Yes.'

'Unpatriotic.'

'Do you think so?'

'I know so. If the world was vegetarian, where would Queensland be? Where would our economy — our future — be?'

'All the world's not vegetarian, Mr Bowditch.'

'Too much of it is. The inferior races. Thank God, the Empire is fixing that. The meat-eaters have the strength, you see.'

'It's a debatable point.'

'Not just physical strength. Brain strength, too. Darwin pointed it out. The apes are vegetarians. Man's an omnivore. Top step on the ladder. The more we evolve the more we need meat. More brain activity required these days than ever. You should know that. Being a city man.'

'Vegetarianism is simply another of the new things the city is trying.'

'Damned dangerous, though. Don't damage yourself.'

'I appreciate your concern.'

'There's a newspaper clipping I have on file. Remind me to show it to you. About those long-distance runners. Very amusing. More brandy? That's vegetarian.'

(They picked their way amongst the litter in the home paddock. Some of the booths had been taken down. A piece of canvas flapped at them. They pointed their guns. It was only the wind.)

'Do you live on Dagworth?' Paterson asked.

'Not really,' Christina replied. 'An extended visit. I am up from Melbourne for a few months.'

'What do you do to pass the time?'

'I have had a friend staying. And I have been making new friends. Including Sarah. Other times I...well...I look at things.'

'Look at things?'

'Yes. Stones, twigs, insects. Dust mainly.'

'Whatever would one wish to look at dust for, I wonder?'

'To see it.'

(They took a course round the front of the house. They kept well clear of the reach of the torch-light from the garden. They knew to keep a watch out for amorous couples straying on the dark plain beyond the house fence. They met none. It was as yet too early in the night for such wanderings.)

To start the dancing, Mr and Mrs Bowditch took the floor. In spite of the thinness of the music they waltzed magnificently. Bowditch was firm and erect, planting his feet with a deft certainty; Mrs Bowditch was a streaming spangle floating from

141

his arms, a tail to her husband's comet. Her dress swung in wild whispers on the floor. Richly they circumnavigated the room, demonstrating how large the dance-floor was, showing there was space enough for a crowd of dancing. And from the rich promise of their dance the violin took heart and the piano was buoyed up until the fulsomeness of the music was a seduction beyond resistance and the couples poured onto the floor with a vengeance.

(They circled round by the dam, avoiding the woolshed where they supposed the police detachment would be stationed. The stars had invaded the sky and the surface of the dam water. They moved along the dam embankment lifting their feet carefully, cautious about sending any of the round stones rolling to a splash in the water.)

Clohesy danced with Christina. Niall noticed that she was not a good dancer. Her body moved well, with an easy, wild grace; but her mind was only reluctantly a part of the pattern of the steps. Niall had the feeling that she would have preferred and excelled at something other than the waltz, perhaps something quite uncivilised, something unimaginably native even, something naked and free. Not this tightness of twirling, this looping measured momentum. Once, when her weight fell against him, he saved her from falling. Her ankle had failed in negotiating a sharp turn away from an advancing phalanx of couples. 'I'm so sorry,' he said, steadying her.

'Not your fault, Inspector,' came her voice at his shoulder. 'You're a wonderful dancer.'

(In the shadows skirting the huts they stopped to take stock of the situation. They had seen no sign of the police detachment. That was a worry. They hoped the troopers were secretly drinking in the dark woolshed somewhere, that they weren't dispersed at stations among the shadows of the outer buildings. Then the two moved, imitating loyal employees who had every right to go there in the lee of the butchering hut by the corner of the stables.)

The music faltered. The old fellow at the piano stood up. He was red-faced and sweating. He raised his hands in supplication, begging for a break. But the dancers were fiery and luminous. They applauded the musicians. They wanted more music. Apologetically, the violinist put down her instrument,

142

dabbing a cloth at the red welt left on her neck.

'Christina'll play,' shouted Macphee.

They all looked towards Christina where she clung to Clohesy's arm.

'Come on, sis,' Macphee shouted.

'Bravo, Christina,' Paterson called.

The whole room joined in. Their encouraging cries and applause blew her unwillingly towards the piano like a storm-thrust ship at a reef.

'I'd prefer not to,' she said. The red-faced pianist adjusted the stool for her. 'I'm afraid you'll all be sorely disappointed.'

'We'll risk it,' they said, delighting in the richness of her blushing.

There was a hush as she sat at the keyboard with her hands clasped in her lap for a moment. Then she looked up and round the room. On her face there was a mischievous grin. 'I hope you can dance to this one,' she said.

'Try us, Chris. Try us.'

'It's a march,' she announced, and immediately dug her fingers into the keys, surprising a sturdy military melody from the depths of the piano's wire and wood, flattening the loud pedal with a delicious stamp of her trim right foot.

(They walked into the gaping darkness of the opening at the end of the stables building, steeling themselves for a challenge from a guard, but none came. They walked along the line of stable gates, smelling the dung and urine, hearing the nervous stampings and snortings, and the heavy collidings of the horses against their stall railings. The first halted, stopping the other behind him. 'Light a match,' he whispered.)

Christina played with an infectious verve, enjoying herself. Occasionally she looked up from the keyboard with a smile to watch the crowd of dancers bob, stride and swerve, enjoying themselves too, it seemed, in the comedy of her choice of rhythm. They were adapting more dancerly steps to the un-yielding swing of her military beat, until they were all virtually marching round the room bright with laughter and triumph.

And though he danced with Sarah, though he held her waist and hands, though she vibrated under his fingertips and looked up into his face with keen, intelligent, vivid eyes, still Paterson's gaze was lured across Sarah's shoulder to the compact figure seated at the blaring piano, and still his ear was seduced by the naked, alert confidence of the tune Christina played.

'I prefer the waltz,' said Sarah, her lips at Paterson's shoulder.

'I imagine a battalion of phoenixes,' he said, not having heard her.

(The lit match gave off a juddering light in the stables. The two men moved forward along the line of gates. They leant cautiously into the stalls to examine the horses. Then the match went out. Another was struck. They moved back again, stopping at last. 'That's him,' they whispered.)

An explosion of applause greeted the last glittering chords of Christina's playing. It continued as she stood and laughingly curtsied, then ran back amongst the engulfing crowd on the dance-floor.

The regular musicians were quick to pick up the fervour with which the room bristled. They launched themselves into a startling jig which had the homestead rocking as energetically as was the workers' mess hut out the back.

Niall found himself lifting and dropping his feet opposite Mrs Bowditch whose hair, when they grasped each other and flew in dizzying circles down the line, whipped past his face in delightful cool gusts. 'I see you are enjoying yourself, Inspector,' she called over the music and panting and laughter.

'Yes. It livens up the old bones.'

'Goonda's famous for that. For giving city people a good time.'

'I believe it.'

They puffed and jangled on, crazy puppets to the strings of the violin and piano. Paterson and Sarah came bobbing by. Paterson called something to Clohesy, but Niall did not catch it. Then Christina and her brother passed in an off-balance spin.

'Are you married, Inspector?' said Mrs Bowditch, clinging in a twirl.

'Yes. I am.'

'Pity,' she called, skipping away as the dance demanded.

(They unlatched the gate and led the horse from its stall. One of them went ahead to peer out the door. He motioned the other to follow. The horse gave a whinny and checked for a moment. Then it allowed itself to be led out into the night.)

They threw themselves down on seats and benches or moved

to the doorways where ragged gusts of cooler air entered. Their expensive clothes were patched with a motley of sweat from their exertions. They smoothed their hair back down on their damp skulls and they fanned themselves with whatever was at hand — serviettes, handkerchiefs, the ends of their coat-tails. Then Bowditch stepped forward and suggested to the room at large that the most generous toasting was that which met the thirstiest throats, so they all lifted charged and glittering glasses and drank deeply in honour of Her Majesty whose sovereignty, believe it or not, extended even this far into the wildernesses of the world.

(When the native trooper came around the corner of the stables they shot him in the left leg, just below the knee. Then they leapt together onto the bare back of the horse and plummeted into the night. They were at the gate and on their own horses by the time Withers, investigating the whereabouts of the disturbance he had heard somewhere in the dark, came across the bleeding trooper stuffing dirt into his wound beside the stables door.)

Just as they were about to toast Mrs Bowditch in the cooling shadow of the monumental toast that had gone before, they were interrupted by the humble but direct entrance of the Sub-Inspector who announced, from a short way inside the door: 'Pardon me, Mr Bowditch, but there's been a raid, sir.'

Marrakesh. Marrakesh.
'Come to bed,' she said.
Marrakesh. Marrakesh.
He paced in the room like a caged thing. From instinct and familiarity he knew where each item of furniture stood, so he did not bump anything in that darkness. He paced, but not up and down rhythmically. He paced in a jagged arc, from one side of the bed to the other, on the circumference of a dark circle for which she provided the centre. Lying there in the bed she kept him on an invisible string threaded out of her will-power. Without her there he would have been thrashing, perhaps aimlessly, in the gidgee-scrub miles away, on his own or with a vast troop of loyal men; it didn't matter. But with her there he was kept in that bedroom, hearing the clock sweat out two strokes in the depths of the house, hearing the erratic tramp and

halt of his own feet somewhere beneath him in the darkness, hearing the crackle of the bed-sheets as she tossed about sharing his anguish.

'Come to bed,' she said. 'There's nothing can be done before daylight.'

Marrakesh. Marrakesh. By Val d'Or out of Bullseye by Conquistador out of La Flèche by The Striker out of Your Majesty by Côte d'Or out of Grace.

'They'll damage him. I know it. If they damage him I'll kill them.'

Who will you kill? Bright at least. The trooper recognised Bright. Bright shot the trooper in the leg. I'll shoot Bright in the heart. Who will you shoot? All of them. The whole camp of them. Crawly, thieving turds. No manners, no morality, no more use to the country than dingoes. I'll hunt them down, I'll skin them alive, I'll use their skins for doormats. Who will you skin? Bright at least. Bright who stepped into Barret's shoes. Bright who is the devil incarnate, whose heart is a glowing ember of hate. Bright who lives on air alone, the foul air of republicanism, who survives on nothing, like an insect, always ready to suck blood and lay eggs. Bright who burns with an unnatural life. He is not human, Bright. He is an abomination sent to plague us. I have not the patience, O Lord.

'They'll not damage him,' she said. 'What would be the point of damaging him?'

They hate me. They hate all that I am. They hate me because I am their scourge and their defeat.

O Marrakesh. Marrakesh. By Val d'Or out of Bullseye by Conquistador out of La Flèche by The Striker out of Your Majesty by Côte d'Or out of Grace.

'They'll hold him for ransom,' she said.

For ransom. What cowards, what philistines! They would hold perfection itself for ransom. And they say it is us who think only of money. They never did a good thing with money in their lives. The filthy, drunken, illiterate savages. But not Bright. No, not Bright and Barret. They could have been men and not animals. They had minds before they were perverted. Are they my defeat, Bright and Barret? Are they the worm for my mind? Never. Not ever. What perfection is it that is built with chaos? What life is it that is sprung out of offal? What daily bread is it that is ground out of dust?

O Marrakesh. O Marrakesh.
I have not the patience. I must wait till dawn? For the
trackers. I know where he is. At the camp? They'll not take him
to the camp. He's a hostage. They'll hide him. I'll track them
myself. In the dark? Not even the troopers do that. Not even the
black men.
'Come to bed,' she said. 'Both Laver and Withers advised
waiting.'
A new ploy, they said. A new tactic. Probably one of desperation. They could have burned down the entire homestead
while they were at it. But it is money they want now. Not
revenge. All this Laver and Withers said. Who are these men?
Who are these men telling me who Bright and Barret are? I
know Bright and Barret. They are the worm in my brain. I know
them like a sickness of my own. I know they still want revenge.
How much will they ask? How much will I pay for the perfection
of Marrakesh? Everything?
*Marrakesh, Marrakesh. O Marrakesh by Val d'Or out of
Bullseye by Conquistador out of La Flèche by The Striker out of
Your Majesty by Côte d'Or out of Grace.*
'I don't trust Laver,' he said.
'Don't be silly.'
'He doesn't eat meat. He smells wrong.'
'That's part of his act. A distracting tactic. A cover. How
could he be on our side and a vegetarian? He's a clever man, is
Mr Laver.'
'Exactly. I don't trust him.'
'Please don't interfere.'
'He needs to be checked.'
'I have checked.'
'Please. Do it for me. Check him again.'
'If you come to bed.'
'I'm not joking. I mean it.'
'So do I.'
*O Marrakesh, Marrakesh. In the subtlety of your form this
woman wanders. In your geometry she swells. In the liquid,
liquid depths of your liquid eye she travels. In the ecstasy of your
mane she floats and wallows. In the gloss of you she gleams, she
thrills, she ferments. In the lash of your tail, she thrives, she
thrashes. In your hip-curve she throbs, in your neck thrust she
startles, in your firm, long flank she simmers. O Marrakesh, by*

147

Val d'Or out of Bullseye by Conquistador out of La Flêche by The Striker out of Your Majesty by Côte d'Or out of Grace.
He rolled over onto his side, turning away from her, and slept.

'I couldn't sleep either,' said Paterson, standing in the fierce starlight beside the bird-bath.

They walked together down the length of the crackling lawn, both men in light dressing-gowns, Clohesy's a plain emerald green, Paterson's blue with a large red bird embroidered Chinese-style on the back.

'Damn bad business,' said Paterson.

'Marrakesh?'

He nodded. 'Damn bad. Worth a packet, I reckon.'

'They'll get it back. Probably have to pay though.'

'Such a pity. What a sour note for a wonderful day to end on!'

They reached the gate and stopped. On one side of the fence was the lawn, the generous garden, the breathing homestead darkness. On the other side, the star-washed wilderness.

'They have a whole world here, don't they?' said Clohesy, looking back at the house. 'Entire unto itself. There'd be no point leaving, once you were settled.'

Paterson leant on the gate looking the other way. 'Don't you believe it,' he said. 'They rely on the city for just about everything. Money, supplies, protection. It's the city that makes or breaks them out here. The city is the market. The city is the government. The drought might squeeze them, but the city sucks them dry.'

'But they're not dry yet. The gracious lady's cumquat squash. The old man's excellent brandy. The excitement of the dancing. I believe Goonda has seduced me. I even ate a piece of liver on Kill Night. Damn good too. Meat that hasn't travelled. A bit like wine, isn't it? Better untravelled.'

The freshness of a gust of wind from beyond the fence stirred around their heads. It carried with it a far-off howl.

'He did well,' said Paterson. 'The warrigal. I saw him all the way, you know. Ablaze he was, with running. A grand sight.'

'I'm afraid I saw little more than the shuddering mane in front of me. What a ride! I don't think I'll ever do that again.'

'And Bowditch was there, right at the end. Dashing like a

demon. If there'd been any grass on the plain he'd have set it alight. They knew which horse to steal, all right. Give it a paint job and take it to Brisbane. That's what I'd do if I were them.'

Clohesy smiled. 'You talk of them as if they were humorous rogues out of a comedy. They're not, you know. They're poor, starving, defeated fools wrapped in the tatters of a finished dream. A not very sensible dream, at that.'

They leant on the gate, their feet in the garden, their eyes towards the wilderness. 'It's this place,' Paterson said. 'It's the outback. It turns men upside down. It's immoral.'

'On the contrary,' said Clohesy. 'It's morality itself.'

Paterson turned suddenly. He was confused and eager. 'What is love?' he said.

'Pardon?'

'What is love?'

'Well, damn me!'

'No, no. Come on. What is it? How would you describe it? How would you, as a man, describe it?'

'Your guess is as good as mine.'

'No, it's not. Not at all.'

'Please. I'm no good at this sort of thing.'

Paterson's face was close to his. 'Have a go,' he said.

Niall struggled: 'It seems to me...that love is a sort of visitation...the descent of a goddess, perhaps—'

Paterson moved back, relieved. 'Thank God for that,' he said.

'For what?'

'Love is something that happens *to* one, isn't it? I thought you might say love was a kind of commitment.'

'Perhaps it is—'

'No, no. Don't say any more. That's fine. That's fine as it is. What you've said is splendid. Don't spoil it.'

'Don't spoil it for whom?'

'Ah-hah, Inspector Clohesy. You are wise to me. Right? All right. Don't be too harsh, sir. Please. This is a divine moment, isn't it? You said so yourself. The warrigal got away, damn it; Marrakesh has been stolen, damn it; but we've had a damn grand day, haven't we now?'

'What the hell are you blathering about?'

'No play-acting, Inspector. I know you're wise to me. Watch

149

me like a hawk you do. But I'm wise to you, too.'
'You are?'
'Of course I am. How's this then: Who killed the swagman?'
'What swagman?'
'You know. Barret.'
'I'm not absolutely sure. It's hard to tell.'
Paterson put his hand on Clohesy's shoulder. 'See what I mean?' he said.
Clohesy looked away into the star-dark wilderness. 'By the way,' he said, 'what did happen to the dingo?'
'The warrigal? Oh, he disappeared.'
'Disappeared? Just like that?'
'Like a mirage. Just like that.'

15th of December

I have conversed. I have danced. I have shown concern and affection. I have been pleasant. I have continued as if nothing happened. Nothing happened. Apart from his coldness. His getting lost. He is a cad. Or I am a fool. I have no experience of love to compare. The sky has not fallen. Not an inch. I will have a good time. Can that be bad? A good time is a good person's right. I will insist upon it. Yet I am disturbed. Opinions disturb me. But I have no faith in others. In their ability to know better than I. Still I know little of love. Except that it hurts. Somewhere in the stomach it hurts. As a vacancy. Does it get better? It does not get better. What is love in a man's view but conquest? What marriage, but possession? And then? The bliss of neglect. The trouble with women is they may marry only men. Then live with the vacancy. Poor men — they get along so well together. I have merely wanted the best. Why must it be so far from perfection?

CHAPTER

8

Two clouds of dust on the river road: a trap and a buggy. Ahead, on the shadeless trap, ride NIALL *and* BOWDITCH, *the latter fretting at the reins, bitter-faced, explosive. Their conversation is punctuated by the lurch of the trap on the road's unevenness.*

Clohesy.   Where did you get to this morning?

Bowditch.   Did some of my own tracking, damn it. Didn't find a thing.

Clohesy.   According to Withers, the tracks led directly to the camp.

Bowditch.   Along this road?

Clohesy.   Straight along. No diversions. No concealments.

Bowditch.   I ended up at Dagworth. Seems I followed the Macphees' horses.

Clohesy.   Withers found nothing either. The tracks were lost right in the centre of the camp. Just disappeared.

Bowditch.   Is that so? Withers ought to pull up his socks. I don't think I'll be trusting Withers for too much longer. Don't think I'll be trusting you, for that matter.

Clohesy.   I'm used to it. Don't worry.

Bowditch.   I do worry. Especially about this bringing the ladies along. It's an unnecessary danger.

Clohesy.   Having the ladies there will be a way of showing you don't intend war.

Bowditch.   I'm not paying a bloody social call.

Clohesy.   I suggest you make it look that way. It would be foolish to provoke them. They hold the trump card, remember.

Bowditch. I remember. Why else would I be pandering to them at all? Just so long as the ladies are kept at a safe distance.

Clohesy. Of course.

Bowditch. How much do you think they'll want?

Clohesy. They've given no indication. What are you prepared to pay.

Bowditch. A thousand.

Clohesy. Pounds?

Bowditch. Guineas.

Clohesy. Do you have all that on you?

Bowditch. I love that bastard of a horse, Laver.

A quarter of a mile behind, under the shuddering canopy of the buggy, the ladies are enjoying a smoother ride. PATERSON *is managing things so that they travel just beyond the unpleasantness of the dust kicked up ahead. He is in his element; his element being a carriage full of admiring women with no male competition around. The artistry with which he handles the driving is, to his mind, superlative. He keeps a steady pace, steers between ruts and pot-holes, avoids excessive swaying of the vehicle, and does it all with a manly nonchalance that would have made himself envious had he seen another performing it.* MRS BOWDITCH, SARAH *and* CHRISTINA *swat at flies. They are enjoying the ride.*

Christina. Bartie is driving so well, isn't he?

Sarah. He always drives well.

Christina. I tend to get seasick driving. But today I feel marvellous. I've never known this road to be so smooth.

Paterson. The road is rough as ever, I assure you, ladies.

Mrs Bowditch. Oh, Bartie. You boaster!

Paterson. I'm sorry. It's hard to be humble when one is so good.

Ladies. Oh, Bartie!

Sarah. Aren't men wonderful? Wonderful clowns, I mean.

Paterson. Exactly. Our only role in life is to entertain women.

Sarah. You have a poor opinion of women's tastes in amusement, Bartie. I suppose that's understandable in a man who has devoted his life to entertaining men.

Paterson.   Please. Leave my poor poetry out of this.

Mrs Bowditch.   I find Bartie's poetry entertaining. Exciting, too. And I'm a woman.

Sarah.   But you are an exceptional one, darling.

Mrs Bowditch.   Yes. You're right.

Paterson.   Being so greatly outnumbered here, I don't expect to be able to force the vote in favour of men. Indeed, I don't believe I'll even try.

Christina.   Go on, Bartie, try. Men are on trial. You'll have to conduct your own defence, I'm afraid.

Sarah.   Excellent notion. Men, you stand accused of being clowns. What do you have to say for yourselves?

Paterson.   Who is the judge?

Sarah.   Not you, that's for certain.

Christina.   Mrs Bowditch is the judge.

Mrs Bowditch.   I'm the judge. What do you have to say in defence against this damning indictment, Mr Paterson? I might warn you beforehand that all the evidence is stacked against you.

Paterson.   Wait a minute. You can't say that.

Mrs Bowditch.   I'm the judge. I can say what I please.

Paterson.   I want a re-trial.

Mrs Bowditch.   Contempt of court!

Christina.   Oh, come on, Bartie. You can do better than that.

Paterson.   All right, then. We are clowns.

Sarah.   Painted grins.

Christina.   Foolish clothes.

Sarah.   Tripping over your own feet.

Paterson.   But we have talents.

Sarah.   For tumbling.

Christina.   For juggling.

Paterson.   For leading the way.

Ladies.   To where?

Paterson.   For creating pleasure.

Sarah.   And chaos.

Paterson.   For telling the truth.

Ladies.   The truth?

Paterson.   Certainly. The roots of our tradition as clowns lie in the blinding truths of the Shakespearean fool.

Sarah.   I object.

Mrs Bowditch.   Objection upheld.

Paterson.   Why?

Sarah.   None of the evidence supports your statement.

Mrs Bowditch.   That's right.

Paterson.   Oh, this is not a fair trial.

Sarah.   Yes, it is. It's patently obvious that the world is full of untruths because the world is full of men.

Paterson.   The world is full of women, too.

Mrs Bowditch.   Contempt of court!

Sarah.   Well said, Madam Judge.

Paterson.   I give up. It's a kangaroo court.

Mrs Bowditch.   I find you guilty, then. And sentence you for the term of your natural.

Sarah.   The criminal was led away from the courtroom broken and weeping —

Christina.   —his greasepaint smudged —

Mrs Bowditch.   —his motley in tatters —

Christina.   —sentenced to life —

Sarah.   —as a man.

Ladies.   Oooh. How horrible!

In his confusion, PATERSON *drives them directly into a mighty pot-hole, so that all their bottoms leave their seats. The ladies come back down with pretty thuds, laughing and hanging onto their sun-hats.*

Mrs Bowditch.   Oh, dear. I'm so glad Eugene can't see us now, laughing and enjoying ourselves. This is the worst day of his life. He loves that horse dearly. It will break his heart if they've damaged him.

Up ahead, in the trap, NIALL *has the impression that* BOWDITCH, *far from attempting to avoid the road's rough patches, is in fact taking a delight in making the journey as jolting as possible. They seem to hit every hole and boulder along the way, and* BOWDITCH *appears to urge the horse faster at just those points where a slower progress is justified — in dust drifts and round corners.*

Bowditch.   Bad suspension. Bad suspension.

NIALL *feels certain that the torridness of the ride is specially directed towards himself. He wonders exactly what it is that writhes in the brain of the man beside him. Then the road takes a series of sharp turns between drooping trees and plunges onto a crossing of one of the far-flung, bone-dry arms of the Diamantina.*

Bowditch (looking ahead). I might as well be frank with you, Mr Laver. I've known some confidence men in my time. Not one of them has ever got anything out of me. I can assure you of that. You may be interested to know that I'm having you checked out.

Laver. Very wise. I do understand.

Bowditch. Tricksters have the advantage over us out here. We're so far from anywhere. You can be whoever you wish to be in the outback. We had a member of the German royal family here last year. Some kind of Prince or Count he said he was. We sent him packing once we knew the truth. We didn't grudge him the few weeks' hospitality he got out of us. We gave the hospitality; he didn't steal it. He was an entertaining chap, anyway. Damn good shot with the rifle. Do you do any shooting yourself?

Laver. Not if I can help it.

Bowditch. That's not in your favour.

Laver. I was under the impression that your wife had already checked me out' as you say.

Bowditch. She may not have checked with the right people.

Laver. I'm certain she has, Mr Bowditch. But do feel free to go ahead. I need your confidence above all else.

Bowditch. Don't worry. You'll get it if it's deserved.

The trap approaches the final riverbed crossing before the camp site. BOWDITCH *stops the horse. The buggy draws up.*

Bowditch. Stay here, Bartie.

The trap moves ahead, with BOWDITCH *and* NIALL *grim-faced in it.* MRS BOWDITCH *speaks to* PATERSON *in a voice no longer girlish with the fun of the drive.*

155

Mrs Bowditch.   We'll go in there after them, when I say so.
Paterson.   But—
Mrs Bowditch.   Just do as you are told. I'd not miss what happens for the world.

At the camp the men are waiting, BRIGHT *to the forefront. They surround the trap as it comes to a halt.*

Bright (sneering).   Left your ladies at the crossing, I see.
Bowditch.   We thought they might catch a disease if they got any nearer.
Bright.   You expected we'd get *that* close to them? (*The men snigger.*)
Bowditch.   Half a mile away is close enough to catch a disease from this place.
Bright.   To tell you the truth, Bowditch, we're all feeling remarkably healthy today. Aren't we, lads? (*The men, about twenty in number, all shout in agreement. One of them belches theatrically.*) But I couldn't say the same for you, Bowditch. You're looking decidedly seedy.
Bowditch.   I want my horse, Bright.
Bright.   Oh, is that all? Sub-Inspector Withers and his band of merry sniffers have been here already this morning. They say we don't have your horse, Bowditch. They looked all over for it.
Bowditch.   I want him back, Bright. He was tracked to this camp.
Bright.   Of course, it was. But did your black snoopers look to see if it could be tracked right out of the camp again? No, they didn't. Interesting, that. We heard a horse ride through here last night. Didn't we, lads? (*A shout of agreement.*) Rode through and disappeared out the back, it did. Funny thing, that.
Bowditch.   I want that horse. I demand that horse, my rightful property, in the name of Her Majesty the Queen. (*A shout of derision.*)
Bright.   Her Majesty, the Queen? Isn't she the fat one with the gin blossoms, Bowditch? I heard she laces her port with whisky. Three groans for the Queen, lads!
Men.   *Groan, Groan, Groan.*

While the groaning is in progress the buggy arrives at a gallop. With a remarkable feat of balance, MRS BOWDITCH *stands up long before* PATERSON *has pulled the horses to a halt. She glares down at the whole proceedings, striking dumb the entire group of men. Her hair stands out in snakes round her head. Her form is stony and massive. She has become an imperious statue of authority.* BRIGHT *is the first to recover.*

Bright. And three groans for the Queen of Goonda. (*The men's response is not good.*)

Mrs Bowditch. Hand over the horse, Mr Bright.

Bright. We don't have the horse, ma'am.

Mrs Bowditch. Then go and get it, Mr Bright.

One of the men sniggers, then pretends to vomit on the ground. His action seems to release the pressure on his comrades. They begin a babble, most of it jibing against MRS BOWDITCH. *Some of the more daring make rude gestures, and the name of Barret escapes a few lips. Then the men seem to realise for the first time that* SARAH *and* CHRISTINA *are present in the buggy. A distinct edge develops on their unpleasantness.*

Bright (*he grabs the hem of* MRS BOWDITCH'S *dress*). Is this the ransom you've brought us, Bowditch? (*He points at the other women.*) Is this what you think we'll take for Marrakesh?

MRS BOWDITCH *is unshrinking.* BOWDITCH *is livid. The women are petrified.* PATERSON *is struggling for the reins which he was dropped.* NIALL *is fumbling for the revolver under his shirt.*

Bright. All right. I'll get your Marrakesh.

And suddenly there is quiet. The men step back, their faces flat as masks. BOWDITCH *fingers the trap whip, trembling with hate, ready to count the damage done to his stallion.*

157

PATERSON, *for some reason unknown to himself, sees a vision of his quiet Sydney office.* MRS BOWDITCH *realises she is sweating all over.* CHRISTINA *feels sick.* SARAH *feels enraged.* NIALL *thinks, inappropriately, that his contract finishes in six days' time.* BRIGHT *goes into a nearby tent and re-emerges carrying a flour-bag. The men let him through. He brings the flour-bag to beside the trap, and by the trap's wheel he empties it out. Onto the ground fall some bones, mane hair, a hoof, and other bits and pieces.* BOWDITCH *goes berserk. He plummets from the trap like a great stone. He tears into the men, lashing out unstoppably, raising blood wherever he swings. The women scream.* PATERSON *drops the reins again.* NIALL *fires a volley from his revolver which stuns them all.*

Clohesy.   Line up. Line up or I'll shoot you.
Bright (picking himself up).   Whose side you on, Clohesy?
Niall.   The side of decency, Bright. Get over there.
Bright.   We didn't steal the bloody horse. Someone dumped a bag of bones in the camp last night. Didn't they, Bowditch? You know all about it.
Bowditch.   Arrest him, Laver.
Laver.   It's not in my power to arrest him.
Bowditch.   I'll arrest you myself, you bastard. By the power invested in me as a sworn Special Constable of the Commission of the Peace.
Bright.   Go to hell, Bowditch. You've got no evidence.
Bowditch.   This is the evidence.
Bright.   That could be the remains of any horse.
Bowditch.   It's my horse, by Christ. What about this?
Bright.   That's the penis, Bowditch.
Browditch.   I'd know Marrakesh anywhere. I'd know my own horse anywhere.

At this point BOWDITCH *breaks into sobs. Genuine, tearful sobs, it seems. He droops to his knees, holding the clotted organ in the palms of his hands.* MRS BOWDITCH *struggles down from the buggy to assist her husband. With the hem of her dress she wipes blood from his forehead and tears from his cheek. Nobody else moves, to comfort or lend a hand.*

158

Then BOWDITCH *gathers up the bones and pieces, in a fumbling way, as if he is blind. Once they are all in the bag he jerks up to his full standing height and slings the bag into the buggy. It lands at the feet of* SARAH *and* CHRISTINA. *They scream. Then* BOWDITCH *hands his wife up to her seat and, once she is settled, gives the nearer horse a whack on the rump.* PATERSON *steers the team away from the camp. Without a further word,* BOWDITCH *climbs into the trap and sets the horse in motion, scattering the men, leaving* NIALL *to his own devices to grab onto the vehicle and, nearly falling, to pull himself up onto the seat. The trap leaves the camp at a gallop. It is a long time before* NIALL *speaks.*

Laver. Are you keeping the bones as evidence?
Bowditch. Evidence be damned.

Up ahead the ladies do their best to keep their feet off the bag. They draw their skirts away from it. They pinch their noses. They look at the horizon. But there is no avoiding it. It wallows on the floor of the buggy. With the swaying of the buggy the pieces inside move round, colliding nauseously.

Christina. I think I'm going to be sick.
Sarah. Why did it have to come with us? Why couldn't they take it in the trap?
Mrs Bowditch (keeping her eyes on the road ahead). It's an accusation. I'm sorry, darlings. Try to think of other things.

They arrived at the waterhole, some time after midday, to find two gaily striped dressing tents already set up in the shade of the coolibahs. A pleasant spot on the bank had been cleared and a group of folding chairs arranged in a circle there. A short distance off, at a point selected with the direction of the breeze in mind, a fire had been started. Beside it, one of the Goonda men was busy with an axe. Amongst the staff buzzing like flies between the tents, the fireplace, and the wagon they had come in, was Mrs Bowditch's favourite Chinese cook, and two of her maids. When the trap and buggy rolled up, one of the maids appeared immediately with the inevitable jug of cumquat squash. All except Bowditch, who went in search of stronger stuff amongst his loyal men, greeted the drink with enthusiasm. 'It's like meeting an old friend again,' said Clohesy, the tart, cool sweetness of the drink laving his throat.

The canvas chairs were not attractive to the young people. They had been sitting too long in the vehicles. They wanted to move around. They wandered down to the water's edge. Paterson looked for a flat stone to skip, but there were none. Sarah and Christina lifted the hems of their skirts gingerly, wary of the mud. Paterson walked, like an eager high-wire artist, out along the thick bough of a tree which grew horizontally across the water. His boots slipped a little. The tree's bark was trodden shiny by previous picnickers.

'Anyone for a swim?' Paterson called.

The women were not interested.

'What about you, old chap?' Paterson challenged.

Clohesy stood rooted to the drier part of the bank. 'I think not,' he said. 'Looks dangerous to me.'

'It is dangerous,' called Mrs Bowditch. 'There are snags under the surface. If you are going to swim you must wade. Don't dive.'

'Looks delightful to me,' said Paterson. He crouched on the bough. He reached down in a risky manner where the bough came closest to the water. 'It's cool,' he shouted. 'It's the perfect temperature.'

'What would you want to swim in there for?' said Sarah. 'It looks like milky tea.'

'You feel it. It's perfect.'

'Tepid milky tea, then.'

Paterson was not to be put off. He came back along the bough as he had gone, arms out-thrust and wavering, keeping his balance. He jumped to the bank. 'I'm going in,' he said. He entered one of the dressing tents. 'You'll be envious,' he called from inside, 'when you see me splashing about.'

Bowditch came back towards the group. As he walked he trampled the dusty bank in the manner of a man bearing a grudge against the earth itself. He had no intention of joining in with the picnic or of being pleasant. He grunted when he saw that his arrival had a generally freezing effect.

'Are you all right, dear?' asked his wife.

'No, I'm not bloody well all right.'

160

He trampled off, swerving towards the buggy parked under the trees.

'What rotten luck! On our picnic day,' said Mrs Bowditch.

'Can we help him somehow?' asked Sarah.

'I think he'd prefer to work it out himself.'

Paterson burst out of the striped tent flap. He was dressed in a royal blue swimming costume. It was a daring outfit. It showed a great deal of his chest. The ladies noticed that the hair there was wiry and golden.

'My word, you do look good, Bartie,' exclaimed Mrs Bowditch.

Paterson was ecstatic. 'I've been waiting quite a while to put these on. Marvellous colour, don't you think?'

He was all lithe movement and action. He didn't want to stand still. His walk was springy and keen. He balanced out along the overhanging bough again. This time his bare feet gripped easily.

'Why don't you wade in first?' called Clohesy.

'Why don't you?' Paterson called back.

'You're being foolish, Bartie,' said Sarah.

'Yes, you are,' called Mrs Bowditch. 'Now please be careful.'

Paterson stood at the end of the bough, as far out as he dared his weight. He took up the stance of a diver ready to spring. He looked back at the others on the bank. They stood separate and frozen watching him. He saw Sarah's disdainful look and Christina's apprehension. He noted Mrs Bowditch's annoyed snapping of the blade of grass she held in her hands, and Clohesy's feigned casualness. Poor Clohesy, he thought.

Then, behind them all, Paterson saw a movement amongst the trees. He realised it was Bowditch taking the flour-bag from the buggy and slinging it over his shoulder. To Paterson, with Clohesy watching him, it was the sight of a single man lifting a nation's guilt onto his back and bearing it off towards an endless horizon. Paterson turned to the water. He dived, and hit the surface with a pink splash.

Bowditch took the flour-bag from the buggy and a shovel from the wagon. Then he headed away from the billabong. He crossed several over-shoots — the rockwork weirs designed to hold back water in the arms of the Diamantina during dry spells. Behind some of them the water was low and foetid;

behind others there was no water at all. When he had come to a wide stretch of barren riverbed — a main channel of the river system — he realised he was sick of walking, sick of putting off what he had to do. So there, beside a tree on the bank, he tossed down the sack and began digging. But it occurred to him, as it might not have occurred to another man, that although this was drought time (seemingly implacable, endless drought time) there would at another time (next month, next year, next decade perhaps) be floods again, when this position might be unsuitable, might be a worry to him. For he knew of the changing of river courses, the erosion of banks, the tearing and scouring of flood frenzies. And it occurred to him, as it might not have occurred to another man (a less religious man), that the digging of the hole there in the shade was too easy, that comfort now would produce discomfort later, that no depth of hole there on the river bank was sufficient to bury the bones in his mind. So he took up the sack again and headed across the barren, burning ground away from the river until he had mounted one of the low, low ridges that together subtly made up the plain; and there, in the sun that fell down on top of him like blankets of disaster, he began the hole again. But as he could have told, the ground beneath the sandy top layer was hard and merciless, bending the shovel rather than yielding, so that he thought: even an opal-miner would move on from here, even an opal-miner seeing every sign of promise would move on from here, and the thought made him stay, continuing to dig with the sun crashing on his back like blistering whips, until he had a hole deeper than dingoes could fathom, deeper than the claws of his own mind could scratch, and there he dropped the flour-bag, the ugly pieces of the beautiful horse clattering about and coming to rest finally. *O Marrakesh.* Then he filled in the grave, in tears and in silence.

Paterson's dive was perfect. The arc of it sprang from the end of the bough like the extension of a new green shoot, and it was repeated, though inverted, in the mirror image on the water's surface where the others saw it downward arcing simul- taneously, and it was repeated again in the dive's continuation under the water where Paterson felt the arc's perfection but the others could only imagine. It was a fine, clean dive, and when the sleek head reappeared above the pinky, opaque water, the tableau on the bank returned to life again.

'Don't you ever do that again, Mr Paterson,' called Mrs Bowditch, relieved.

'I thought I might be diving in myself for a moment there — to save him,' said Clohesy.

'And then we could have had two broken necks,' said Sarah. 'I mean — I would have waded in.'

Paterson was laughing — splashing round and ducking under the water.

'You gave us the horrors, Bartie. It's not funny at all.'

'Why don't you all come in?' he called. 'It's absolutely perfect. The water's so *soft*.'

'He's incorrigible,' said Mrs Bowditch.

'He's a writer,' said Sarah. 'Writers will do anything for an audience.'

'Near kill themselves?'

'If possible.'

'It *was* a good dive,' said Christina.

'Don't you dare tell him that.'

Suddenly Mrs Bowditch wanted to be punted. Suddenly she had an urge to be excessively pampered, and punting was the way it would be done. She called for the men to carry the punt from the wagon to the water, and she had the pole placed in Clohesy's hands. 'You will punt me, sir,' she said, laughing. She was handed into the flat-bottomed boat. She sat with her skirts around her and a parasol shading her head. 'One always holds a parasol in punts. If one is female, that is.'

'Yes, ma'am,' said Clohesy, pushing away from the bank.

They were gliding out across the billabong. Soon the bottom was too deep for the pole to be useful, so they drifted. Still in the water, Paterson swam around them. He dived under the boat and came up the other side. 'We are ignoring you, Bartie,' said Mrs Bowditch.

He did it again and resurfaced, grinning. He grasped the side of the boat. 'I am sorry if I frightened you,' he said, flicking the water out of his eyes. 'I was just finding something out.'

'Oh? And what was that?'

'Nothing much. Just what it's like to leap in here. That's all. It was an experiment.'

Mrs Bowditch was not pleased. 'Kindly save your experiments

163

for a time when people who love you are well out of the way. Pole on, ferryman.'

It was superb on the water. All that was seen on the banks was of another world; it seemed to demand a suspension of disbelief to allow it to belong to the same dimension they punted in. From the middle of the billabong it was difficult to think that the rest of the world was soiled, exhausted, spattered with blood. Along the bank Sarah and Christina moved, keeping up with the punt, bending now and then to gather items of interest. In their white dresses they shone. Paterson swam languidly to the bank. Back by the tents he emerged from the water and began towelling himself dry, glistening. Laver stood erect, the perfect ferryman. At the other end of the punt Mrs Bowditch gleamed beneath her parasol, giving off waves of light like some dream-object.

'You are very good, Mr Laver.'

'At what, Mrs Bowditch?'

'At everything, I suspect.'

The punt kept drifting.

'I don't believe I'm doing well at what I was sent here for,' Laver said.

'Patience, patience. We will prevail.' Under the parasol, Mrs Bowditch's face was netted by lacy shade. 'We are not quality, are we, Mr Laver, you and I? Not quality. We are far too dishonest for that. And that is why we will prevail. Now, Bartie—he's a different matter. Being quality, he sees no need to take care of himself. He's so honest, and such a fool. Sarah? She's quality. Chris? One of us, I'm afraid. And my poor husband, my poor dear Eugene...exceptional quality....'

They drifted on. Niall was fascinated by her radiance. 'Your husband doesn't trust me,' Laver said.

'Of course not. Why should he? I don't trust you myself. If I trusted you, you would have to be predictable; and if you were predictable there would be nothing for me to admire. I would pity you, that's all. One can't admire what one pities.'

'You don't admire your husband?'

'How could I? He is quality.'

'But you love him.'

'They are both love: admiration and pity. Bartie will find that out, I am sure. He admires Christina and pities Sarah.'

Laver laughed nervously. 'I told him love was the descent of a goddess.'

'Or god. Admiring love is. When the god or goddess ascends again what is left is pitying love.'

They had reached the far end of the billabong. With the pole Laver manoeuvred the punt around and set it gliding back again.

'You have been enjoying Goonda, Mr Laver?'

'I have, indeed.'

'It always happens. There's a magic about the place.'

'I don't know about the magic. I believe it is something very down-to-earth that has captivated me. Something to do with the essentials of survival, I would say.'

'Things are clearer to see?'

'The complexity of things is clearer. I used to subscribe to the notion of a divorce between the city and the bush. Now I am not so sure. I feel I have simply come to another part of the network.'

'How often have you been in the outback, Mr Laver?'

'Never. City born and city bred.'

'Surely you are only as amazed at our survival as we are at yours? I can take the city only in the tiniest of doses.'

'Like medicine?'

'Like an immunisation. We have to know about the city. That's part of our surviving. But we don't have to let it strike us down.'

'They say the Australian will look at himself in the future and see a city man.'

'Then, he'll be using the wrong mirror, Mr Laver.'

The punt nudged up to the bank at the picnic spot. With the slow sucking sound of the muddy water beneath her, Mrs Bowditch was returned by outstretched male hands to the dry land. They found Paterson dressed and bursting with energy. He was being very attentive towards the mud Christina had gathered on her shoes during the walk along the bank. She lay back in a canvas chair, plucking at the strings of a simple zither-like instrument. Paterson was down on one knee, his trouser-leg in the dirt, scraping at her shoe with his nailfile. Sarah lay back in a canvas chair beside them; she had been careful to get no mud on her.

'What was that tune you played at the ball last night?' Paterson asked.

' "Craigielea" it's called,' Christina answered. 'I heard it at a

165

race meeting once. I've never been able to forget it. That happens to me sometimes. Some tunes I can't get out of my head.'

Clohesy looked out at the ridiculous flapping flight of a white cockatoo on the other side of the billabong. 'It was a catchy tune,' he said. 'I almost remember it myself.'

'Play it now,' said Sarah. 'Can you play it on that?'

'I don't really know what to do with this thing,' Christina said, but she struck off several chords which were immediately recognisable as an introduction to her famous tune, and everyone assisted:

'That's it,' they said. 'You've got it now,' they said.

Christina played 'Craigielea' by the billabong. On the zither it had a weird, fuzzy quality, not at all like the brazen march of the previous night's piano performance. This was more like the reverberating ghost of the last night's tune, strangely metamorphosed by the new setting, slithering from the buzzing strings in a strangled, unearthly manner; no longer a triumphant march, but a Gothic, nervous dirge.

'This is not really the instrument for it,' said Christina. 'Or at least, I'm not the one to play it well enough.'

'Nonsense,' said Paterson. 'It's very effective. Somehow ethereal.'

'Do you know what I think, Bartie?' said Mrs Bowditch. 'You ought to write words to that tune. It would make a marvellous song.'

Christina was asked to play the tune again, from the beginning. Paterson hummed and muttered along, enjoying the looks of expectation around him. One of the maids came by with a trayful of meat from the barbecue, but no one was much interested in eating.

'All right, all right,' said Paterson. 'I think I've got something. *Da capo*, Chris. . . . How's this?:

> 'O, once a sorry bagman
> Wilted by a waterhole
> Blistered and sore from the sunburnt track,
> And he cursed as he searched
> For an ant inside his trousers:
> "Who'd hump a flamin' bluey in The Great
>   Outback?"' '

166

The reaction from those around him was not good. Sarah and Christina burst out laughing; Mrs Bowditch was non-committal; and Niall, refilling his glass with an amused grin on his face, watched Mrs Bowditch's reaction from the corner of his eye.

'OK. That's just a first draft,' said Paterson, obviously piqued. 'The final version won't necessarily be anything like that. But it's a start, it's a start. Now, how does the chorus go again?'

They were interrupted by the return of Bowditch. He stumbled into the picnic site appearing more than a little sunstruck. His face was distinctly pale beneath the heavy tan. The wound on his forehead, suffered in the camp melee earlier in the day, had begun bleeding again. They all leapt to his assistance. They grasped him and settled him down in a chair. His wife attended to his face with a handkerchief cooled in the billabong water. Paterson went off to find the flask of strong spirits that existed somewhere amongst the Goonda men who had gathered in the shade beside the wagon. Encouraged and fortified, Bowditch eventually shook himself free of the concerned attention. He looked around for something to eat. The tray of cooked meat lay there under a gauze cover, gone cold and virtually untouched.

'Were you waiting lunch for me?' Bowditch asked, nonplussed at the extensive range of cuts on the tray.

'None of us was very hungry,' said his wife meekly.

'Jesus Christ!' he said. 'You're going to let that good flesh go to waste?' He stuck the point of a knife under the gauze and speared a chunk. He lifted it to his mouth and tore the meat from the knife's point. He filled his mouth to overfull, working his jaws extravagantly.

They sat around him, not knowing where to look or what to say. They heard his jaws creak in their chewing, and they heard the fabric of the meat tear as he pulled it apart, as he pushed it by hand into the side of his mouth where the molars could do the biting work. They sat there, not daring to sing or play again, their heads desperately empty of an appropriate conversation opening.

'Well? Go on, then,' he said through a mouthful. 'For God's sake do something.'

The punt came to Mrs Bowditch's rescue again. 'Why don't you all go punting?' she suggested, mock-eagerly. 'It will hold four, won't it?'

'How should I know? I suppose so,' said Bowditch. He looked straight ahead, with hooded eyes, at a point somewhere deep in the billabong of his own mind.

'I believe I've had enough punting for the day,' said Clohesy. 'You take the girls, Paterson. I'd prefer a walk.'

So the punt glided out once more and when it reached the centre of the waterhole Paterson made Christina strike up the tune again on the zither while he stood in the stern singing and composing like a gondolier on the canals of Venice. But he was a gondolier especially happy because his own two loves sat there before him, his passengers and his audience.

On the bank the Bowditches continued in silence, Mrs Bowditch knowing that her husband was unapproachable, wandering somewhere in the wild wastes of his tortured imagination. Farther along the bank, Niall picked up another pair of delicate mussel shells, similar to those he had found on his previous visit to the waterhole. One of them broke as he fitted them together in his hand.

In the punt Sarah wrote on the paper Paterson took from his pocket with the pencil he also gave her. She wrote and crossed out as Paterson dictated, as Christina played:

> 'O, once a droughty boozer
> Rested by a riverbank
> Under a branch of the blue gidgee-scrub,
> And he prayed as he probed
> For a trickle in his whisky flask:
> "Lord, don't let me drop before I reach the
> next pub." '

'Too much a cartoon,' said Sarah. She crossed it out with a line from left to right.

> 'O, once a bleary blanketman,
> Lying by a billabong,
> Dreamed of his family in the city's sweat:
> Of his kids in the streets;
> Of his dear wife in a factory—
> "Surely this is not how life was meant to get." '

'It doesn't sing well,' said the critic. She put a line through it.

'Just what is it you want to say in this song?'
   'I'm not sure yet,' said the poet.

> *'O, once a starving swagman*
> *Sat down by a riverbed*
> *In the scanty shade of a stringybark-tree,*
> *And he sighed as he searched*
> *For a crumb in his tucker-bag:*
> *"The squatters and the unions are the death*
>   *of me.*

> *"Squatters and unions,*
> *Squatters and unions,*
> *Squatters and unions won't fleece me*
>   *when I'm dead";*
> *And he sighed as he searched*
> *For a crumb in his tucker-bag:*
> *"No one needs a card to shear in God's*
>   *woolshed." '*

'Too provocative. Too direct.' Sarah crossed it out.

> *'O, once a dying swagman*
> *Lay by a riverbed*
> *In the lonely shade of a baobab-tree,*
> *And he sang softly, watching*
> *His last campfire burning:*
> *"O, who'll come a-humping the drum with me?"' '*

'Too tragic,' said Sarah. 'The tune's not tragic.'
   'Don't cross it out,' said Paterson. 'I want it tragic.'

The Bowditches left in the trap. The Goonda men took down
the tents and packed them on the wagon, with the chairs and the
punt. The fireplace was covered with dirt and the waterbags
taken down from the boughs of the trees. Then the wagon
left.
   'It's desolate,' said Sarah. 'Without the picnic, it's desolate.'
   'Don't be like that,' said Paterson. He climbed onto the
buggy, and sang:

> *'Once a jolly swagman*
> *Camped by a billabong...'*

169

The others climbed onto the buggy. It moved off. Clohesy stood on the step, hanging on. He looked through the trees across the plain. 'Let's find a pub,' he said.

'Let's find lots of pubs,' said Sarah. 'Let's do a crawl.'

'What's a crawl?' asked Christina.

'City talk,' said Paterson. 'It means drinking too much without getting bored with the scenery.'

'Between here and the North Gregory,' said Clohesy, 'there are at least three pubs that I can think of.'

They began at the Dagworth Hotel. They drank there, then set off again across the vast flat plain with the vast flat sky above them. They sang and sang:

> *'Waltzing, Matilda,*
> *Waltzing, Matilda,*
> *"You'll come a-waltzing, Matilda, with me."'*

They rattled and bumped across the plain in the glorious hot afternoon.

'Stop, stop,' said Christina. She got down from the buggy to tear the blue branches from a scrubby tree just off the track. She carried a sparse armful back. 'We must decorate the buggy,' she said, smiling up at the others from beneath her flapping broad hat.

They drove and drove. The branch-festooned buggy flapped across the plain like a clumsy, flightless bird. Clohesy hung precariously from the side. He sang at the top of his voice:

> *'Down came a jumbuck*
> *To drink at the billabong,*
> *Up jumped the swagman*
> *And grabbed him with glee...'*

They drowned the rattle of the buggy with their singing; drowned the jangle of the chains and the clatter of the hooves and the skirring of the wheels in the sand. They gulped down the wind blowing in their faces and sang it back out again, a gay shower of song on the sunny plain.

The Dick's Creek Pub was next. They drank again and sang. A couple of old-timers joined in, waving their glasses at the sunburnt girls:

'Waltzing, Matilda,
Waltzing, Matilda
"You'll come a-waltzing, Matilda, with me."'

Then they left the wide-eyed pub and bounced onto the plain
again, and Paterson pushed the horses, standing with the reins,
singing:

'Up rode the squatter
Mounted on his thoroughbred;
Down came the troopers,
One, two, three...'

They passed brolgas dancing in the riverbed, and emus racing
away with spurs of dust; they swerved by lizards waddling
desperately, and they scattered flocks of sheep into fussy panic.
They sang with roaring voices to the plain, and the plain was
theirs. They claimed it so. It belonged to youth and gaiety and
the alcohol spurring in their veins. So Paterson drove the buggy
harder and they threw back their heads, exposing the strong
white of their throats, spreading the plain with happy laughter.

'"Where's that bloody jumbuck
You've got in your tucker bag?
You'll come a-waltzing, Matilda, with me!"'

At the Twenty Mile Hotel the girls did not wish to go inside.
The place was full of shearers come across from Gloucestershire
Downs. Just payed off, they were, and full of fun. The girls
refused to budge; they would wait in the buggy, their drinks
could be brought to them there. No one would hear of it.
Paterson and Clohesy begged and wheedled them; the lusty
shearers spilled from the pub doors and surrounded them. They
would not move. So they were lifted by strong hairy arms from
their seats. Still in their sitting positions, screaming delightedly,
they were carried into the bar and set up on seats on rough
tables.

'Waltzing, Matilda,
Waltzing, Matilda,
"You'll come a-waltzing, Matilda, with me."'

171

The shearers sang the song. They clapped their hands. They toasted the girls and danced round them. As if they had never seen girls before; as if Sarah and Christina were the two most beautiful women in the world; as if these two goddesses had materialised through the iron roof of the pub as a special divine dispensation. And for Paterson, who owned both women in his mind, the occasion was an inspiration. So he shouted the entire mob of shearers to a round of drinks, and when they had finished it he wanted to buy them another. But they refused, and he almost got angry arguing over their refusal because he was having such a marvellous time. Then he made a new verse of the song for them, the shearers, and they all joined in, every gruff-throated one of them. And with them he knew that the swagman had not suicided, that that story was all wrong, because he was a shearer, and no shearer intended ever to die:

'Up jumped the swagman,
Sprang into the billabong.
"You'll never catch me alive," said he...'

So if he had died, he was murdered, a sacrifice for their cause; and if he had been killed, the shearers should rise again for him, pointing the shear-blade of justice, crying out for him the name he cried from the other side of the grave, the name a corpse will tell:

'And his ghost may be heard
As you pass by that billabong,
"You'll come a-waltzing, Matilda, with me!"'

The shearers hailed Paterson as their very own minstrel. They put another chair on a table opposite the girls, and they lifted Paterson onto it so that he stood, because the ceiling was not high, with his head cramped down on his shoulders. They made him sing the song again and they joined in fiercely. They had food and drink tight in their bellies; they had work and the promise of work, for while sheep kept living there was wool to clip; they had happy wives writing them weekly letters; they were ripe for song and poetry, these shearers with work; for them the experience of the fly-blown strike camp months before was turning in memory to a misremembered adventurous holiday, a source for boasts and tall stories, something that might now be sung about with bravado. The song their poet sang rushed to their hearts as the alcohol rushed to their brains, and it set off tiny, useful explosions there, just as songs of battle often fired the hearts of those who had forgotten, or never known, the fighting. The song was something that filled a vacancy in them: it monumentalised and clarified; it soothed; it assuaged guilt and it cooled hot pride; like a stirring speech above a grave, it laid the corpse of a great era to rest—they could all go home now and forget what the corpse had died fighting for. The song immortalised the rebellion, while comfortably killing it off.

To show their appreciation, the shearers each bought Paterson a drink, and as a good joke they opened the bottles and crowded them onto the table below his chair, so that he stood there, crushed against the ceiling, prevented from descending by a table-top full of frothing brown bottles encircling the plinth, the perch on which he had been placed. And they handed the first of the bottles up to him, cheering him on, as if he might have to drink the lot before they allowed him down. When he drank it, spilling it down his chest, they were delighted.

'But I'm not at all a drinker,' he protested.

'Don't give us that,' they shouted in reply.

The hairy, tattooed arms that had lifted the girls to the altar of womanhood and the young city man to the throne of the arts had no equivalent way of dealing with Clohesy. He was, to the shearers, uncategorisable, and therefore untouchable. He seemed to them an observer, so they let him observe, leaning against the rough counter, though out of courtesy to his relationship with the celebrities not allowed to buy his own drinks. Thus left out, Niall wondered what it was that drew men together. His own experience of intoxication was, as ever, that it highlighted his individual place in the world, not his team spirit. This dispersed, shared, anonymous revelry playing itself out grandly in front of him did not conform to his notion of a good time, which was something other, something personal and sharply focused, something unwelcome to the brawny, exposed limbs of these healthy shearers, something suspicious in the vast, naked geography of this developing land. The image that took his mind from amidst the singing and the female laughter was one of the coast, of a lonely stretch of the coastline with cliffs for ever towering north and south over a narrow strip of pure,

173

bright sand, now and then collaged with rocks and rock-pools where tiny marine lives prospered. There, on a wave gently swollen for the occasion, was delivered to him a stunning woman on a papier-mâché dolphin.

'We really must go,' shouted Paterson. 'You've all been too kind. We appreciate it. Now, how the hell will I get down?'

The shearers could not relent. They had a hero and two goddesses captive; the elastic bounds of politeness could be stretched further yet. 'You haven't finished our shout, Banjo,' they said. They were enjoying themselves.

Then Christina stood and took off her sun-hat—the big floppy hat she had kept on her head all this time. She held it in both hands and pulled at it with all her might, distorting its shape until its straw ripped. Then she began to tear it into small pieces which she threw into the air. As they fluttered down, big red arms grasped for them. As the pieces were caught they were kissed, or thrust into pockets or the bosoms of shirts so that they would rest close to the strong hairy bodies. When Christina's hat was gone the shearers wanted something from the other goddess, before she too could be released. So Sarah found, on searching, a page of rice paper under her sash, and when it was torn to confetti, it fell in a shimmering petal shower over them so that they wore it in their greasy hair and under their collars. Well pleased, the shearers relented. They carried the girls out of the pub and deposited them on the cushions of the buggy. They carried Paterson out too, and they shook Clohesy's hand amiably. As the buggy drove away they offered up three generous cheers.

Waving back through the dust, Sarah said, 'They must think us odd sorts.'

Christina answered, 'I think they think us brilliant.'

'We are brilliant,' said Paterson.

For old Jarvis, festive periods were a source of delight and gratification. No matter what the occasion—Christmas, Easter, a birthday, a funeral—he treated the pleasure they gave as his personal due. He reasoned that as a man who had spent so much of his life alone in the wilderness he now deserved complete indulgence in crowded, civilised gatherings. He had had so many lonely Christmases in his life—at outstations in the

174

Himalayan foothills where the big white monkeys came down from the forests like Santa Clauses, at Fijian lagoon posts where yuletide hurricanes delivered their seasonal destruction, in isolated Papuan villages where news of an ungodly cannibal feast might interrupt his solitary celebration of a sacred day meaningful to no one within a fortnight's contact. On at least two occasions which he could recall and recount at length he had celebrated his own birthday on the wrong day: once after his entire stock of personal and government gear had been stolen, including his clothes, horses and diary; and again after an almost fatal bout of malaria during a protracted patrol on which he had lost track of time completely. Ironically, the legacy of those obscure days of near-fatal delirium was a miniature bout of malaria each evening at 7 p.m. on the dot, regular as clockwork. Of course, on all the important calendar days during his life he had been surrounded by faces. But they were black faces, and could not be counted as company. There had been no festivity in the vacant looks and the belated, courteous smiles those faces gave when many a lonely glass he had raised to them, saying: 'Merry Christmas' or 'Happy New Year' or whatever ritual toast his own culture had prescribed. So to the old Police Magistrate Winton was by comparison with his previous postings neither isolated nor uncivilised. He felt now so close to the hub of events that mattered, where formerly he had been so decidedly on the rim, that he entered into each occasion of gathering — from the simplest quiet luncheon to the rowdiest crowded ball — with the abandon of one making up for a life of lost time.

Thus it was that with the arrival of the 'colts and fillies' (as Jarvis thought of those younger than himself) he again responded to an unspoken and entirely imagined call upon himself to entertain and thereby be entertained. Having supposed, on his return to society some years before, that his decades of wilderness seclusion had not only provided him with a constant supply of fascinating anecdotes, but had also somehow sharpened his wit, he tended to run off at the mouth in festive table conversation as incontinently as he did in the act of eating itself (the stains in his beard bore witness). And if he was not so thick-skinned as to be unconscious of mainly boring those who listened to him, he still believed that, as an old man who had given the best years of his life to the march of civilisation amongst the primitives, he was owed a debt by civilisation, a debt that could be most easily paid off in the form of audiences for his tales of memorable isolation.

And thus it was—the story of the bush hotel crawl having been delivered by Paterson and bellowed and tittered over by the swelling pre-party group at the Rowleys—that old Jarvis struck up a very long and complex story-cum-history about possibly every cave, hut, tent, shack, cabin, galley, kiosk, cell, brothel, boarding-house, mansion, palace, where he had ever had a drink. His whole life had been a sort of pub crawl in the never-never, he claimed. His thirst for the story's continuation beyond multiple chapters seemed unquenchable. An alternative entertainment was finally sought by the others in the Rowley's main room. With some urgency, young Ramsbottom was called upon to sing.

Young Ramsbottom was of a grazing family that took the cultivated life seriously. The father had spent a great deal on his son's education, especially his musical education. The son had repaid the father by singing solo with facility at the Brisbane Opera House, and by getting into difficulties in a duet with a young man from the chorus line in a less cultured establishment farther down Queen Street. The young man had been handsomely paid off. All the dangling ends had been tied up by a clever solicitor. Young Ramsbottom had been brought home to work off his loan from the family fortune with a stint of hard riding on the family property boundaries. But on return to the fold young Ramsbottom had found that his singing career was not at an end. On the contrary, his father continued to encourage it with a freedom greatly resented by the son. Every Hospital Benefit, Woolshed Dance, Pastoralists' Association Women's Auxiliary Luncheon, almost every indoor function on the Winton area calendar, provided old Ramsbottom with another opportunity to show off the better side of his son's musical education, and to get just a little more mileage out of the punitive sojourn to which he had sentenced the young man.

While old Ramsbottom took his son's musical education rather too seriously, young Ramsbottom took himself rather too seriously. He considered his father a tyrant and his term in the outback an unjustly hard and sweaty labour. He tended therefore to seek a measure of revenge by singing flat notes or messing up the timing, or by choosing songs of which his father would never approve, given foreknowledge. The number of times a flustered accompanist found himself or herself called upon to play a roaring ballad where the item set down in the function programme was one of the Lieder, had quickly become legend. Called upon at short notice to sing to the Rowleys' assembled guests, young Ramsbottom chose a ballad that perhaps betrayed some unfilial wishful thinking. Certainly the experience described in the song was not his father's own experience, nor was it likely to be. Nevertheless, the son sang it with a ferocity which was easily mistaken for rage against the droughty season, thereby pleasing everyone in the room. Christina knew the tune — 'The Little Old Log Cabin in the Lane' — so she played. Young Ramsbottom stood beside the piano, immaculately dressed in formal evening wear. During the introduction, he said, 'I humbly dedicate this song to my absent father.' Then he sang:

> I'm a broken-down old squatter,
> My cash it is all gone,
> Of troubles and bad seasons I complain;
> My cattle are all mortgaged,
> Of horses I have few,
> And I've lost that sprawling freehold on the
> plain.

> The woolshed's gone to blazes,
> The plains are barren dust,
> I've pleaded with the mortgagees in vain;
> My wool it is all damaged,
> It isn't worth a crust,
> And I've lost that sprawling freehold on
> the plain.

> I commenced life as a squatter
> Some twenty year ago,
> When fortune followed humbly in my train;
> I built myself a mansion
> And I chose myself a wife;
> We were happy on that freehold on the plain.

> So I thought I had sufficient
> To last me all my days,

177

I thought I'd have no reason to complain;
But I speculated heavy,
Never counting strikes or drought,
And they scorched me on that freehold on the
plain.

> *Oh, the woolshed's gone to ashes,*
> *The plains are barren dust,*
> *I've pleaded with the mortgagees in vain;*
> *My wool it is all damaged,*
> *It isn't worth a crust,*
> *And I've lost that sprawling freehold on*
> *the plain.*

Old Jarvis applauded long and hard. He cleared his throat loudly, as if he himself had been the singer. He praised young Ramsbottom lavishly, on his projection of voice, his manly stance, his graceful gestures. Having no sense of irony at all, old Jarvis also praised him on his choice of song: 'A fine popular piece upholding the traditions of endurance common to all civilised men,' he called it. Luckily there were no squatters present — they were all at a Pastoralists' Association meeting in the billiards-room of the North Gregory Hotel.

While Jarvis, the self-appointed critic, continued with a lecture on the anthropological significance of differences between civilised and primitive singing styles, Clohesy drew Paterson aside to whisper in his ear. It had occurred to him during the song that young Ramsbottom's singing talents might be put to good use amongst the jollities planned for the North Gregory Hotel later in the evening. Paterson was in agreement, and was perfectly happy for Clohesy to tutor the singer in the interpretation to be given to the first serious public performance of the swagman's song. Eventually there was a huddle round the piano which included Christina and young Ramsbottom, and there was a search through an old chest full of moth-eaten clothes. There was also the gathering together of miscellaneous items from the pantry, the servant's room, and the shed out the back. All of this was done conspiratorially, with much exchange of winking glances and muffled grins. They were devising a little entertainment for the Winton high society. Clohesy said, using a colloquialism from the city, he hoped they would find it 'catchy'.

Old Jarvis in the meanwhile had lost control. He had made the mistake of mentioning the songs with which the natives of the Niger Basin call down the rains to begin the wet season each year. This had allowed others, including Mr Rowley and Mr Henderson (the latter was the secretary of the town's volunteer fire brigade), to carry the conversation beyond the boundaries of anthropological musicology, to which old Jarvis had believed he strictly adhered, and into the more fanciful area of rain-making dances for the Winton district. For Jarvis's benefit it was suggested that a collection should be taken up to ship a group of the Yoruba tribesmen out from Africa to the Winton area in the hope that they could break the drought. The suggestion was seriously considered by Jarvis, but before he could lay before his audience an itemised list of objections to the proposal, the debate was taken over by the turgid accents of a German, the newly appointed site engineer for the Colonial Boring Company, who said that the town's artesian probe, already at the 2,500-foot mark, had still not reached water. 'Good water always runs deep,' was Jarvis's confident comment on the situation, but the German engineer was not so sure. In his experience, the water below that mark was unfit for drinking: 'Too many minerals,' he said, rolling the 'r' unpleasantly, as if he had already a mouthful of the dreaded stuff. 'Nonsense,' said Jarvis. 'We'll get used to it. That's why we've come so far already. It's our race's adaptability that has set us to the fore in the world. Look at what I've had to put up with in the name of progress. Some of the water I've drunk! Not fit for a rodent. Yet look at me. Strong as an ox.'

It was time to go. They climbed into traps, jinkers, gigs and buggies for the brief drive round the block to the main street.

CHAPTER

9

It had been arranged that everyone should arrive at the function hall of the North Gregory Hotel at eight o'clock. This was to coincide with the expected conclusion of the meeting of the Pastoralists' Association begun there earlier in the evening. When the guests arrived, however, the Pastoralists were still in conference behind the locked doors of the billiards-room. So the guests, without their male hosts, were obliged to fend for themselves amongst the trestle tables and decorations, waiting for the emergence of the gathering's leaders from the adjacent room.

It was close enough to Christmas for looped paper chains and tinsel lanterns to be hanging from the ceiling of the hall. The same festive note was added to the food on the tables. Amongst the plates of sausage rolls and mince tarts there sat cakes with icing script which read: 'Season's Greetings' and 'Mary Christmas'. The cakes also bore sprigs of marzipan holly with blue leaves. The town's Chinese baker had made the cakes.

In the circumstances it was the Pastoralists' wives who took over the hosting duties. Thus while Bowditch, old Ramsbottom, the Macphee Brothers, and the other graziers, continued with the pressing items on their meeting's agenda, the guests in the adjoining room settled down to a pleasant pre-performance gossip. In spite of the informality which took over in the absence of the evening's Master of Ceremonies, Mr Campbell, it was agreed that Mrs Bowditch be elected Temporary Mistress of Ceremonies. She gave a very pretty speech which welcomed them all and reminded them that the world had the comfortable habit of continuing to turn even when her husband and his confrères were indisposed. The audience greeted this observation with, in the main, uneasy disbelief, though there were some men who showed polite amusement and some women who applauded covertly. The town's society was used to adapting itself to the policy decisions made at the Pastoralists' Association meetings; any suggestion that the town was not in fact obliged to do so struck an unfamiliar chord. The townsmen — the merchants and the government officials — whose livelihoods depended upon the growth of the area's pastoral industry, were not free to accept too literally Mrs Bowditch's charming irreverence. For the women present, however, the matter was different. They had done what had to be done when their husbands were laid low with broken legs or gout or sandy blight, and on those occasions they had discovered certain aspects of station management previously kept secret from them, the most important being that the job was not beyond their capabilities. There were women present who had organised and ridden musters, overseen shearing, supervised slaughters, and directed tank-sinking. And if their husbands, on rising from their sickbeds, or returning from whatever called them away, had found abundant cause to complain about the levels of mismanagement during their absences, it was generally conceded, amongst the women at least, that the men did so only out of spite and a concern for self-preservation. So Mrs Bowditch's speech caused a little thrill of self-congratulation amongst the women. One of them, ample Mrs Campbell, who always took up two chairs at a gathering, extracted a Guinea Gold from her bag and lit it as a form of celebration, causing old Jarvis and others to tut and mutter. Mrs Bowditch sat down. The gossip continued. The tardiness of the Pastoralists was proving a marvellous opportunity for general communication.

Severely outnumbered, the men in the hall did their best to avoid conversations which began as incomprehensibly as: 'I must give you a cutting of the antigonon, my dear. It grows like a weed', or 'There's been absolutely nothing in Brisbane since Miss Achurch played Nora Helmer in *A Doll's House*.' The men formed a tight scrum all their own and discussed the latest polo or cricketing or real-estate disasters. But two of them, Clohesy and young Ramsbottom, stood on the sideline, the latter keen to

181

hear news of Brisbane concerts, of which the former was able to deliver a critical account. Yet as he spoke Niall kept his eye on the locked door to the billiards-room. His mind travelled beyond it, trying to guess what kept the graziers occupied so overlong. Was it himself they were discussing? Surely it was. Had they broken through his ultimate devices, the final by-passes he had placed in the 'channels', the supervision of which he had left to his assistant back in Brisbane? Now that his contract time was close to expiry, and there had been no reply to his pleas for an extension, for how long could he rely on the loyalty of those agents placed strategically along the lines of communication? He might have become the spider trapped in his own extensive web. The only way he would find out for certain would be when he was told by the enemy that they knew exactly who he was. He sensed there in the decorated hall, with the Christmas cakes and the ominously closed door, that he was about to be exposed. And he had not yet completed his mission. There was still time, he reminded himself, time to succeed. He did not have to be under contract to fulfil the contract's terms. If he had to continue the operation as a private citizen, not as an agent, then he would do so. There were yet ways to deflect complete exposure. He felt the heavy weight in the holster strapped close to his body, under his left arm. He could defend himself, if necessary. Niall watched the closed door until eventually it opened.

The graziers moved into the hall self-consciously. They tried to shake off the aura of their meeting by pursuing little rituals such as opening and closing their watches, smoothing back their hair, fingering the knots in their ties — all in the attempt to step smoothly from one dimension to another without giving any indication of what it was that had detained them in the holy of holies of their particular world. Niall noticed that none of them looked directly at him, and he counted that a bad sign. He was also perturbed to see the postmaster slip from the room amongst the graziers: the postmaster was a loyal link in the Pastoralists' network. The meeting had undoubtedly been debating his own future, Niall decided.

'You are looking glum and dejected, Inspector Clohesy.' Bowditch had come round behind him and now offered him a glass of sherry.

'Just exhaustion, I expect.'

'Yes, it takes it out of one, the dry heat here. Totally enerva-
ting. We've just been discussing you in our meeting, old chap.'

'Oh?'

'I believe the Association is on the verge of making you a
proposal. Nothing too handsome. But it might help you out.'
Bowditch took a sip at his sherry. 'Drink up, Clohesy. Sherry's
probably the best cure for outback weariness. It's sugary and it's
wet.' Niall gulped down the small glassful in a single toss.
'There's a good chap,' said Bowditch. Then he leant close, and
under the buzz of the talk in the room he said, 'We're not sure
that you were the right man for the job, Laver. Perhaps too
sensitive. That's not to say that the job doesn't demand sensi-
tivity. But you've not progressed far, have you?'

Laver replied nervously. He was not certain of the import of
the conversation. 'The job is a big one,' he said. 'I think I've
progressed fairly.'

'Of course you do. But you've not yet made any report.'

'I shall when I know who killed William Barret.'

'Don't give me that. You know already. Everyone had a finger
in it. It's where you pin the blame that counts.'

'I know he was killed by a many-headed Beast, Bowditch. It's
the heart of the monster I don't yet know. It's in the heart that
guilt and innocence are separated.'

At the end of the hall there was a simple raised stage and
behind it a back-drop used on some past occasion by the
Dramatic Club. The back-drop was faded and peeling. It had
been originally executed with a minimum of painterly talent. It
depicted a coastal scene: a round bay with sandhills, some
palms amongst the salty scrub, and a line of cool blue mountains in the distance. Beyond a foreground of water and gentle
breakers, a group of stick figures, Aborigines apparently, were
standing and sitting on the shore. A wisp of smoke rose from
their camp-fire. The scene seemed intended to present the view
from the boat approaching with the first white migrants arriving in Australia. Slanted across one corner, in red cursive
script amongst clusters of crotchets and quavers, were the
words: *Bound for Botany Bay*. At the top a hole had been cut in
the canvas and a piece of gauze inserted so that a light could be
placed behind. Whether it was meant to represent the sun or the

183

moon was not clear. The thing that struck Niall about the scene was that the Aborigines were depicted as being serene and comfortable. Judging from this artist's impression, the First Fleeters might have been forgiven for thinking that they were arriving in a truly idyllic land.

Mr Campbell stepped onto the stage. His weight made the boards complain. 'Ladies and gentlemen,' he announced, 'we have kept you long and we apologise. We hope that the evening's amusements will soon put you in the mood to forgive us. Our justification for postponing your entertainment tonight is, as you surely know, that our land is a great one, and decisions concerning our advancing it and realising its promise are not to be made without concerned and informed discussion. The drought is our biggest challenge now, but we will defeat it if we act with care and imagination. We will defeat all our problems in this way. We will advance Queensland, and Australia too, if we — as they say in the classics — knuckle down, put our nose to the grindstone, and stick to our guns. So with that plethora of proverbs, I take pleasure in presenting tonight's first item. By golly, it's the lovely voice of Oorooma's own Miss Clara Dobbs.'

There were songs and recitations, violins and a French horn, a mellifluous barber-shop trio and, for light relief, a magical act by an old veteran of the area who had to be assisted when a penny he deposited under a hat on a table reappeared stuck between his shoulder-blades where he could not reach it. There was also provided, as a surprise from the hotel management, a wild animal trainer who had arrived that morning bringing a big, lanky cat in a cage strapped on the roof of the coach. He set up a pen on stage and went a few desultory rounds with the unhappy black monster. The poor creature looked cowed and moth-eaten, and the trainer, a small man with a black moustache, did not look much better. But they excited the audience immensely, and someone said the puma was the world's most ferocious cat, and another said it was therefore a credit to the trainer that he had reduced it to such tameness.

Part-way through the programme's second half it was announced that The Banjo of the Bush was present in the audience and that he had penned a song specially for the occasion with the help of the lovely 'Daughter of Dagworth' (alliteration taking priority over strict truth), Christina Macphee. Young Ramsbottom then came on stage dressed as a swagman. He walked across the water of Botany Bay as all the performers had done before him, unconcerned about the inappropriateness of the back-drop. He trudged about a bit, his billy jangling from his swag and his waterbag limp in his right hand. Good-humoured jibes were flung at old Ramsbottom concerning the values of an education and the success he had made of his son, but they quieted when Christina began to play and young Ramsbottom sang:

O, once a jolly swagman camped by a billabong
Under the shade of a coolibah tree,
And he sang as he watched and waited till his billy boiled,
"You'll come a-waltzing, Matilda, with me!"

"Waltzing, Matilda, Waltzing, Matilda,
You'll come a-waltzing, Matilda, with me."
And he sang as he watched and waited till his billy boiled,
"You'll come a-waltzing, Matilda, with me."

Down came a jumbuck to drink at the billabong,
Up jumped the swagman, and grabbed him with glee,
And he sang as he stowed that jumbuck in his tucker bag,
"You'll come a-waltzing, Matilda, with me!"

Up rode the squatter, mounted on his thoroughbred,
Down came the troopers, one, two, three:
"Where's that jolly jumbuck you've got in your tucker bag?
You'll come a-waltzing, Matilda, with me!"

Up jumped the swagman, sprang into the billabong.
"You'll never catch me alive," said he.
And his ghost may be heard as you pass by that billabong,
"You'll come a-waltzing, Matilda, with me!"

Niall did not watch the performance; he watched the audience. He studied the faces of the men: Campbell, Dobbs, the Macphees, Tregilgas, Shipley, Connor, McIlwraith, Bowditch. They were all squatters and they all thought the song marvellous. They sipped their sherries and laughed heartily. They scratched themselves unselfconsciously. They looked at each other and at their wives without communicating doubt or fear or guilt. They joined in the choruses and sipped more sherry, and when the song was over they stood to applaud. Only then, with the applause rattling around him, did Niall notice Mrs Bowditch looking at him with a triumphant smile on her face.

While Niall examined the squatters, Paterson examined the figure seated at the piano. It was only then Paterson realised how much the song was hers. Her ear had captured the melody. Her hands had set it free again. Her liveliness had inspired the transcendent vitality of the words he had written. It was — after all the politics and the history were said and done with — a love song. It was an outback romance — a plea by a wanderer for the filling of the vast mirage-girt plain within himself. Who'll come a-waltzing, Christina, with me?

And as if a ghost from the future called him, he saw himself parading at Randwick with Christina, promenading at Bondi with Christina, waltzing at Government House with Christina. And in his vision she vibrated on his arm like something shimmering made of music and light. And she captivated the crowds in his vision, and they responded to her as to some perfect, shimmering chord they all recognised from a song their hearts had sung once, then lost. And in the midst of the crowds in his vision she leant up to his ear and whispered to him to make him see some tiny, ignored thing, saying, 'Isn't it perfect?' and he learnt by it some tiny, ignored fact that eclipsed the world of crowds and mirages. Oh, you'll come a-waltzing, Christina, with me!

They stood to applaud. Paterson was clapped to the stage to accept the ovation with Christina and young Ramsbottom. The song had been an enormous success. The congratulations flew from all parts of the audience. In the fervency of the situation Paterson kissed Christina on the cheek amidst a gale of whistling and laughter and delighted hooting.

Sarah left. She simply picked up her neat straw bag and walked quickly to the hall's main door. Up on the stage, Paterson was one of the few who noticed. He dropped Christina's hand and charged through the audience, flinging open the door which Sarah had neatly closed behind her. Christina was left bowing with young Ramsbottom. She was flushed in the face and also across her bare shoulders — from the success and the heat, the audience thought.

'A difficult act to follow,' shouted the Master of Ceremonies; 'but here is the one to do just that. It's everybody's notion of the perfect gentleman—Jack Tregilgas—to sing for us "The Piebald Winner".' Niall crept away, too, as the perfect gentleman launched into a lively song about a horserace and a drunken judge. He climbed the stairs wearily to his room. He had caught no one in his trap. So much for the ghost of Billy Barret being heard, he thought.

Sarah walked briskly down Elderslie Street. A cool, black breeze, formed somewhere in the pools of night sky above, fanned her face. She felt no fear, in spite of the silent stares she received from stockmen and miners lounging in dark groups along the street. She was inviolable, she knew. In fact, she felt the loungers to be allies rather than threats; they would rise from their loose, comfortable groups to her assistance, should she need it. She felt that each of them, too, was alone in the night like herself, alone and free.

She had to be careful where she trod in the unclean street; yet she continually raised her eyes from the ground to the sharp glister of stars above, as if she navigated by them. She recalled that her father had, only days before he died, opened the case in which he kept his old sextant, the major item of dearness from his youthful days at sea. He had found that the instrument was broken. The glass of its lens was scattered in slivers and chips across the plush lining of the case. She had come under the house and surprised him there. In tears he was, the case open before him. She was fourteen then, just days off being fifteen and fatherless. She was now thirty-one. She had lived more than half her life without his guiding hand.

When she looked up at the star-splashed sky it seemed to her, at first, a God-painted chapel dome. Then she realised that was wrong. It was not religious or moral, the night sky, not God-fashioned or God-ordained. But it was God-loved. It was the hot, dark womb of Lilith, the cavity in salt flesh that God had been tempted to fill, in which He had left the bright glitter and wriggle of life. To Sarah this was a revelation of her own independence. With Lilith, she could take and leave the God-embrace, she could carry on with the God-knowledge and

God-spatter inside her; it made no difference. She would leave the walls of her own womb star-studded, like Lilith. Nothing would come of it, she knew.

She had turned the corner into Oorooma Street when Paterson caught up with her. He was puffing violently in the night. She did not look at him. She kept walking.

'It was nothing,' he said. 'What's the matter with you?'

'I'm afraid you will have to grow up, Mr Paterson, before I find interest in your conversation again.'

'I didn't mean anything. I was carried away. It was a very happy moment for me. You know how I am with an appreciative audience.'

'Take your hand off me, Mr Paterson. It was not the behaviour of a gentleman.'

'A kiss on the cheek? What the hell is a kiss on the cheek? Come on, Sarah. You are acting as if I've committed a crime.'

'I cross the road here, Mr Paterson. If you'll kindly step out of my way.'

'All right, I'll apologise. I'll beg you for a pardon. If that's what you want. But I maintain that I've done nothing to compromise our love. I love you, Sarah.'

'You are shouting, Mr Paterson.'

'I know I'm damn well shouting. I'm trying to get through to you. Don't you understand?'

'I cross the road here, Mr Paterson. Please let me by.'

'Doesn't what we've shared mean anything to you? I came here all the way just to be with you.'

'And I came here to get away from you.'

'I don't believe that.'

'Believe what you like. Nothing matters now.'

'Everything matters now. I love you, Sarah. I want to marry you. You know that. You've already agreed to marry me. You can't change your mind.'

'Men have such a low opinion of love. You are no exception, Mr Paterson.'

'Listen. Quit this "Mr Paterson" nonsense. I'm serious, Sarah. This is the most important moment in our lives. Don't let's spoil it. Don't let's be fools. For God's sake, Sarah. Kiss me.'

She broke away and ran across the street. When she reached the house she fumbled with the latch on the veranda gate. He

188

caught up with her there on the steps.

'Sarah, I'm sorry. I promise it will never happen again. Now that I know how it hurts you. I wouldn't mind you being kissed on the cheek by another man. It's modern, Sarah. That's all. It doesn't hurt. How can it possibly hurt? But I'll not do it again, Sarah. My darling!'

'Good-bye, Mr Paterson.'

She moved towards the door. Paterson went with her, crabwise at her side. Then they were standing on the star-washed veranda, face to face. Sarah absolutely still. Her hand on the door latch. Waiting for him to leave before she opened it.

'Good-*bye?*' he said, suspicious.

'Good night and good-bye.' She said it without emotion, without regret or despair, without any sense of loss. She said it as a tutor would to a slow learner. Then she held out something in her hand. 'Here is your ring,' she said.

She entered the dark house and closed the door on him.

Paterson stumbled down the veranda steps. He was in a rage. He got as far as the front fence, then turned and yelled at the house: 'I'll get you, Sarah. I'll hound and pester you until you give in. Until you get reasonable again. I've done nothing wrong. You're stupid acting this way.' Then he spun round and headed determinedly along Vindex Street.

Turning the corner into Elderslie Street Paterson could see a gig drawing away from the North Gregory Hotel. He knew by the team of greys that it was the Macphees' vehicle. It came down the street towards him, the horses jostling to get into stride, their heads dipping in the wash of starlight, their bodies jerked sideways in the harness. They came on towards him, their motion visible before the sound of it reached through the black-flecked air to him; their pace unknown, for they came head-on, pounding on the road at full trot but in the one place, without forward progress. They came on towards him, the street dust squirting star-caught at their hooves, not getting closer, just looming larger and larger, with the growing threat of a juggernaut's implacable approach. And fixed there in the street, his feet grown roots into the dust of the street, Paterson felt the tremor of the vehicle's approach rise through his feet, and the thunder of it broke in his brain, and he did not budge an inch as the horses passed within a hair's-breadth of him so that he even smelt them, the close-up smell of horses, as they passed so near and yet a thousand thousand miles from him, and yet again he could not tell how close they passed. And as they passed he saw on the gig the Macphee brothers smiling a polite greeting or waving a congratulatory salute — or did they fail to see him at all? He did not know, for he saw Christina sitting between them ignoring him on purpose. That was definite. Among all the other aspects of the vast night of which he knew nothing, or only little, this was the definite thing, the one definite, ineluctable fact: she ignored him. She did not look down at him, yet she knew he was there, and she wanted him to know it, that she was ignoring him standing there in the road like a beggar, star-struck, woman-struck, passion-struck, struck mad by rejection and loss and the thunder burning along the labyrinth of his veins. And she wanted him to know how well she ignored him, how perfectly ignored he was, and he knew it.

When he looked down the street the gig had gone. That end of town was quite empty of movement. He felt for a vast moment empty too, until there crept on him the weight of the night sky, creeping on him, moving on him, rushing on him, until its pressure was the full weight of the star-laden darkness and he flung himself down on the road with total abandonment, not caring for the hurt or the dirt, not caring for the scene that he made or didn't make, not caring for an audience or his total aloneness, caring only for the complete, mind-cracking aban-donment of the flinging, aiming himself at some point deep inside the earth and colliding with the intervening ground with a gratifying, bone-jerking, flesh-bruising shock. Then he lay there with the rage bleeding from him into suffocating pools.

An Aboriginal stockman bent over him. 'Are you all right, sir?' he said.

'Get off,' said Paterson.

Niall was in bed. By drawing the curtains and manoeuvring a chair against them he had been able to make the room virtually secure against the insidious starlight. At just one or two chinks it penetrated, hardly noticeable. He lay on his back, trying to empty his head of the day's events, trying to encourage himself towards the precipice of unconsciousness, towards the plunge

190

into sleep. By lying on his back — he knew from past experience — he invited dreams to come. They would be memorable if he stayed on his back. They would lie with him, on him, if he opened himself to them. They would remain with him in the morning, perhaps they would wake him, but only if he lay on his back, his face away from the earth. Only that prevented them from sinking back into the depths of unconsciousness. Floating on his back in sleep he would save his dreams.

Of course, the dreams he wished to keep and savour were of the woman who now in waking memory slipped like mercury through the interstices of his grasping mind. He could no longer picture her face. He could not fix it in memory, not even when his mind sneaked up behind her form and surprised her. On turning, the face darted away like a wild thing, or melted into a confusion of features that he dreaded because it was a collage of so many women, and especially those around him now: Mrs Bowditch, Sarah, Christina. He wanted nothing of these. He felt betrayed by some part of himself when, not craving these women at all, his mind presented him with their images more readily, more clearly, than that of the woman who truly excited him, to whom he found little difficulty in being loyal. Yet there was one image of her form he could call up at will, and which stayed as long as he willed it: the dead image of her. The image of her frozen by the guillotine-snap of the photographer's shutter. That unwanted, haunting image of her astride the dolphin at Humpybong. He did not want to remember her like that. That was her public image, the property of every male in the world. It could live in every lewd and lusting mind that had contemplated it. A threepenny postcard was all it took to own that aspect of the woman on whom he had spent his soul. Yet it was the delicious, pornographic ensnaring of her that his mind could reproduce in every grain of detail, while his memory had failed to hold the completeness of the flowing, vivid moments of his own shared life with her.

Lying straight and flat on the bed, he dropped from the cliff-height of consciousness. It seemed only moments later that he was woken by a light close above his head, a lamp it was, held in a gloved hand, a white glove holding a lamp above his face, and from beyond the dazzle of the lamp close above his eyes, a voice, a soft, woman's voice, saying something, something he did not hear at all at first, except that he knew a voice had spoken.

'Who is it?' he asked, softly. Then frightened, he shouted, 'Who is it?'

From beyond the light juddering on his eyeballs came the voice: 'Don't call out, Hammond Niall.'

It was the first time he had heard his own name in a woman's voice since Brisbane more than two weeks ago. He immediately recognised that the head-start he had had was whittled away completely. His true identity had caught up with him, as had been inevitable. A thousand miles it had come and he had outrun it. But now, like a shadow, it attached itself to him, and could not be denied. There was no surprise left in his attack. Yet it was not the fact of his identity becoming known that alarmed him so much as the fact of the identity betrayed by the voice which now spoke it. He lurched his hand out at the lamp, and it swung away. The burning smell of the paraffin invaded his nostrils. 'Don't be silly, Mr Niall,' said the voice; 'you'll cause an accident.'

'I must warn you, Mrs Bowditch,' he said to the light, 'that I have removed my clothes. If you'll kindly allow me the time to dress —'

'On the contrary,' came the voice, 'I am pleased to hear of your nakedness, Mr Niall. It suits my purposes admirably.'

She sat herself down on the edge of the bed, still waving the lamp over him. He drew the sheet up tightly around his throat.

'Your eyes, Mr Niall!' She laughed. 'They are sticking out like organ-stops — bloodshot organ-stops.'

He brushed her amused observation aside. 'How did you get in here?' he asked.

'Locks are for honest people, are they not?'

She placed the lamp on the bedside table and began removing her gloves. The first smooth hand to emerge, slightly yellowed by the flickering lamp flame, was her left hand.

'Just what is it you want of me, Mrs Bowditch?'

'Well...you'll be relieved to hear that I no longer want to know who you are. I've found that out at last. Clohesy...Laver ....Niall. It was like peeling back an onion. Or better still: it was like one of those gifts you get from a waggish five-year-old nephew — multiple layers of wrapping paper, each layer having another ribbon with a complicated knot to untie. It gets boring

192

after a while. And usually, at the centre, there's nothing of importance — nothing of much use. But one must continue with the farce to humour the child.'

Both gloves were off and lying amongst the folds of the sheet. Now her hands were up at her head, untying the ribbons.

'So, now that I know who you are, Mr Niall, your identity interests me no longer. Instead I now want to know what you know. It is only what people know that makes them important, not who they are.'

Having arranged the fall of her hair over her shoulders, she began manipulating the ties which held together the lace at her neck. The collars of her dress started to open like petals, exposing the white of her throat under the slender working of her fingers.

'This is too bizarre, Mrs Bowditch. I suggest you desist at once.'

The two halves of the front of her dress fell apart, revealing her naked bosom. She took her breasts in her own hands and lifted them towards him, squeezing them softly so that her thumbs and forefingers ran down gently to the nipples, which she pinched, drawing the fingers back so that the teased nipples were left pouting at him.

'Oh, God, Mrs Bowditch. This really is too ridiculous.'

'Stop me, then, Mr Niall.'

'How can I stop you? I am trapped here. You are taking advantage. It is quite improper of you.'

'In that case, your memory is exceedingly short, Mr Niall. Have you not just finished a remarkably similar attack on an entire roomful of people? Wasn't your little mouse-trap play equally obscene? Certainly when one considers obscenity to be the invasion of the privacies that another holds dearest. However, I will be perfectly content to desist from my present behaviour if you answer me truthfully. What did you discover from the trap you set for that roomful of innocents?'

'You saw for yourself. Absolutely nothing. No one reacted at all.'

'You disappoint me, Mr Niall. I did see for myself. Everyone reacted.'

'I saw nothing. There wasn't a guilty face or gesture in the room.'

She leant forward over him. Her breasts loomed in front of

him. They swung burning arcs into his brain. 'You are being difficult, Mr Niall. I am only asking for the truth.'

'Then you must want a different truth from the one I know.'

She reached both hands out and pulled at the edge of the sheet held at his throat. He gripped it from underneath, his hands feeling the pressure she exerted. She drew the sheet down to his waist. As she leant forward over him he fancied the fragrance of coolibah leaves pouring down from her hair.

'You really are a fool, Mr Niall. I killed Barret. Isn't it obvious? I was responsible for his death. Perhaps that is a better way of putting it. But to tell the truth — you like peeling back onions, don't you, Mr Niall — to tell the truth, perhaps I should say that I was the reason why he suicided.'

She had begun a torture of caresses on Niall's naked chest. She ran her fingertips round his pectorals, pulling at the hairs growing there, delving and pressing between his ribs, manipulating along and over his clavicles, and down onto his biceps. She massaged his chest as if she were gently kneading dough, toning up the surface of his body like a taxidermist preparing for a mould-taking.

'Certainly it is true my husband would have shot Bill Barret had he not decided his own fate. I had to tell Eugene who it was cuckolding him on that occasion because by that time Barret had become a nuisance and a liability. His information was unreliable: he was inventing intelligence so that he had excuses to see me. Unreliability is not appreciated in the outback, as you probably know by now. We shoot what we cannot trust, Mr Niall.'

She leant her head right down to his chest so that her breasts pressed on the sensitive skin around his navel while her lips formed an 'O' over his left nipple. She ran her tongue on the nipple several times, then gave it a firm, stinging bite.

'Jesus!' he gasped.

'Yes, he loved me too much, Barret did. Too much for his own good, that is. I am not presumptuous. Other men have done silly things because of me. Men will always do silly things because of women, Mr Niall. Out here especially. Out here where Matilda is the most popular whore, and a dry old one at that. Most men need more than a bed-roll and a fertile imagination. My husband puts bromide into the workers' ration tea, Mr

194

Niall. You might like to add that to your secrets list.'

She placed her hands on the sheet at his waist. With irony, she smiled. She said, 'What do you think of my confession so far, Mr Niall?'

'It has its merits.'

'Of course it does — seeing it is no confession at all.'

She drew the sheet down over his thighs. His penis was not erect. She watched his genitals' reflex movement there in the creamy lamplight. 'See how your testicles roll of their own accord. Like clouds forming. Like a storm brewing. All men's testicles move like that, Mr Niall. There's nothing special about yours.'

She closed her lips over his penis and took the whole softness of it into her mouth. It lay in her mouth like a witchetty-grub for a moment. Then, without his permission, it began to swell. It kept swelling until it had pushed most of itself out from between her lips. She raised her head and sat up. She looked at his penis reared to full height. Then she put her hands to the ties at the front of her dress and began doing them up.

'But I cannot take all of the blame or credit for poor Barret's death. I shall only take my share. Everybody killed him. Everybody had a hand in it. Everybody in the colony. You included, Mr Niall. Because Bill Barret was something we weed out in this country. We call him Anarchy on the stations, Mr Niall, but others around here call him Rebellion and New Thinking, and you might call him Creativity or Individualism. But no one calls him Security, or Religion, or Tradition, Mr Niall. And even those who call him Freedom wouldn't call him Certainty. And those who see him as Hope or Promise know they fool themselves when they mistake him for Insurance. He was a threat to everybody, one way or another, and by meaning so much to so many he became the enemy of all. But he thought he had an ally in me.'

The collar of her dress was secure. She now took her hair up, winding the tresses round the slimness of her right forefinger and gathering them with the ribbons.

'I have his letters here. If you like, you can read them. I have no way of proving to you that they are genuine. However, a true love letter is difficult to forge. In fact, they are not unlike your own letters.'

195

'My letters?'

Her hair was in place. She now drew on the gloves. 'Don't worry. We've sent them all on. They were held up somewhat, however. They caused us a great deal of trouble. We thought they were in code.'

'Serves you right. Of course, I trust you've not interfered with my wife in any way.'

She drew the sheet up from his knees to his neck. 'The quicker you go home, the sooner you'll find that out. Quite a sensational little piece, I noticed. 'The Humpybong Girl.' Aren't our private lives amusing? Love is so dreadfully levelling. It turns us all into such children.'

She stood and took up the lamp in her white-gloved hand. 'I think we understand each other now, Mr Niall. I'm pleased we were able to achieve it in such a pleasant way. The Pastoralists' Association has been so generous as to donate your return fare to Brisbane, plus some pocket money. They've even gone to the trouble of booking the tickets for you.' She took a small envelope from a purse hanging at her waist, and threw it down on his sheet-covered chest. '*Bon voyage,* Mr Niall,' she said.

'And if I don't choose to leave?'

'In that case I can merely inform you that you will be no longer welcome here. I won't guarantee your safety after the coach departs tomorrow morning.'

She moved and opened the door. 'Good-bye, Inspector Clohesy,' she said. He expected her to draw the door to gently, but she slammed it. The sound startled him so greatly that he felt he had somehow been shocked into a new awakedness. The room was as dark as it had ever been, the corridor as quiet. He was there on his back as he had been before falling asleep. It occurred to him that if he got out of bed and tested the door-handle, he would find it locked, as it had been after he had turned the key, and before he had blown out the lamp, an hour or so ago. He rose from the bed, his body as clean as it was before lying down, his mind as taut as it had been. He put his hand to the door-knob and turned. The door opened. Strange, he thought, that at the moment when he was closest to her he was farthest away from everything he had aimed at. He went back to bed and set his miniature alarm clock for an early wakening.

During the night the stars went out. The process began in the west. Those lowest on the horizon disappeared suddenly, as if blown from the edge of the night sky. Then those higher up took on a fuzziness, faltered, and were buried beneath the dark explosion of clouds ascending. The air turned thick and dense. It weighed on the ground. It pinned the earth with its swollenness, stifling rebellious eddies of dark dust, clamping down on the excited twitching of knowledgeable leaves. There was rain coming. Everything smelt it and smelt of it. There was rain coming in the pockets of wind-gust. There was rain coming in the stillness of insects and the silence of watercourses. There was rain coming in the cracking of roofs and the twanging of empty water-tanks. There was rain coming in the closeness of the darkness.

And in the clouds' unfurling and swinging and building fold upon fold to towers there was a tangible sense of the impossible happening, as if the earth had begun to roll a different way, bringing by miracle a healing raiment of cloud over this leprous stretch of the earth's body, and under the swerve and unfurling the dry earth awaited the reward of its dusty faith, quivering with expectation for the healing slap and smother.

And when it came at first it came in drops the size of eggs, that broke on the hard ground like eggs, and splattered rolling on the dust like the meat of eggs, accompanied by the thudding, cracking sounds of eggs bursting. Then the individual shocks of drops bursting grew to one great symphonic shudder of bursting, and those who woke in the night said to themselves, 'It's raining', and some of them woke others, and some of them rose from their beds and went to verandas to feel the rain's realness, and some of them could hardly believe it, and others simply turned over and slept again with unusual comfort, and yet others could not sleep for excitement or gratefulness or, in a very few cases, annoyance.

But the rain, having no consideration for individual reactions, fell in one massive blanket on rooftops and fence-lines and tennis courts and roadways, and it fell in one great trampling plunder on splitting grasses and tearing branches and shying dust and steaming rocks, and it fell in a heaving, downward mass on ragged dogs and jerking horses and shambling sheep and scuttling lizards and surprised water-birds, and it fell in a gouging torrent on thickening sand-drifts and rotting timbers and softening clays and caving banks and turgid waterholes, and everything it crashed on it muddied or damaged or broke or danced to a frenzy or made to sing wildly.

So water moved on the land again. And it moved with a brash rush, no John the Baptist trickle showing it the way. It moved in walls and sudden waves, hesitating nowhere, asking no directions, knowing the land like the back of a hand. And it barrelled down its courses, ever-meeting, ever-swelling, tipping objects from its path, ever-skeining, ever-plaiting, hooting in the night like an escape of lunatics, ever-meshing, ever-ravelling, until it ran across the land like veins in the backs of a crowd of hands.

And in the morning there were fans of water on the land, all knit together, isolating the interspaces.

CHAPTER

10

Niall woke with a pounding head. He reached for his clock in the darkness, thinking he had woken before the alarm had sounded. The clock showed 8 a.m., but it had been set for 4. It had run amuck in the night, he thought. Then the pounding began again, and Niall realised it was nothing in his head, but a knock at his door. When he opened it he was greeted by an oddly dripping and muddied Paterson who pushed through from the half-light of the corridor, setting loose a flood of frantic words that reverberated unpleasantly on Niall's sleep-webbed brain.

'The roads are bogging up already. The Diamantina is flowing for the first time in seventeen months. Elderslie Street's a quagmire. Look at this! I sank to my ankles right outside the hotel. What a place! They're certainly not used to rain here.'

'Rain? What do you mean: rain?'

Paterson whipped back the curtains from the window. 'Good God, old chap. Where have you been all night? It's been bucketing down.'

Something vague stirred in Niall's awakening brain. 'What about the coach?' he said.

'The coach? It left all right, but God knows how far it will get. You should see the roads. Well, you can't see them, that's the point. The roads have turned to rivers, basically. They'll be impassable soon. Everyone will be isolated. But no one cares. They're so damned happy because it's raining. There are idiots down there outside the Commercial Hotel smearing mud all over themselves. And dancing in it. I saw a woman drinking from a bucket and pouring it over her head. The whole place looks as though it's got the jumps.'

Niall looked out the window. Elderslie Street seemed all of a slant with driving gusts of rainy wind. Paterson was right. There were sodden people dancing in it.

'Sorry, old chap,' said Paterson, 'but I've really come barging in here to ask you a favour. You couldn't spare me just a little of your time, could you?'

Niall had no idea what he could or couldn't do. The morning had burst on him in a totally unexpected way, and he had not had a chance to consider what he should do. He had missed the coach, that seemed certain. In spite of the greyness of the light outside it was obviously well after daybreak, and equally obvious that his clock was telling the correct time. He had missed the coach, or at least missed the opportunity to decide whether or not to take the coach. He did not yet know what status he held in the town, or the extent to which the situation was dangerous for him. If things were really bad — that is, if he was trapped in the town — there was not much point in dramatic action yet. The bee that struggled excessively in the spider's web, he recalled, risked enmeshing itself more firmly. Subtle action was the art of the escapologist. But here before him was Paterson, clearly frantic with some desperate escape plan of his own, asking him for his time and assistance. To aid him might supply just the sort of subtle diversion he needed.

'I'll help you on one condition, Bartie.'

'Anything, old man.'

'That you listen to me for a few moments now.'

'But time is of the essence —'

'It's my only condition.'

'OK, OK. But please hurry.'

'It's simply this. You know me as Clohesy, but my real name is —'

'Yes, yes. Everybody's heard. Announced last night after we left. Caused a stir, apparently. Hammond Niall, isn't it? I'm very pleased to meet you, at last.' Paterson put out his rain-wet hand. It was odd their shaking hands as if they had just met. 'It makes no difference to me,' Paterson continued. 'I trust you. In fact, you're the only person I would turn to in my predicament. I feel you're the only one who could understand.'

'What is it I should do?'

'All I need is for you to go and talk to her. Sarah Rowley, I mean. Go and try to talk some sense into her. She won't speak to me. She's locked herself in her room and refuses to budge. At Vindex Street, of course. She's locked herself in and won't see me or hear from me. If you could just deliver my apologies and plead with her to come out to talk the matter over with me reasonably and sensibly. That's all.'

'And what matter will I be referring to?'

'We had a spat last night. Over me kissing young Chris on stage. She's just being the jealous woman, but I can't get through to her. Do you think you could do it, old man?'

'I'll give it a try. If you'll just wait till I put some clothes on.'

'No, old man. I won't wait. I've got to fly. Got some other urgent business. That's the problem, you see. So if you don't mind, I'll skedaddle.' He rushed to the door, then turned and said, 'This could be the tragedy of my life.' And was gone.

Niall dressed without hurrying. He shaved calmly, careful not to nick himself. He removed the false moustache and tossed it away. He did not oil his hair down flat, just combed it back. He tidied his bag and straightened up the room. Clohesy's spectacles he left by the lamp on the bedside table where he had put them the night before. The cane he left propped in the corner.

He went down to the dining-room. It was empty, a white silence of tablecloths and napkins in rings, dull cutlery, and chairs pushed in under tables. He sat in the far corner of the empty room, and waited. There was a single trail of muddy footprints across the floor where someone had traipsed through from the rain outside.

Eventually a member of the staff came by. Her footsteps and voice echoed in the room's vacancy. 'The breakfast's over. I'm sorry,' she said.

'I only want a boiled egg,' said Niall.

The woman left, but came back immediately with two cold boiled eggs and five slices of unbuttered toast. 'Sorry. That's all there is,' she said.

'Marvellous,' he replied. 'Enough to feed a multitude.'

When he had eaten the food he left the empty room and stepped out into the street full of rain. He walked towards Vindex Street. He drew his coat up over his head to keep his hair dry. He stepped cautiously to avoid the deeper puddles. When he reached the Rowleys' house he was told by the maid that Miss Sarah was indisposed and would see no one.

Gently, Niall pushed past the girl, smiling at her reassuringly. 'Which is Miss Sarah's room?' he asked. He was shown to it. The door was closed. Niall knocked.

'Who is it?' came Sarah's voice. She sounded distressed, as if something like tears were choking her.

'I've come on Bartie's behalf, Sarah. He has asked me to represent his good intentions to you.'

'That's very noble of you, Mr Niall, but I am not leaving this room until Mr Paterson has made a permanent departure from this town. Nor do I intend to entertain any deputations on his behalf. He is a cad, and I don't wish to think of him further.'

'But surely you are being hasty?'

'Not at all, Mr Niall. You yourself present further evidence of his unreliable character. The man he sends to represent him is an unashamed impostor — very fitting, I must say. I overheard last night's talk of your exposure, Mr Whatever-Your-Real-Name-Is. And I have had ample evidence of your character through viewing your aiding and abetting of Mr Paterson's interest in Miss Macphee. I have no wish for further involvement with him or with his faithless accomplice. Anyone may play a melody on fickle instruments such as yourself and the wanton Banjo, Mr Niall. And never is the tune true to pitch. If you think my metaphors desperate, then you perceive correctly. So, if you wish to do something truly gallant in your life, you'll leave me immediately and save me from further emotional torment. Good-bye, Mr Niall.'

Niall looked at the door. It was divided into four panels, with a cross described between them. It annoyed him that he had noticed.

'Good-bye, Miss Rowley,' he said.

Paterson rode like a madman. In the frenzy of his mission he hardly noticed the sting of rain on his face, the spreading damp across his chest and down his back, the clag of mud on his legs. He gunned the horse against the wall of rain, heedless of the regular skid and stumble as the driving hooves sought out the solid ground beneath the slush. There was an exhilaration in it, though that too, like the unpleasantness, registered only in a minor way on Paterson's consciousness. What he thought about, as the rain whipped like bullets around him, was the girl ahead. The wild, perfect girl, probably mooning now on some bare corner of the Dagworth veranda, looking out across the rain-whipped plain, waiting for him.

The road he galloped out along was the same that had brought them back to town the previous day: the river road, then vibrant with heat and mirages, now sodden. As he rode he relived that gay drive: the processional grandeur of it; the mad ballet of it; the drunken stagger of it; the buggy team prancing like a fairytale through a dreaming landscape; the women lifting their heads and holding onto their sun-hats; the laughter flowing unimpeded to the horizons; even Clohesy (Niall it was now) enjoying himself like a schoolboy truant from some hard lesson. Yes, it was that scintillating opal of experience Paterson rode for now, that sun-splashed, vivid afternoon of colour that he rode to retrieve. And looking back on that gay drive, from the grey enclosures of rain he rode through, was like looking into a glowing stained-glass window — all reds and oranges and blue-greens gleaming — from inside a cathedral gloom.

But haunting his ride all the way was a booming never far off. It was constantly there in the background, the booming rush of the river according to which the road wound and bent. He had not yet been forced to tackle a major crossing: the road followed obediently on the north-eastern side of the main channel for most of his way. But there were crossings ahead, and if he thought of them at all it was in the context of his own perfect belief in himself and in the elemental rightness of his mission. He had, he knew, as much right to surge ahead as did the flood. He was riding for the master-stroke of his life. He was riding for his past's cure and his future's consummation. He was riding to the salvation represented by a woman he hardly knew but, in his feverish passion, believed he could know better than any.

The Twenty Mile Hotel came and went beside the roadway. It was haloed in wreaths of rain-splatter. Although he saw horses tethered there, he saw no people. He pressed on, his body's irritations from rubbing against wet clothing hardly recorded in his brain. He was little more than a live, lone mind conveyed across a grey anonymity. He was little more than his feverish vision, an ember protected by a skull, conveyed across a storm-smothered plain.

When he came to the first crossing of the Diamantina's main channel he knew immediately he was beaten. It was not a matter of failing courage, or fear of death, or a matter of his burning passion being suddenly quenched by the flood-flow tearing at the banks there. It was a matter of his recognition of his own unworthiness. He sat on the horse, enveloped in rain, watching the flood-fierceness, thinking with a thought as formidable as the river itself that he simply did not deserve the perfection he had envisaged. It was no weakness in his vision or his determination that allowed him to see his failure so readily; it was the merciless eloquence of the river's fury. His realisation did not come as a blow might come to stagger with its unjustness. It came as a sentence should after a trial: with a vivid inevitability.

He did not know how long he stayed there, hypnotised by the sinuous sweep of the river. It might have been a long time, for he recorded every detail as if this impasse were the vision he must now bear into the future in place of a transcendent happiness. He saw and drew into himself the fall of clods from the ripped bank, each clod a universe of individual grains falling to become part of the river's rush. He saw a sheep's skull bowled by, a trophy of the drought. He saw bubbles of froth clinging in desperate embrace, spun and dizzied by the water's tyranny. He heard the deep growl of the river, as if the earth's depths spoke in it. When he knew the river would run like that, exactly like that, in him for the rest of his life, he turned the horse away, feeling fully for the first time how his body itched and burnt in the wet clothes, feeling the hot bite of the rain on his cheeks and the swampiness of his feet in their boots. Then slowly he rode back to the Twenty Mile Hotel and tethered his horse with the other sodden beasts at the rail outside.

Inside there was a fire blazing. A dozen or so men sat before it, drinking rum. They welcomed Paterson as they would have welcomed any mud-spattered, anonymous traveller. They were labourers en route from one station to another. They were not unhappy with the rain: it provided a holiday. A glass was filled for him. He took off his coat and hat, and hung them by the fire. In doing so he found he was shivering underneath. Cold had become such an unlikely phenomenon he had almost forgotten how to recognise it. 'Get this inside you, mate,' they said. He drank the rum down, not too quickly, but determinedly. They filled his glass again and asked him his name. 'Chance,' he replied. 'Will Chance.' He settled into the warm ring of men by the fire. It felt good. He had known he would get drunk here the moment he turned back from the river, had wanted it; but it was nice to find such welcome warmth to do it in. These weathered men were friendly and unsuspicious. The rains had thrown them into a pub where they might have to stay indefinitely. They would never have asked for much more than that.

They began singing, well-trodden melodies that Paterson joined in on. Then one of the group suggested the new swagman song, and set out on a verse and chorus. But the singing faltered. The singer did not know the words.

'Ever heard of that one, Will?'

'No, mate. It's a new one on me.'

'A couple of coves and two lasses came in here singing it yesterday. Damned if I can remember it all now. Bloody good song, though.'

They sang something else instead.

Paterson drank on, unremittingly. Some time during the afternoon, before he passed out, two children playing by the fire showed him a fossil they had discovered and kept. 'Plenty down on the flat by the river,' they said. Paterson held the slab of ancient, petrified mud in his hands. On it was the imprint, faint but discernible, of part of a bird—the curve of the head and leading edge of the wing—captured by the mud as it pitched forward to death. From the shape of the head, the position of the eye, the general size of the imprint, Paterson recognised, in spite of his warm drunkenness, that it was the cast of a seagull—but an ancient seagull, with a useful-looking hook on the end of its beak. 'An inland seagull,' he said, marvelling.

'You can keep it if you want,' said one of the children.

Perhaps they were surprised at his thankfulness. He counted it the most important of gifts.

'Unexpected surprise seeing you still here, Mr Niall.'

'I want to send a telegram.'

The postmaster leant on his counter and looked at Niall from behind his bottle-end spectacles. He had bushy side-burns and a gold tooth.

'Well, isn't that a coincidence, Mr Niall?' he said. 'There's a telegram waiting here for you.'

He passed it over from the bank of pigeonholes. Niall opened it and read to himself.

'Bad news, Mr Niall?'

'I don't suppose I need tell you.'

'Ah. Ever suspicious.'

'Listen, Morse. I can do quite well without the charade of your conversation, thank you.'

The postmaster picked up a pile of letters and began sorting them. 'Only doing my job,' he said.

'Some job. You're a disgrace to your public office. And to your namesake.'

'Forbear, Mr Niall. Forbear. Samuel Morse was my grand-uncle on my mother's side. The name's the same because my mother and father were cousins. The family boasts a proud reputation in the field of communications.'

'Little good it did you. Postmaster in the-middle-of-no-where.'

'Best place to be postmaster, Mr Niall. I know I'm needed. Oh, by the way, that telegram you have there is perfectly genuine. Came through from the Amalgamated Workers' Union headquarters in Brisbane this morning. Sent yesterday afternoon. Not bad news, I hope.'

'Oh, shut up, Morse. And kindly send this telegram from me marked "Urgent". I suppose you will do it without any tampering or interference?'

'Confidentiality is my job, Mr Niall. Now, if we are lucky it will go through before these storms bring down the line.' He counted the words. 'Two and eleven-pence.'

Niall paid. With a characteristic flourish of the wrist developed over years behind the counter, Morse placed the penny change in Niall's hand. 'If only your great-uncle could see you now,' Niall said. 'He'd turn in his grave.'

'On the contrary, Mr Niall. I'm sure he'd pat me on the back. I'm a primary link in the country's communication network. I'm like the nerve at the tip of your index finger, Mr Niall. It is me who tells the brain when the finger's burning.'

'Then you won't have much to do if the weather persists in its present inclemency, Mr Morse. Good day.'

Mrs Bowditch did not normally allow herself to sit in front of her mirrors at this hour of the day. Afternoons were usually reserved for activities of greater sociability. But this afternoon was different. Not only had the rains completely enveloped and isolated Goonda, restricting virtually all activity to indoors, but also, in the shadow-subtle light of the grey day, she had discovered the appearance of a new wrinkle on her neck. She worked at it with creamy fingers, gently massaging the vulnerable skin of her throat.

Her husband stood on the veranda outside the bedroom door. He felt against his face the fine spray from the rain sweeping under the roof's overhang. He was thinking about the homestead's plumbing. 'The system's coping, I reckon,' he said.

He looked back at her through the doorway. 'Why don't you come out here?' he said. 'The rain on the face. It's marvellous.'

She raised her eyes to him. She smiled, fingering her throat. 'I'm casting a spell,' she said, 'to ward off age.'

'Ah, yes. You're doing a brilliant job.'

'Not brilliant enough,' she said ruefully, looking back at the mirrors.

'Of course you are.' And he came up behind her, putting his big hands over her shoulders, letting his long, roughened fingers curl around her throat, massaging with a surprising gentleness. His sun-dark hands on the paleness of her skin, teaching her the beauty of her throat to him, so that she leant her head back against his body and closed her eyes, letting the warmth run in supple waves between them. Then from behind her closed eyes she felt his mouth come near and press into hers, upside down, as he leant over and kissed her. 'That's not a wrinkle,' he said, kissing over her chin and down her throat, 'that's just the mark of another season we've survived.'

They went onto the veranda. They lay back in the planters' chairs drawn to a comparatively sheltered spot. They threw their legs over the leg-rests. The rain surrounded them, spinning gusts of spray across them. It made them laugh. The water splashed in great jungle drops and miniature cascades down the leaves of her garden. The plants opened themselves unfearing to every drip and spatter. The boards of the veranda floor shone wetly. The waves of grey rain boomed in the paddocks beyond. The paddocks themselves writhed with the drive of it.

'Good management,' he said. 'Good planning and management. Courage, foresight, imagination....' The list went on but there was no need for him to continue. 'We deserve a toast,' he said.

He had the port there, one of the treasures he kept in the coolest part of the house. He poured two crystal glasses full. They raised the glasses towards each other. Their eyes sparkled warmer than the crystal. Their glances intertwined exclusively, as conspirators. 'To the future,' he said.

'To our future,' she corrected.

The glasses touched with the teeth-edge caress of crystal. Then the Bowditches drank together. They pushed their heads back. Their faces were finely sprayed with the rains. Their hair and clothes were finely dampened. On their own veranda, in their own rain-spun world, they drank together. And pushing the glass from her lips Mrs Bowditch let out a great laugh. So the port spilled from her mouth down the bosom of her white dress.

On the road to the strike camp Niall passed a bogged bullock team. The drovers worked in the rain, manufacturing a corduroy from amongst the timbers they carried as a load. Niall drew up to see if he could be of any help. He was assured (not without vivid cursing) that the situation was under control. The dray was heavily laden with materials for the building of a hotel. Apart from the posts and boards there was roofing iron and even a billiard table. The latter had been saved from spoiling by a tarpaulin. En route to some godforsaken, hotel-less place farther out, the load was. On its way to become an oasis in the desert. But at the moment the notion of an oasis was irrelevant. The dray had bogged down almost to tray level. The bullock team wallowed belly-deep. The men who worked around the stricken vehicle were often sucked thigh-deep by the voracious mud.

One of the drovers called to Niall through the beat and slash of the rain: 'Bit of a soft patch here, mate. Don't for God's sake come too close.'

Niall accepted the advice. He rode on, keeping to the safer-looking stretches of the road. He looked back just once at the picture of ultimate optimism portrayed by the sinking dray and its mud-wading salvagers.

At the strike camp the men were drinking rum. Niall was greeted at the flap of the men's shelter by an emergent arm holding a pannikin into the rain. Niall pushed back the flap to find Bright on the other end of the arm.

'Take what you can while it's there,' said Bright. He drew in the pannikin and sipped the rum and rainwater.

'Especially if it's rum,' said Niall.

'I was referring to the water,' Bright replied.

They sat at the mess bench. Niall declined the offer of a drink. Through a section of the canvas raised on the leeward side he could see the gully rushing with water beyond the camp's tent line. He could also see the smaller floods coursing through the camp site. They divided it like ribs in a fan, cutting eroding slashes through the sandy ground.

'I've wired again for a renewal,' Niall said. 'It was worth a try.'

'Why should they be sympathetic?' asked Bright, coldly.

'There's all the evidence. Surely they know I can hold out on them with that.'

'Perhaps they don't want it any more. Perhaps what you've got's not worth anything.'

'How can that be? I'm closer than ever to a solution now.'

'But you're also further off than ever. You're sprung all over town. Didn't take long, that didn't. You're useless now.'

'I'll wait for a reply, just the same.'

Bright drank deeply from the pannikin. He was a bit drunk. The drunkenness allowed the edge of his disillusionment to show through. 'There's not much point in you staying on,' he said. 'Barret was a traitor and a double-crosser. He let a woman turn his head. There's no place for men like that in the movement. Better to let his memory fade. He doesn't make a good martyr.'

Niall didn't answer. There was no point in arguing.

There was a tray of meat on the table, under a piece of tar-paper. Bright took off the covering and invited Niall to eat. Niall declined. 'It's genuine mutton,' Bright said, smiling bitterly. 'Fresh, too. A jumbuck strayed into camp this morning, didn't it? One thing floods are good for — straying stock.' Bright stabbed at the meat with a knife. Bloody juice spurted over his hand. 'The rain put the fire out before it was properly done,' he said, almost sadly.

In his cups Bright was cynical and unfriendly. Niall's presence in no way jollied him. He had already added the triple-barrelled name of Clohesy-Laver-Niall to the list of philosophies, causes, and individuals, in which he had lost faith. At times like this he felt the length of that list to be particularly daunting. It read like a paean to impotence: all the squashed rebellions, leaky revolutionary theories, and unrisen martyrs. It was an inventory of all that he had been robbed of. It was a list much longer than the sheep or horses he had duffed, the rum he had looted, the bridges he had tampered with, the woolsheds he had fired. He had so little left, apart from bombast, and even that was running thin. 'Don't worry, Niall,' he said, winking, 'I'll make a war — somehow. All we need is shear-blades and hatred. Shear-blades and a bit of decent, moral hatred.' He put his head down on his arm and appeared to fall asleep. Niall drew on his cape and hat and pushed through the flap into the rain.

On the way back to town Niall found the dray still stuck fast, but the activity surrounding it had been abandoned. Instead of further attempts at dislodging the vehicle, the teamsters had removed part of its load. At a short distance from the road, on higher ground, they had set up an elaborate, homely camp, in which it seemed they intended a lengthy stay. The billiard table, too, had been removed from the dray and situated under a large tarpaulin fly. When Niall rode up, the drovers were standing around the table, chalking up their cues.

'Could be here for weeks, we could,' said one of them to Niall. 'So we're starting a championship. Is ball your game, mate?'

The fire was homely, the tea hot and strong. Niall stayed.

For Christina, at Dagworth, the strum of the rain on the veranda's iron roof was not unwelcome. It provided a soft cocoon of sound in which she could rest and catch up with herself. Her life over the past fortnight had been too public, she felt. It was a relief to settle down alone, to find out what was happening in the private recesses of her own consciousness. She took up the letter which had lain for several days unopened on the writing desk in her room. There on the desk's rich rosewood the letter had gleamed as a source of guilt, rather than as the prospect of pleasure it should have been. She opened the envelope, noting the Melbourne postmark. She knew the handwriting's particular cramped curl. It was three weeks since that hand had caressed her. In this very room. She unfolded the letter, and read.

By the time she had finished reading there were tears in her eyes. She had wiped at them with her fingers and the backs of her hands. Their moisture had smudged the ink in places down the margins. She re-folded the letter and immediately began her reply.

Dagworth Station
17th of December

My darling fool,

        I have only just read yours. It arrived three days ago but — you know me! — I have been so busy having a wonderful time, I let it lie, waiting for a private moment. Now I am desperate for having done so. My poor, sweet, loving fool! How can you be so faithless? How does that wonderfully intelligent mind of yours conceive such foolishness? I forbid you ever to propose such a stupidity again — ever! — because it hurts my heart horribly to think of you thinking that way. And it frightens me to think of what I should do without you, my darling, darling fool!

        So please listen to me, with your ears and your heart. I love you with every breath and pulse beat. I have had a marvellous time here since your departure, but I missed you horribly. Everything I have done, I have done with an imagined you — and with that aching emptiness inside, which can only be filled by my sharing experiences with you. I will tell you all that has happened, but first let me soothe your poor, silly, fragile, frightening mind!

        My strongest hope, on reading your letter, is that you are quoting the lines of some character you have played, rather than truly meaning what you say. Surely, my precious, wonderful man, you cannot believe in such juvenile nonsense. Suicide does not become you! You are far too valuable for that. And knowing how precious you are to me, you do me the greatest dishonour even to suggest that I neglect you. I am sure you do not mean anything of what you say. It is flattering to me that you should say it, but it frightens me too much. And with a stockwhip! I do not believe you even have a stockwhip. Besides, that is just too boring — it has been done before. I know that if you really intended anything of the sort you would do it with imagination, originality and style. There — I am laughing now, but I was crying before. The thought of you dying is too upsetting to me. You must not conceive of such an idea ever again, not even as a protestation of your love for me.

Now, my brilliant, silly man, let me tell you about what has been happening here. The Bowditches of Goonda put on a spectacular Gala Day. It was such a colourful bustle of activities and humorous characters. The highlight was a dingo hunt, but you'll be pleased to know, as I was, that the poor creature got away. Then followed a homestead ball where — how embarrassingly awful! — I was made to play a waltz. But you would have been proud of me, my love. I played a march instead! You should have seen them trot! It was most amusing. One of the guests was the poet, Banjo Paterson, whom I know you admire. Did you tell me you had bought a book of his, *The Man From Snowy River*? He found the tune 'Craigielea' (I heard it at the Warrnambool races with my parents last year) to be an inspiration, so he wrote some words for it — about a swagman who (perish the thought) suicides because he has been caught stealing a sheep. The song has been very popular, but I do not think many people see what a sad tale it relates. Sarah Rowley and I, with the Banjo and his friend Mr Niall (some sort of private detective who has been upsetting people around here) sang the song to a group of drunken shearers and they liked it so much they would not let us depart. Sarah and I had to tear up our hats and give them the pieces (as the currency lass did in that play you mentioned) as mementos of the occasion. So, as you may imagine, we've been having a very gay time, but constantly I think of you, my darling, and look forward to the end of your wretched play's season when you can again join me here.

Robert and Angus have indulged me in every way to make my time here delightful, and Mrs Bowditch has been extremely kind, but they cannot make up for your absence. On some occasions, such as when I watched the turkey hens huddling to protect their chicks from the hawks at Goonda, I have thought of you — of us — with such deep emotion that I wanted us never to be apart again. But we must not become so dependent upon each other that we are tedious to friends or to ourselves, my darling. I want us to live creatively; I want ours to be a special relationship, one composed of independent survival and mutual loyalty. Brother Robert says the dingoes live like that—they are mates for life, but each of them, the male and the female, must take care of his and her own survival in a world dedicated to poisoning them.

And that (by a roundabout train of thoughts) reminds me of the most dreadful incident to occur here recently. Poor Mr Bowditch had his champion stallion stolen by strikers and—you will not believe this—they ate him! How can men be responsible for such a horror?! I remember the eyes of that horse (Marrakesh was his name—you saw him once—do you remember?), such a deep, luminous, liquid black they were. Mr Bowditch was so upset he dug the grave for the bones himself. With his bare hands, he said. I felt deeply for the man in his tragedy. It was as if he had lost a member of his family.

Well, my darling, I cannot end this letter on such a tragic note, so I will mention the marvellous news that the drought has broken here and everybody is quite ecstatic about the torrential rains. And even though I am cut off from you by a thousand miles, and probably a thousand rushing rivers, I have the thought that perhaps it is raining in Melbourne too, and therefore you and I are together under the one magnificent, teeming stormcloud, and if I put my hand into the rain now it will be wet with the same perfect water that falls on you, my darling.

So, no more desperate thoughts, my love.
Your very own,
Chris XXX

J.W. Street & A.B. Paterson
Solicitors
———
Box 788, G.P.O.
Telephone 1197

Waltham Buildings
Bond Street
Sydney, ...18...

Still in the wilderness

My Perfect Angel!
Just a quick note on a borrowed piece of Bartie's stationery, to tell you that I am alive and well and battling on, though it has all become rather pointless now.

They have exposed me and all but defused me—how vulnerable one is when naked in this deceiving land!—but there might yet be a word I can say, as a private citizen, to make a difference.

Vain hope? I must admit the future looks solidly in their possession. If I had beaten them, might there have begun an Australian Dream of the spiritual, rather than of the material, kind?

They all killed the swagman, Rowena. I killed him too, by failing. We will all keep on killing him, I fear. To kill off that which dreams and loves is to be Australian, it seems. Bartie has written a wonderful song about it. But I have seen them singing the song lustily, joyously, with never a damn for the words.

Australia or myself? I believe I will opt for myself. Our love is the antidote I will rely on. The future is sick. Terminally so.

I am sorry for depressing and worrying you. Keep the bed warm for me.

With all my love,
Ever Your True Mate,
Hammond.

20th of December

I have calmed sufficiently to write. I will never calm sufficiently to forget. Or forgive. I will take steps to ensure that my hurt, my bitterness, my prejudice, never die. I have before me his book, *The Man from Snowy River and Other Verses*. I see now the features of the Bartie I know in these pages. In his verse as in his life he has made muscle his muse; enshrined the crude beauty of toughness and action; pursued the hollow aesthetics of fighting and winning. Behind those puerile attachments to courage, heroics, violence, there is the vast hypocrisy of the insecure egotist. Behind that superficial forthrightness and modesty there is the disastrous ignorance of the man who knows only the masculine. I can see them all now, those lonely, lonely men sitting round campfires, poaching off each other's stories, singing louder to beat back the fertile dark, making their music and dancing together, waltzing each other through manly ballads. And he is there where he belongs, among those shameless firelit phantoms abusing the true heart with their substitutes. Damn the man from Snowy River! It is the woman from Snowy River who must stand for the best in us all.

CODA

It was Christmas Day, and the first morning for more than a week that the coach was able to leave. It was not a particularly early departure: the driver was concerned about the state of the road. He had no wish to set out until full daylight, especially considering the weight of his load. He was going to have two passengers on the splash-board and another on the roof. There was a caged cat, too, on the tray at the back. In addition, the rains had brought on a bumper crop of mail. All the town had taken up pens as the torrents descended. So there was an extra mail basket to go as well.

As the coach was loading outside the North Gregory Hotel, two well-dressed, proud men shook hands. 'She's a woman of her word,' said one of them. 'She's not emerged from that room yet. Not for me or anyone. She speaks to others, though. But not to me. Seems she's serious.'

The other put his hand on the speaker's shoulder, consoling him. Both men had dark circles under their eyes, but the non-speaker's face was particularly haggard. Its drawn quality seemed to indicate that he was being called upon to buoy up his friend's emotional state when his own was dangerously sunken. The two of them stood for a while, locked in that arm's-length embrace, finding nothing else to do but watch the loading of the coach. Then the haggard one spoke: 'I'll stay on a while longer,' he said. 'There are still things I can do here. And I'll see if I can talk to her again. She may come round. I'll think of something, and I'll keep you informed.'

'You have my address?'

'Yes, I have it here somewhere.' The haggard one went through the pockets of his coat, bending forward slightly, staring at the ground, all his consciousness focused at the ends of his fingertips as they felt in the deepest corners of his coat's recesses. 'I thought I had it,' he said.

'Never mind,' said the other. 'I'll write to you first. Anyway, I don't expect you'll have much success with her. She's a stubborn woman. It wouldn't surprise me if she never speaks to me again. Do you know, she told me she had come here to get away from me? Good of her to mention it, don't you think? I'd have stayed in Sydney if I'd known.'

'She couldn't have meant it.'

'I believe she did, old chap. I suppose it's ungallant to say so, but I think there's something wrong with her head. I mean a brain weakness. Pity she's not talking to me any longer, otherwise I'd convince her to see a specialist. Oh, well. By all means go and talk to her if you can, but don't bust a girth-strap over it. There are plenty more fillies in the paddock, aren't there?'

They shook hands again. Then the one who was leaving — the athletic, smooth-skinned one — climbed into the coach and took his seat. The one farewelling him stepped back into the group of well-wishers surrounding the coach. When the wheels first began to move, they picked up gobbets of Elderslie Street's mud and carried it round to the tops of their arcs. There it drooped and fell, spattering the axle hubs on its way to the ground. As the coach picked up speed, it began flinging the mud out behind in a streaming wake, like a paddlewheeler progressing through a muddy sea.

When the coach turned out of Elderslie Street, heading towards the clearing eastern horizon, there emerged from its wake a mud-covered figure coming into the town, a sodden, clay-splattered man pushing a mud-caked bicycle. He was greeted with a cheer by those who had just farewelled the coach and by others who were in the street. He gave the impression of having been suddenly born out of the mud of the land itself, bicycle and all; or of being the lone survivor of a disaster in the desert rains, limping now into a remote but civilised port, still clinging to the unlikely piece of machinery that had kept him miraculously afloat.

As he came on up the main street, others of the town

216

appeared at doors and windows. They cheered him heartily. In the mud on his face there appeared a crack, and a smile broke through. Then someone called: 'Three cheers for Pastor Frank!' and received a booming, triple response. Two men came round the side of the hotel with buckets of clean water. They pitched them over him, bike and all. When the mud had washed down, there stood a beaming man dressed in simple black with a royal blue bicycle. To the back of the bicycle was lashed a swag, and from the handlebars there dangled a parcel wrapped in leather. To the delight of the growing crowd, the man unwrapped the parcel and, in a street full of shouting, he lifted a pair of boxing-gloves high above his head.

Then there was a great bustle. The crowd, mainly men, funnelled through the main door of the North Gregory Hotel. They escorted the man with the bicycle right through the hotel to the rear yard. In the hotel's billiards-room the tables were pushed back against the walls. The score-boards were covered with the coats of some of those present. The space of the room filled up with the sitting, squatting, and standing forms of a significant percentage of the local male population. Shearers, miners, rouseabouts, boundary riders, tank-sinkers, drovers, packers, scourers, storekeepers, saddlers, troopers, drunks, and sundry others, even the town's sub-inspector of police — all waited meekly and with expectation for Pastor Frank to appear.

Meanwhile, in a stable behind the hotel, Pastor Frank leant his bicycle against the wall. He unrolled his swag, and took out the battered Bible and Book of Common Prayer which were his constant travelling companions. He also changed his clothes. He shrugged on a surplice and a green chasuble. Then he pushed the wet, thinning hair back over his head, using his hands to flatten it down and make it stick to his scalp. All this done, he picked up his books and his boxing-gloves, and headed for the billiards-room.

'Dearly beloved Brethren, the Scripture moveth us in sundry places, to acknowledge and. . . .'

The congregation was extraordinarily attentive. Pastor Frank's voice seemed to move over and among them like a special dispensation. All those grubby, gruff, flash men; all those boasters and yarn-spinners; all those swearers, drinkers and gamblers; all those ungodly, irreverent jokers who scratched just exactly where they itched—they all sat meek as lambs listening to the unintelligible prayers and supplications, conscientiously putting matters to right if any drunk snored off or any immature one of their number found cause to titter or guffaw. They gave Pastor Frank their undivided attention, those distractable men. They did so with impeccable politeness, those ill-mannered heathens.

Then when it came to the sermon—a brief analysis of Jesus's role in the advancing of the Australian bushman's lot, with special reference to the place of privilege accorded the Shearer's Union at the manger-side, deftly handled by Pastor Frank, and being mainly a sequence of good jokes lifted from the *Bulletin*—the men were all ears and smiles. And when they rose to sing the hymn, with a great clatter of muddy boots on the floor, their voices were hearty if not glorious, and resonant if not pure. And as if a religious experience of real splendour were drawing nigh, the strains of 'Onward Christian Soldiers' (an Easter hymn, but who cared?—it was the one they always sang) were worked to a crescendo until the final 'Amen' crashed in the hotel billiards-room and all of Winton heard it and knew Pastor Frank's service was progressing well, as usual.

After the hymn, the men sat again, and Pastor Frank put down his Book of Common Prayer. With the aid of two of the congregation, he removed his vestments and stripped down to just his baggy black trousers. Then he bent and retrieved his boxing-gloves from beneath the improvised altar. Turning to the congregation with a smile, he announced: 'Now, boys, it's time for a bit of recreation.'

The front rows shuffled, clearing back a little. The local champion was pushed forward and supplied with gloves. Pastor Frank danced about, limbering up and jabbing at the air. The crowd muttered and called happily. And all was ready for the fight.

It hardly went a minute, but the crowded billiards-room savoured every exciting second of it, every dancing, weaving, flaying, staggering second of it, during which Pastor Frank was battered, bludgeoned, spun about, and knocked down. And after the count had gone to ten and the local bruiser's hand was raised above his head, Pastor Frank still lay there, cold. So, as usual, they tipped a little water on him and he came round, and

218

they supported him as he got up, and the smile on his puffed face showed he was quite pleased with himself; and the complete lack of resentment in his body as it got working again spoke like a sermon itself, stating lucidly that if one believed in something, then one would choose to be battered for it.

They called for drinks and Pastor Frank was shouted. They crowded around him as if he were the victor. The adversary who had just floored him was now part of the crowd slapping him on the back. As he sipped from his mug, Pastor Frank's face beamed. On it was the expression of a clergyman totally fulfilled in his ministry.

'You're a good old bastard, Pastor,' one of the crowd said, and Pastor Frank knew it to be the closest any minister was likely to get to the drawing of a witness of conversion from amongst these artless men.

GLOSSARY

Ascot—a wealthy Brisbane suburb
Billabong—waterhole formed when the arm of a river system is
    cut off from its main flow
Billy—can for boiling water
Blighter—ne'er-do-well person; a nuisance
Bloke—man
Bludger—one who won't work; a lazy person
Bora-ground—traditional Australian Aboriginal sacred ground
Botany Bay—the first landing point of white settlers in Australia
Breakfast Creek—creek in the Brisbane area
Brisbane—Queensland's capital city
Coo-ee—traditional Australian bush call of welcome
Coolibah—a variety of Australian eucalyptus
Drover—teamster in charge of a large team of steers or horses
Fortitude Valley—sleazy area of Brisbane
Galah—parrot
Gidgee—blue-leafed shrub of semiarid Australian regions
Goanna—large lizard or iguana
Grazier—cattleman or sheepman
Grazier's Contract—shearing according to the sheep owner's rate
    of pay
Grog—liquor
Heremai Lasi—Have you no shame? (Motu language, Papua, New
    Guinea)
Hump a Swag/Hump a Bluey/Hump the Drum—carry a bedroll, or,
    be an itinerant worker
Humpybong—seaside area near Brisbane, popular in 1890s

Ithaca Creek—creek in the Brisbane area
Jackaroo—young man gaining work experience on an outback sheep or cattle station
Jumbuck—castrated male sheep
Kanaka—South Pacific islander
Larrikin—wild young man
Martin Place—center of the city of Sydney
Matilda—see *Swag*
Moleskins—trousers
Myall—an Aboriginal tribesperson
Never-never—wilderness
Pannikin—see *Billy*
Pastoralist—grazier; sheep station owner or squatter
Pawpaw—papaya
Randwick—Sydney racecourse
Ringbarking—method of tree killing where a three-inch band of bark is removed from the circumference of the tree trunk
Saltbush—semiarid region shrub
Scab—non-unionist worker
Sheep Station—sheep ranch
Shout—buy a round of drinks for others
Spring Hill—an inner Brisbane suburb
Squatter—one who having made a claim to a piece of undeveloped government land undertakes to clear and use it
Surfers Paradise—Florida-style resort on the south Queensland coast
Swag—bedroll or sleeping bag
Swagman—bedroll-toting itinerant worker searching for employment in rural areas
TAB—Totalisator Agency Board (horseracing)
Trap—horse-drawn vehicle
Trooper—policeman
Tucker—food
Waltzing Matilda—carrying a bedroll or, being a swagman
Warrigal—dingo
Willy-willy—whirlwind